Chasing Christmas

A Holiday-ish Novel

Alex Winters

ONE

SHAY

"Treesgiving?" Benjy makes a face. His soft brown eyes are dubious in the shadow of his faded red ball cap.

I make one back. "What? You've never heard of it?"

"Of course, I haven't." He looks at me over the rim of his plastic Pig-Out cup. The logo is a pig with wings. A pig with wings wearing a cap very much like the ones on our young, tired heads. Meta much? His long fingers grip the cup lazily, like they always do. "Because it doesn't exist."

I jut out my chin. "Does too."

He chuckles. A soft, crooked smile. Bashful and boastful at the same time. "Then how come I'm just hearing about it now, huh?"

"Cuz you're lame and don't ever listen to a word I say?"

"Accurate." He still looks clueless, though.

I cluck my tongue. "I mean, I've only been talking about it since Halloween."

He sighs impatiently. Nudges my foot under the patio table. I shiver, not unpleasantly, at the touch. Wither under the curious gaze from his gentle eyes. Enjoy the flattering shadows that drift across his light-skinned face under the

1

string of exposed bulbs gently waving in the soft breeze above us. Drink in his long, gangly body, so enticing and smooth even in just his workaday uniform and wish, for about the millionth time, I could be happy just staying in *The Friend Zone*. "Just tell me what it is already, Shay."

"It's just a little party I throw every year on the day after Thanksgiving." He looks unimpressed so I keep spinning, really selling it the way I would the dinner special to an unsuspecting party of five. "It's all very super cool like. We put up the tree, string the lights, hang the ornaments, drink hot cocoa spiked with peppermint schnapps, eat Christmas cookies by the dozen and—"

He's totally not having it. Yawns and stretches and gives me all the body language at the same time. "I so call bullshit on this whole thing."

"What? You can't call bullshit. You weren't even listening to what I was saying."

"Was too!"

"Was not! I could see your eyes glaze over five words in."

His face is vaguely apologetic before he shrugs. "Cuz you were being super-duper extra, that's why."

"I was, wasn't I? I felt as if I leaned in a little too hard, but I'm just really very excited about it so... no apologies here."

Big frowny face. "No one's ever been that excited about anything, Shay."

I pout, vaguely hurt. Why is nobody, literally, nobody, excited about this frickin' brand-new holiday I invented? Not my manager, not my neighbor, not my coworkers, not even Cash, the creepy dude in the dish pit who typically hangs on every word I say, can seem to muster up any enthusiasm for this thrill-a-minute holiday of mine. I mean, everybody I tell about it, when they stop running away from me long enough to actually listen to me, that is, kind of gives the same "meh" reaction. "Well, I am. I'm extremely excited."

"Well, can you explain it without all the fireworks and hand waving and no crazy eyes this time, please? You're making me hate it already before I even understand it."

"No, Benjy, I can't, actually. A holiday this special deserves fireworks and hand waving, even crazy eyes for that matter."

He chuckles and takes a long, luxurious sip of his shift drink. Cheap well vodka and cranberry, like always. I forgot I even had one and do the same. Life is so much different since we both turned 21 last year, opening up a whole new world of shift drinks, lazy times after work, cheap vodka buzzes and the lingering, simmering temptation of sitting across from Benjy with a belly full of booze.

He sets down his pig-covered cup and narrows his chocolate brown eyes at me, a winning complement to his smooth bronze skin and lazy, crooked smile. "I've known you for how long and I've never heard of this faux holiday before. That's why I'm calling bullshit."

"Well, I mean, it's my first year in the new apartment, so..."

He lights another cigarette. Expresses his dissatisfaction by exhaling soft, warm smoke all over me. "So, you just... made it up?"

I glance down at the lighter stacked on top of his crumpled pack of cheap cigarettes. It's got a picture of a hula girl on it. Perfect. "Sort of, yeah."

"So, what are you sitting there making me feel like an ass for if no one else in the world but you knows about it, either?"

"I dunno? It's pretty easy, though."

He sputters out a cough-laugh, staccato cigarette smoke scattering across the littered tabletop like tiny smoke signals. Glances toward the French doors leading out to the side deck. Sits up a little. "Let's suppose I do come to your fake holiday."

I feel a little gurgle of anticipation. This is it. This is the moment I've been waiting for. This…this could actually, possibly, maybe be happening. I bluff just the same. "There's no supposing. You are coming. That's a fact. Get used to it."

"Fine, but how you gonna fix both of us having the day off after Thanksgiving?"

I shrug casually, like I haven't been pulling the strings on this covert operation for literal days at this point. "Glenda always says whoever works Thanksgiving is off on Black Friday, or vice versa. So…you in?"

"I'm down with working Thanksgiving, I guess." He shrugs back, mulling it over. "You gonna put the 'day off' request in for us?"

I nudge his foot back under the table. The cheap vodka and cran are gently kicking in and I let my toes linger there a smidge longer than I usually would. He doesn't notice or, if he does, doesn't seem to care. "Would you be mad if I already did?"

He beams at me from under his weathered Pig-Out ball cap, that simple smile making all the hard work I've put into this totally worth it. "Frankly, Shay, I'd be disappointed if you hadn't."

We chuckle lazily. Familiarly. Overhead the country music oozes softly from carefully angled speakers hidden in the rustic wooden rafters above us. Over the years, we've learned to ignore it almost completely. The clang and twang are at such distinct odds with the generally breezy, reggae style, salty vibe of our otherwise tropical little seaside Florida town.

We sit in comfortable silence for a few moments. Gaze past each other at the vacant patio attached to the main restaurant. Hardwood tables are a little small for four but just right for two. Black wire mesh chairs that are especially comfortable after another long shift. A few rows of exposed bulbs swaying gently overhead. Sip the last of our free shift drinks. Jiggle the ice at the bottom of our red plastic pig-cups to get the last of the slushy vodka and cranberry goodness. Speak over each other at the same time:

"Anyway, I think it should be a good time…"

"You ready, Shay?"

I stand abruptly, as if summoned. The chair makes an awkward sound as it stumbles out with me. Try to hide my disappointment at his abrupt signoff. I could have stayed like that, chill and swoony, buzzed and blushing with my toes inches from Benjy's, for another hour at least.

Maybe even two. Who am I kidding? Definitely two, girl. Come on now.

I don't know why I still get so surprised when he does that. Benjy's always ready to go before I am. Whether we're at the movies or just grabbing sushi after work, when he's done that's it. Up and at 'em and out the door. I wonder, idly, if he's like that in bed, too. Cara's never said. Thank God for small miracles, I suppose. "Yeah, just lemme get my backpack first."

He unfolds himself from the deck chair, all gawky limbs, and sharp angles. Quickly. Like he's been ready to go forever. Grabs his own backpack, ancient and tattered and covered in concert pins for bands he was all hot on once upon a time but probably hasn't listened to in ages. Wags it at me as I tidy up a bit. "Told you to get it when we came out here. Why don't you ever listen to me?"

I wave a hand. "Yeah, yeah…"

He watches me reach for the door. Bites his lower lip. "Meet you at the bike rack?" He sounds uncertain. Like maybe I won't. Like I'll actually skip it this time. For, like, the first time ever.

I give him a reassuring grin instead. Linger as our eyes meet, full of all kinds of things we've never had the guts to explore. "Duh."

TWO

SHAY

I go into the liquor room. It's just inside the French doors that lead to the side patio. It's late. After hours. The big, cavernous barn of a restaurant sits idle, the only sound the constantly twanging country music crooning overhead. I listen to it for once, savoring the moment of having the restaurant to myself. It's a woman. Good voice, actually. Strong but feminine, the way I like to think of myself sometimes. Something about a cheating boyfriend. A puppy dog. And boiled peanuts?

I smirk and grab my backpack from one of the hooks hanging over the shelf full of Kentucky Classic, our vaguely expensive sounding but actually quite cheap-ass house whiskey.

Back out of the closet. See the dim light glowing from inside the kitchen. Groan and sigh and drift closer to the swinging metal door even though every fiber of my being wants to run, sprint, in the other direction. Push through anyway. Hear the tapping of a keyboard and drift toward the kitchen office. Tap on the open door gently. "Anybody home?"

Glenda glances up from the keyboard, ebony skin shiny in the unflattering fluorescent light of the closet sized office. "Says the home-wrecker."

"What?"

She waves a pencil toward the corner of the computer screen. A little square from the security camera reveals a vaguely blurry video feed of the side deck and, specifically, the table Benjy and I were just sitting at. I blush and sputter and take an involuntary step forward to peer more closely at the blotchy square of live camera footage. "Glenda! You were spying on us?"

My general manager looks me up and down as if to see if my virginity is still intact. Sorry to break it to her, but it hasn't been for quite some time! "I prefer the term 'watching out for you,' but...yeah, I suppose I was."

I blanche. Can't imagine what she might have seen. Or heard. God, I'm always so obvious, coy, cheesy, and saucy when it's just Benjy and me together. And add an extra-strength shift drink on top of it? I feel nauseous. Thank God the camera doesn't have x-ray vision to see me grinding his toes with my sneaker beneath the table. Or that heat seeking stuff to see the micro-flare in the crotch region of my dowdy work pants. "Does that thing have a microphone?"

Glenda chuckles merrily. Enjoying herself immensely, unapologetically, as she watches me squirm in the doorway. "Wouldn't you like to know, you brazen-ass hussy?"

"Come on, Glenda. That's rude *af* and you know it."

She wriggles in her chair a little. Not because she's uncomfortable with committing several privacy act violations while closing the restaurant, just to get more comfortable before she lectures me a tad. Crosses her arms over her shelf-like bosom and gives me her best "harrumph" face.

"Ruder than not inviting me out there for a shifty with you two after work?"

I roll my eyes. Slip on my backpack. Still half-in, half-out of the doorway. Knowing Benjy's out there at the bike rack, wondering what's taking so long. Knowing, too, that I should enjoy playing a little hard to get for once but fearful all the same that he'll just bail on our ride home together and I'll miss out on fifteen more minutes of harmless flirting before our night together ends.

"Like you'd ever come if we did ask you, Glenda."

She waves at a disgruntled pile of wrinkled spreadsheets and scribbled on work schedules, all bearing the flying pig in a hat logo in the top left corner. "I would once my paperwork is done."

"Yeah, in two hours."

"You can't wait that long?"

I chuckle. "I'll be in bed by then, lady."

She swivels in her chair. It squeaks under her considerable girth. Fixes me with alert, pointed eyes and a vaguely maternal expression. "I just hope you're in bed alone tonight, girlie."

I blush some more, as if there's any left. "What does that even mean?"

"You know what that even means."

Of course, I do. But still. Now? We have to do this now. "Come on, Glenda. This again?"

She waves her hand. Pencil still wagging her disapproval. "I'm just sayin', Shay. You know Cara's probably coming home for Thanksgiving, right? I just worry she'll see how cozy you've gotten with her boyfriend while she was away at school this semester."

I stiffen as if I've just heard another verse from the boiled peanuts song. "I'd hardly call it cozy."

She makes a "harrumphing" sound to accessorize her harrumphing face. Turns slightly in her chair as it creaks in helpless protest. I can tell she's eager to get back to work, but not so eager she can't resist one last guilt trip before I go.

"And besides," I add hastily. "Obviously we were talking about her. Mostly."

"Uh-huh, that's how it starts. Talking about her. Drinking with him. Another drink or two, you start talking about each other. Inhibitions are down. Hormones are up. Then what?"

"Then I go home and take a cold shower like every other night, that's what!"

She chuckles. Big, bold, and pure. Everything's okay with us again. She still has her back turned, but I can tell just from her puffier than usual cheeks she's smiling. "Just make sure you do, Shay. I've got enough drama around here without entertaining home-wreckers like yourself."

I roll my eyes. Reach for the light switch. The other hand on the doorknob. "I'll show you home-wrecker, boss lady!" Turn off the lights. Shut the door. Hear her screaming-laughing from half-a-kitchen away as I beat a hasty retreat across the slippery floor tiles on my non-skid sneakers.

THREE

BENJY

I slip my phone out of my pocket while Shay's inside, dragging her ass as usual. Fire off a quick text to Cara while I've got a few minutes.

BENJY:

'Sup?

Put the phone down on the wooden railing by the bike rack to see if she'll respond in a timely manner. She doesn't always lately. At least, not right away. Used to be she was writing back five seconds after I texted, but that was when she first went away to school. Now she's busier, apparently. Classes. Mid-terms. Lectures. Labs, blah, blah.

Those are her usual excuses, anyway.

I unlock my bike while I'm waiting. Shay's too. Her lock combo is the same as her clock-in number, the same as her phone password and pretty much everything else in her life: the last four digits of her social security number.

5-6-0-7.

Pretty sure I could hack her whole life if I wanted to. But I don't need her whole life. Just her heart. I shake away the cheesy thought and click her lock open instead, swirl the neon blue chain in a loop and hang it off her left handlebar the way she likes. Smile to imagine the way she'll bound out of the side-deck door in another few minutes, backpack slung over one shoulder, pretending to be surprised like I don't do that for her every other night or so.

My phone bleats. I jump a little, surprised. Forgot I even wrote Cara for just a second. Glance at the screen-saver pic of us together, beaming in bathing suits on the beach. Her hair is swept back. There's a slight glow to her face. Lips thin across her crooked smile. Her green bikini top is crooked, the hint of tan lines just beneath. She's on my lap.

I'm wearing the stupid pineapple baggies she bought me for my birthday. My faded Pig-Out cap is crooked. I'm slightly buzzed and trying to nibble her ear, and not just for show. She's got her hand on my bare chest to steady herself. Or keep me at bay. Neither would surprise me, frankly. Two seconds after she snapped the selfie the cheap beach chair, we were sitting in toppled over from our weight, and we laughed and laughed as we struggled to right it in our sandy hands.

I think it's the last time I saw her laugh. And we took that picture like, two years ago. I wince to read her text because I know it's just going to be one of her long string of random excuses and I'm not disappointed.

CARA:

Beat from study group. You?

I roll my eyes and tap out something clever. At least, I think so anyway.

BENJY:

> Beat from work. We should just copy and paste this thread since we're on repeat every night.

Think twice before sending it because there's a thousand different ways it can go sideways. Send it anyway because, with Cara, it'll probably go sideways no matter what I write. Or how long I think about it after I send it.

It does. She writes back right away. Never a good sign lately. I wince some more, realize my stomach is all tensed up, the way it usually is whenever Cara is involved lately.

CARA:

> You sound bored. With us. Is that it?

I have to chuckle because of how quickly she went from zero emotion to full on high drama.

BENJY:

> No babe, just...we're both tired. That's all.

CARA:

> I guess. When we catch up, it'll be different.

I grin. A glimmer of hope in a long string of excuses.

BENJY:

> You mean like over Thanksgiving break?

I string a bunch of winky-face emojis along just to show her I won't be disappointed when she denies me. Again.

CARA:

Baby, listen...

BENJY:

Just kidding, boo. I miss you. Is all.

She writes back right away, as if she's already composing her text halfway through mine.

CARA:

Me too, babe, just listen, I've got study hall in a few minutes so gotta cut this short, but...

BENJY:

Thought you just got out of study hall???

Yeah, I go heavy on the question marks because, wtf??? I check the time on my phone. It's just past eleven. My phone bleats with another flare up.

CARA:

We're doing this again?

BENJY:

We're not doing anything, just...it's late, that's all.

I sigh and see movement just beyond the French doors. Grin a little with anticipation and fire off a quick thumbs up emoji before silencing my phone and slipping it in my backpack. I'm sure I'll get 4,000 angry texts in reply by the time I check it again, but it feels good getting the last word in for at least an hour or so.

Shay bursts through the door grinning, chestnut brown hair buried beneath her Pig-Out ballcap except for the sexy little ponytail sneaking out the back. "What's so funny?"

She shrugs, rounding the railing on her long, coltish legs until she's on the other side with me. Nods at me, her cheeks aglow with a mischievous little smile. "I should ask you the same."

"Me? Why?"

"You're grinning like you heard the best dad joke ever."

I lie, just a little, because she always gets hinky whenever we talk about Cara. "I'm just imagining you, sitting around in your apartment, surrounded by index cards and high-lighters and notebooks, coming up with this Treesgiving BS, that's all."

She buys it. Looks at her bike and grins. "I'm gonna have to change my combination one of these days."

I slide on my bike seat and back it out of the rack. "Well, first you're going to have to remember how to unlock it yourself."

She chuckles, smile big and broad. "Well, if you weren't always unlocking it for me, maybe I could."

"Well, if you would listen to me for once and bring your backpack out with us for shifties, you wouldn't always have to go back inside and end up chatting with Glenda for an extra ten minutes while I sit out here twiddling my thumbs."

I can see her mouth moving with another reply, full lips frosty and smooth with her favorite cherry lip balm. Then she gives up, green eyes tired and smiling at the same time. "I got nothing…"

She grunts and gets on her bike, steadying herself as I take long, lazy circles in the parking lot. I watch her every time I glide by, ripe and curvy where Cara is slender and firm, giggling as she struggles with her kickstand, carefree and slow as she beams up at me from beneath her Pig-Out cap. I look away before I can say something stupid, hearing her seat creak as she finally climbs atop it.

"Wait up, Benj. Jesus!"

I grin, glad she can't see how happy I am to have her by my side. "Sorry, you're so slow."

"What, you're in a rush to get home?"

"Not exactly, but I'll be glad when I'm away from here."

She catches up, small hands steady on her handlebars. "Same," she huffs, all in a twitter from boarding her bike. Like we don't do it every night.

We coast along, side by side, passing the other restaurants in the dining complex on the north side of town known as Restaurant Row. Besides Pig-Out, there's Molly's Mexican Cantina, bright and cheery with its mariachi music and winking Christmas lights. Next to that is Papa Pepperoni's Pizza Parlor, then Jade China's Imperial Pavilion and, at the very end of the circular Cove district, the Bait Bucket Shrimp Shack.

We glide past each one, the parking lots empty, the doors locked, only the dishwashers and closing managers drifting through the back doors as they close up for the night. You can see the red winks of flame at the end of their cigarettes and hear bursts of husky, kitchen laughter as they drift away from each other and over to their respective, shitty cars in the employee parking lot.

It's the best time of night, as far as I'm concerned. Quiet and simple, mellow, and alone, just the two of us and the ten- or so-minute ride home. Shay by my side, smiling at her own private thoughts, quiet when there's no need to talk, chatty when we want to talk.

Like always, tonight is a little bit of both. When it gets a little too quiet, I try to think of something to say. If only because I know our ride will be over far too soon and I don't want to waste a minute of it.

FOUR

SHAY

"So, do I have to bring anything?"

"What?" It takes me a minute of slow, distracted pedaling to assimilate Benjy's seemingly rando, out of the blue question. "To what? Treesgiving?"

He nods, slim and sturdy atop his ratty ten-speed. It creaks and shimmies beneath him. Pretty sure he got it back in high school and has been riding it into the ground ever since, but that kind of tracks with the rest of his personality. If it ain't broke, why fix it, right?

I shrug. Stifle a sigh of frustration at his suddenly needy ass. The kid can remember the orders for three tables in his head, no pad necessary, but he can't wrap his head around one casual holiday get together. Even if it is fake ass and we both know it? "I mean, that would be the polite thing to do for a human being in actual society. Yes."

He chuckles, that big smile lighting up his whole face and half the street while he's at it. "Like what, tho?"

Let up my reins and sigh just a little. Hoping he gets the point. A quick glance shows he hasn't. "I dunno. Whatever Christmas-y thing you're in the mood for that day."

"Christmas-y?" He makes a face like I've just asked him to put pineapple on his pizza. It's still pretty cute, though. "In November?"

That's it. I let the sighs out, hot, and fast, one after the other. "Jesus, Benjy. You act like it's July and I'm telling you to wear a Santa suit."

"I mean, practically. We just took down the Halloween decorations at work, is all I'm saying."

I roll my eyes. Wonder why he's making such a big deal out of things. It's not like he's Scrooge or anything. He's actually pretty festive, given the opportunity. And here I am, giving him the opportunity! "You'll see. It'll be fun."

"Oh, I'm sure. It's just...have you ever heard the term 'chasing Christmas,' Shay?" He winks at me, as if answering his own question.

"Stop." I'd shove him, but we're both on bikes and I'm not quite up for a visit to the ER tonight.

"But for real though?"

"I have heard of it, Benjy, and...this isn't that."

"You sure, cuz sure sounds like it."

His voice trails off. We pedal slowly through the quiet streets of our hometown. It's late November. The air is soft and, in this tiny seaside Florida town, still sticky and warm. It's fine. You get used to it.

I swerve my bike gently closer to his. Spook him just a little. Grin at the spasm that crosses his smooth, handsome face. "Listen, if it's gonna be an issue, why don't you just bring some nice, non-Christmasy sausage and cheese, okay?"

His whole body literally sags with relief. "Phew. Good. Fine."

"Maybe throw in some basic, non-holiday shaped crackers if you're feeling it?"

The additional look of extra relief on his face is almost comical. "Yes please!"

"God. Have you always been such a Scrooge?"

He looks vaguely offended. "Not during actual December."

"It'll be days away by then, Benj. Literally. Days."

"I know, but still…"

I sigh and drift from one side of the wide, empty sidewalk that runs along Ocean Drive to the other. He follows suit. We don't have far to go to my apartment complex. Instinctively, we both slow our roll a little bit. Stretching out the trip before it ends all too soon.

Or maybe just I do. I can never really tell with him. He's hot. He's cold. He's clingy. He's aloof. Impatient if I'm five seconds late to the bike rack after work, but also just fine if we're not on the schedule together for a shift. It's almost like he's the girl in this often-one-sided relationship that isn't quite a relationship, after all. I have to keep reminding myself of this fact from time to time.

I listen to his pedals creak as we weave our way through town, leaving the Row far behind us. Fill the soft, silky silence with the inevitable. "Think Cara will be home by then?"

I mean, I have to ask. It would look like I didn't care if I didn't at least inquire about his significant other. And I do care about my friend. His girlfriend. I just care about Benjy more.

I'm not proud of it, obviously. And it wasn't always this way. Things have changed, since Cara went away to college. They were always bound to, I suppose, the dynamic shifting from three to two, but not this much. Not this profoundly.

Before, back in high school, Cara and I were friends. Good ones. Best ones, actually, if only by default. Cara was

20

the popular one, the polished one, the glitzy one, stylish and fashionable and cool and hip and with it. She had a ton of acquaintances, but once she and Benjy started dating, toned down her act and kind of just stuck with the two of us after a while. A vaguely quiet tomboy outcast, I was pretty honored they chose me to be in their quiet little circle. And we had fun, together. Did all the things, shared all the time, said all the words, laughed all the laughs and, now it's just Benjy and I, carrying on the tradition. Differently, now, obviously.

If only to me...

Benjy's face remains placid in reply. Neither high nor low. Doesn't flinch or frown or smile or beam. He hems quietly, his normally fun and goofy voice subtly lowkey and downtempo. "Not sure. I can't get a straight answer out of her."

I play the devil's advocate even if my heart's not in it, because the last thing I want to be is the BFF always whispering in his ear about how horrible his girlfriend is, especially when she's not exactly around to defend herself. "Well, she's busy, you know. Classes. Exams. She's not in our hurry anymore."

He's still wearing a placid, vaguely cryptic expression that borders ever so slightly on a frown. I stifle the slight, totally irrational but undeniable feeling of relief I get that he's not exactly copacetic with her at the moment. He will be, again, for sure. But for now, tonight, it's just us and a little part of me is secretly stoked about that.

He turns slightly toward me and is definitely frowning. "Still. It's Thanksgiving, right?"

"I know, Benj. I know..."

He looks vaguely wounded, bordering on helpless. The kind of helpless that makes me want to reach over and hug his big, broad shoulders. "She should want to come home, right?"

I nod, trying to stay noncommittal. "She should, sure. But like I said, she's not in our hurry anymore, Benj. And we're not in hers. She may be feeling pressures we're not at the moment. Exams coming up, papers due, what do a couple of townies like us know about all that stuff?"

"All the more reason to come home then, right?" His doubtful tone makes it clear he's asked himself this question a thousand times before.

I nod anyway. "You would think so, Benjy, but maybe staying on campus is the best choice for her right now. She's there and we're here and things might be a little weird until she graduates in a few years. We...we kind of knew this when she went away this year."

He nods. "I know," he blurts, like he really, truly doesn't. "It's just knowing it and feeling it are two different things, you know?"

I don't, not exactly, but I nod just the same. He smiles as if that means something and, gradually, both our faces turn back toward the road, familiar beneath our bike tires.

The sign for the Salty Seagull looms just off in the distance. Faded blue and pink lettering benefits somewhat from their neon glow, a sketchy beacon that signifies the end of our post-shift journey. I lean into the inevitable and pedal for home. He's right by my side.

I cruise up to the bike rack. It's just on the other side of the pool fence, bordered on either side by a cluster of scraggly palms desperately in need of a trim. Hear the quiet trickling of pool water being displaced over the sound of Benjy's squeaky bike seat. Hide a satisfied grin. Dismount and slide my trusty beach cruiser into place. He straddles his trusty ten-speed, blocking my back tire as if I might change my mind and peel out for somewhere else. Wrists bent at the joint of the handlebars, long fingers hanging down.

I sigh. Wait for the inevitable. And there it is. "Work tomorrow?"

I nod, inevitably. "Dinner shift. You?"

He frowns, eyes downcast in the same weak street-lamp that towers above the rickety bike rack. "Lunch."

My belly does another irrational drop to think we won't share the same shift together. "Well, that sucks."

He brightens slightly, eyes aglow beneath the weak orange streetlamp. "At least I'll get to say 'bye' to you."

I stand near my bike, halfway between Benjy and the pool gate. "Well, that's something."

He nods. Like he always does. Pauses. Like he always does. I grin as he creaks back onto his seat, preparing for a slow getaway. "Say 'Hi' to your mom for me."

Rolls his soft brown eyes. "Yeah, like she'll be up at this hour."

I nod. Forget not everybody considers midnight prime time the way we do. "Well, in the morning, then?"

Rolls his eyes but nods just the same. Benjy and his mom have a complicated relationship and I try to tread lightly whenever the subject comes up. "Will do, ass kiss."

I snort self-consciously. He knows me so well. But it's not my fault, either. His mom's never quite warmed up to me, and it's always fairly irked me that I can't quite get through to her. Benjy says few people can and, considering what she's been through, I get that. Truly, I do. Cheating husband? Single mother? No child support? Doing it on her own? Trust issues anyone? But me? I'm pretty likeable, I think. But she's always preferred Cara's smooth, polished Insta-life to my rough, tomboy edges and smart, sassy mouth. She should hear her son sometime. "Anyway, I'm just being polite."

He pauses. Gives me a look as if just now realizing this. "I know. You're always that."

He looks so serious, or maybe just so vulnerable. I slug him on the shoulder and peer gently up at him. "You're polite too, Benj. A good boy. A good son. You know that, right?"

"Tell her that," he huffs, a little wisp of family dysfunction bubbling up to the surface unannounced. Well, it is the holidays, after all. No better time for that, I suppose.

"She knows that, Benjy. I know she does."

He seems to sag a little, like maybe all the fight's just gone out of him. "I guess, the holidays, seeing you in your new place this year, and Cara in her dorm room, and me? Going home to my old bedroom like some shmuck, I'm just feeling a little defensive is all."

"I can see that," I tease, trying to joke him out of his sudden funk. "I mean, hell, living at home? No rent? No bills to speak of you, your bank account must be big enough to choke a horse by now, right?"

"Sure, yes, I can move out anytime, I just…"

"You just what, Benj?"

He nibbles his lower lip for a minute, glances over my shoulder then back to me again. "It sounds weird, her being so successful, looking so successful, putting ads in the paper in her fancy blue dress, sending out mailers here, there, and everywhere, all the deals she's making and talk about a bank account? But after what Dad did to her, the way she still raves about him, feels wounded and betrayed, I just feel like she's got these issues. Big ones," he adds, as if I don't already get it.

"Abandonment issues," I huff, knowing them all too well. "Tell me about it, Bud."

He nods almost excitedly. "Yes, exactly, and, well, independent as she is, and as constantly as she's always telling me to move on, move out, go to school, get a life, I'm not so sure she really means it, you know?"

I can see that. "I'm sure she sincerely wants that for you, Benjy, but also, maybe...doesn't as well. But that's not your fault. You can't stay just for that."

"No, obviously. I get it." He nods, pauses. Smiles wryly. "I know that. And I'm not alone, but also, I am, you know? It's like, we share the same house, but live separate lives. She's working 24/7, on the go, never sure when she's gonna be home, and I've got my schedule, and you, and pop in at home and crash there and then it's right back to the grind. And it works, for us. Dysfunctional as it sounds, and seems sometimes, I feel needed there and the thought of leaving is harder than the thought of staying. Does that make sense?"

I nod, surprised he's being so forthcoming. Here. Now. Maybe it's a holiday miracle after all. "It does, and I know she loves you. And needs you. And probably feels bad for needing you because, as a mother, I'm sure she wants you to have the freedom to make your own choices, too."

He nods. Glances somewhere just over my shoulder again. "She does. I know that, obviously. She's got her friends at work, her career she's so invested in, more money than she's ever had, than we've ever had, but ever since Dad left, I'm the only family she's got left, now."

I brush his shoulder gently with my hand. "I know you feel like the man of the house ever since your dad left, Benj, but in all that sometimes I think you forget that she's the only family you have left, too. Right? I mean, it's only natural you want to stay and protect her."

He nods and glances back my way wryly. "I know what you're thinking, Shay."

"Doubtful."

"You're thinking I'm sitting here, complaining about my own mom when...you know?"

I slug him playfully. "You mean, when my mom's off in California crashing with some aunt I've never met and probably won't send me a Christmas card this year either?"

I try to keep the bitterness out of my tone but can't help it. Muscle memory, I suppose. Try to think of the last time I spoke with my mom and struggle to come up with a date and a time, only an emotion. Mom, sounding vaguely drunk and thoroughly needy, asking how I'm doing and when I say "fine," just to make her feel better, her getting irritable and asking, "No, dear, how are you doing, financially speaking?"

I got the hint and asked her how much she needed. Insisted she didn't need any money but, if I was in the mood, could send her a few hundred for "incidentals." After that I changed my cell number and haven't heard from her since. Doubt she has the address for the new apartment, so doubt I'll be getting a card this year, for sure.

Wish I could say I miss her, and do, if strangers ask. But Benjy? He knows better. We both do.

He snorts shyly, probably regretting bringing the topic up in the first place. "Something like that, yeah."

"I'm happy you still have a mom to be close to, Benjy. I don't confuse your situation with mine. I've made peace with being on my own. With keeping the friends I have close and not making much effort to make new ones. And besides, I have my chosen family around, like you." I slug him again, trying to get the playful vibe back.

"I know, and that's nice, but real family is too, right?"

26

"Who says you're not my real family, bud? I mean, if you think about it, you probably know me way better than anyone actually related to me. Like, way more."

He nods and grins, easing his bike gently back as if we've already said too much. "Guess I could say the same about you, Shay."

"And Cara?" He's inching further back, wriggling his front tire playfully as if he wants to leave, but also maybe doesn't, too.

He chuckles, giving me a quick going away present. "Hell, I doubt that girl would know where I still work if I wasn't wearing my Pig-Out shirt whenever I *FaceTime* her!"

And then he's gone, leaving me standing there wondering what the hell *that's* supposed to mean. I watch him inch toward the middle of the street. Wait for him to turn around. Like he always does. Wave happily, like he's surprised I'm still watching. Like I always do. Watch him, actually, until he's turned up Palmetto Street toward home in the safe, cloistered suburbs on the other side of the street. Then he's gone and all that's left are the tattered surf stickers splattered over the street sign like shotgun pellets.

I sigh and grab the rustling plastic Pig-Out sack from my bike basket and open the pool gate, belly slightly aquiver in anticipation of the second part of my nightly ritual.

FIVE

SHAY

"Well, that was awkward."
I chuckle. Drift toward the shallow end of the pool where Hub Crawford leans, casually, hip deep in the tranquil, trickling water that laps at his narrow waist. His salt and pepper hair, surfer bro, tan skin and tattoo vibe fit the scene so perfectly he might as well be a pool accessory, like the "No Diving" sign screwed to the pool fence behind him or the big net affixed to the long blue pole just above it. "Yeah, it's been like that ever since Cara left for school in the fall."

He grins. Drinks me in like he always does, trying not to be obvious and failing miserably. It somehow manages to be more flattering than creepy, despite the obvious age difference between us. His eyes finally settle on the crinkly takeout sack in my hand. "I've noticed."

I sit on the edge of one of the deck chairs. Slip off my non-skid work shoes and stiff, sticky socks. Get back up and sink down onto the blue and pink tiles that surround the edge of the pool. Hand him the sack. Sink my feet in the shallow end while I watch his eyes light up at the bounty inside.

"For me?"

Snort. "You don't have to ask that every single time, bro."

He grins like he already knows that. "Sure, I do."

"No. You don't."

"What if one time it's not for me?"

I glance around the empty pool deck, silent save for our words and the gently lapping water. "Why would I ever want to bring takeout for anyone else?"

He frowns. Fiddles with the knot on the plastic bag. "Ever is a big word. Ever is a long time."

I groan. "Seriously, Hub, not tonight with the buddha zen bullshit philosophy bumper stickers, okay?"

He looks vaguely hurt. Or amused. Or surprised. Or just plain stoned. I can't really tell anymore. He's mostly always ever stoned so all his looks are vaguely stoned-ish so you can never really tell what he's thinking which is all part of the allure. If you can really call it that? I guess. I don't know. I always feel vaguely stoned when I'm around him. "Not tonight what?"

"I'm not up for a philosophical discussion right now."

"Time isn't philosophical. It's fictional."

I wag a warning finger, damp from the pool deck and my gently splashing feet. Scowl for emphasis. "That. Right there. Not doing it. Not having it. Not tonight."

He chuckles. The bag opens. The not entirely unpleasant odor of fried green beans fills the otherwise chlorinated air. "Oh. Wow." He opens the to-go box. Beams even more. "You've really outdone yourself tonight, Shay."

I snort, wriggling my sore, wrinkled toes in the cool,

tranquil water until they eventually plump up back to normal after being squished inside my boxy, non-slip shoes all night. "You say that every night."

He winks. "Well, not every night. You don't work every night. And you only bring me food on the nights you work, so…"

He sees the look on my face. Stops his rambling. Nods to the little cooler behind him. "Help yourself."

I reach for it eagerly. "Thought you'd never ask."

Inside is a smattering of random and assorted but all yummy tall boy cans. His favorite Angry Andy's Ciders and mine, Tempting Teas. It's a little tradeoff, barter, good neighbor thing we do where I bring him home food from work and he always has a few adult refreshments at the ready as we sit and unwind together in the soft, humid darkness after the rest of the world is silently sleeping. At 21, I could easily buy my own booze any day of the week, but free booze always just tastes better, I suppose.

I crack one open and feel the gently carbonated spray tickle my nose. Take a long, heady sip as the worries and the wants that usually accompany a ride home with Benjy begin to gently slither out of my brain. "Ah!"

He waves a long, battered green bean toward me. "At least have one."

I make a face. Give him a palms out "go away" gesture. "Trust me, I had plenty tonight."

He asks, "How come?" through a hefty mouthful.

"It was the nightly special and you think any of our fat ass redneck guests wanted something with a vegetable inside of it?"

He chuckles, taken by surprise, I suppose, with the vehemence of my reply. Though I don't know why. I sound like this every night and twice on Sunday. "You don't seem to think too highly of your clientele, Shay."

"No shit?" *See what I mean?*

He cocks one eyebrow in typical Hub lecture style. "I mean, work should be a happy place. If you don't like your guests—"

"Oh, like you love the customers at Thrifty Dollar?"

He visibly recoils. "What? Those assholes?"

We chuckle together, soft, and familiar in the deep dark of night. I sip my Tempting Tea and reach for a green bean when he's not looking. He catches me anyway. Winks. Hooks a greasy thumb back toward the bike rack. "So, what's going on with Benjy?"

I sigh. Wriggle my toes in the pool. Glance away. Up to my apartment door. Then over to his. The one right next door. He's still got a paper disjointed skeleton hanging on it from Halloween.

Lazy ass stoner.

He taps my knee with something cold. I glance down to find it's a fresh Angry Andy's can. Chuckle. I glance at the long, agile fingers clutching the can. Then quickly away before I can start to admire them. "So, spill the tea."

I shrug. "Nothing's going on with Benjy, I guess."

He nods. Sips gently, ripe lips on the top of the can. Soft, salt and pepper stubble around the lips. Waves his tall boy like a baton. "And that's the problem, huh?"

"I guess."

He grins. Pushes the laugh lines up around his gentle, tender hazel eyes. I press my toes against the side of his Hawaiian print baggies, feel the hard, firm man flesh of his hip just beneath. "What's so funny?"

"Oh, nothing. Just to be young and in love."

"Who said I'm in love?"

"You don't have to say shit, kid. It's written all over your face. Your posture. Your tone. The way you guys linger at the bike rack every night. The low, steady, familiar murmurs of two people who have quiet, private things to say to each other that just can't wait. The way he makes sure you're home safe before he leaves for the night. The way you watch until he pedals out of sight. Then watch for just a little longer, out in the middle of the street, as if he'll turn around and come back to you."

"That's not what he's doing."

"Making sure you're safe? Sure, he is."

I avoid his eyes and watch my feet trill around under the water, magnified beneath the surface so they look to be a boy's size 13. "I live on his way home. I'm a pit-stop. That's all." I glance up, to see if he's listening.

He looks vaguely dumbfounded above the lip of his tall, cheery red cider can. And not just in the usual stoner Hub dime store philosopher way. "You can't believe that, Shay. Please tell me you don't believe that. Please tell me you believe you're special enough for someone to make sure you get home safely every night."

I sigh. Slump a bit. Set my tall boy down on the pink square of pool tile by my side. Wriggle my toes in the soft, gently lapping water and try to ignore his hard, lean torso gently aglow from the shimmering pool light. "I guess I do. I just…it's easier to think otherwise."

He nods. "I can see that. But you'd still be lying to yourself."

I glance away again. It's late and I should be tired but instead it might as well be midday. It's always like that after work. After a ride home with Benjy. After a tall bright yellow can of spiked tea with Hub. He splashes me gently.

Wakes me out of my anxious reverie. "So, what are you going to do?"

"About what? Benjy?"

Nods. Then shakes his head. Covered in trendy salt and pepper stubble to match his gritty five o' clock shadow. I grin to myself. Benjy calls him the Silver Surfer and I have to admit, it's a pretty good nickname. "About being in love?"

I frown. "It's not love, exactly."

"No?"

"More like lust."

His turn to frown. Eyes smoky and judge-y like I just gave the wrong answer to a pop quiz only he knows the answers to. "Don't be like that, Shay."

"Like what?"

"Toss your feelings away like you just want to get laid."

I shake my head. "It's not like that. Exactly. Maybe I used the wrong word. I don't feel it in my pants as much as I feel it in my heart, you know?"

"Not really, no."

I sigh and try to explain. "It's more like...forbidden lust." His face still looks placid, gentle, and blank like the deep end of the pool. I can tell he's waiting for more. Might as well give it to him. "Like, I know I can never have him, so lately Benjy is all I want, you know? So, everything about him, every gesture, every word, is amplified because he's so high up there on my emotional radar."

Hub finally nods. Smiles. Leers is more like it. "I know that feeling very well, little girl." He lets that little cryptic tidbit hang soft and gentle in the air. Then: "But why can't you ever have him?"

I stare back, dumbfounded. "Cuz Cara, duh?"

Wrinkles his brow. "Cara. That's the brunette with the

tight little..." He nods toward the drippy wet pool tiles beneath my basic khaki work pants.

I chuckle. She does have a pretty nice badonkadonk. "Gross, but yeah."

"The one who went off to real college after getting her Associates degree here first?"

I'm vaguely impressed he's retained so much knowledge about our sordid love triangle from just our nightly sessions at the pool. "Uh huh."

He nibbles another fried green bean with his wet pool fingers. Then two or three more as he sorts things out in that always working noggin of his. "So, then, it was the three of you up until, what... fall? Of this year?"

I nod again. Sip my spiked tea. Grin to discover it's almost empty already. Set it down and lean back, soft and buzzed and chill under the sultry grey moonlight. Prop myself up on the pool deck with both hands while I gently kick my feet up and down beneath the water's surface. Watch him watching me. Wonder, not for the first time, what he sees when his eyes drift along my body like they do. Lazily. Curiously. Almost, clinically. Our eyes meet and, somehow, I'm the one who feels most embarrassed.

"So, everything was status quo until, say, August. The three of you hung out and you were fine being the third wheel. But now, a few months later, you and Benjy are suddenly, a couple."

I snort, surprised by his insightfulness. Maybe he's not *always* stoned after all. "Not exactly, but yeah. Sure."

He shakes his head as if arguing with himself. "I mean, I don't remember you and him riding home together until a few months ago, so...right?"

I do the mental math and nod with a reserved smile on

my face. I've never really thought of it that way before. He nods, too, as if agreeing with himself.

"So then, the dynamic has changed. From third-wheel, to friend zone, to couple who rides home and…"

"You could def say that."

"I know. I just did."

I let one of my feet escape the surface of the water and splash him playfully. He grins that cocky, older grin that makes me wish I was wearing a bikini. A really, really small one. I blush and move my can just out of reach, so I won't be tempted to finish it and maybe lose any more inhibitions than I already have. "Anyway, it's complicated."

"I imagine." He stands there, waist deep in the pool, torso lean, and glistening and smattered with tattoos both exotic and seemingly random at the same time. "So what's gonna happen when she comes home for Thanksgiving?"

I bite my tongue and look away again. Listen to the crinkling of water as he moves before I feel the gentle ripples along my shins. Glance back to see him tugging himself effortlessly out of the water and onto the damp pool tiles. Grin to see his lean, fit body before he catches me, the baggies slipping slowly down his narrow hips to reveal just a glimpse of soft white tan line glow beneath. His voice is husky and low and knowing. "See something you like, little girl?"

"Gross, Hub. Stop."

But it's too late. He knows. He's always known. Ever since I moved here in January. I guess we both have. Stands up in all his shimmering, glistening glory, hard and glinting and masculine. Offers me a hand up. I take it. Long, calloused fingers wrap themselves around mine. Tugs me to a standing position with little help from me.

We stand, face to face, features bathed in soft shadows

under the even softer moonlight. He's taller so I glance slightly upward. He winks. Shoves me playfully away, bare feet splattering on the wet pool deck. We chuckle, almost gratefully, as if relieved for a break in the not-so-subtle sexual tension. I try not to watch as he towels himself off with slow, sensuous motions.

He glances up after knotting a thin, ratty beach towel around his narrow waist. "You ready?"

SIX

SHAY

"Do you ever wear a shirt?"

He glances down at his bare torso. Hairless. Tan. Covered in a smattering of random, disjointed, sexy tattoos. Skulls next to butterflies. Hearts next to dolphins. Looks back up. Winks. "Not if I can help it."

We're outside my door. But it's like my ride home with Benjy. Neither of us seem in any big hurry to leave just yet. He leans with his back against the walkway railing, the pool area below still wet with our footprints. A hand on either side of him. Watches me watching him.

"Does it bother you, Shay? Me not wearing a shirt?"

I shrug. "Not particularly. Must be nice, is all."

"To what? Look this good?"

I snort with a jolt of unexpected laughter. "Okay, sure. I meant it must be nice to go topless all the time."

He grins sheepishly. Waves one of his hands at me. "By all means, be my guest!"

"You know what I mean, stoner."

"Hey man, listen. I wear my buttoned up green collar shirt all day at work. Mr. Assistant Manager, that's me when

I'm on the clock. But when I'm home, I'm home, you know?"

I hold my hands up in surrender. "I get it. Just sayin'."

He waves another hand at me. "Look at you, anyway. Khaki shorts and a t-shirt to work in. Must be nice."

"You act like you wear a suit and tie."

"Feels like one most of the time."

We both chuckle lazily. I finally slide my backpack off my shoulder. Fiddle with my keys. He still clings to the walkway railing across from my door. Watching me. Lingering. "Well?"

I pause. "Well, what?"

He grins. "Are you going inside or what?"

"What do you care?"

Grunts audibly. "I can't relax until you're in there safely."

"Since when?"

"Since you moved in, silly."

"Okay, and what if I let myself in, wait for your door to close and come back out and walk the streets all night? Hit up all the crack houses and tattoo parlors and opium dens in town. Then what?"

He waves his hand dismissively. "Well, that's on you. At least I've done my part."

I slip my key in the door. Twist the knob. Push it open. "Okay, well…"

"Was that so hard?"

"Kind of. I mean, with you watching and all…"

He waves a hand. Gently unfolds from his perch along the railing. The takeout bag wrinkles in his hand. "Well, goodnight."

"Waddya mean?"

"Waddya mean, what do I mean?"

"I'm gonna stand here until *you're* safe inside."

"How you gonna do that?"

I speak slower this time. "Stand here. Until you're. Safe. Inside. Your place. Now, go." Make little wave-y hands to indicate it's time for him to scoot his narrow little ass back over to his doorway.

Hub chuckles his dry, smoker's cough. Shuffles away in his flip flops. Glances back over his shoulder every few steps. It doesn't take him long to reach his door. They're not very big apartments, after all.

He waves. I wave back, but don't move. Rolls his eyes. Twists the doorknob, no key required. I'm not sure he's ever locked his door in the eleven months I've known him. "Night now."

"You too."

"Go in now."

"You first."

"Jesus. Every night with this, Shay?"

"Hey, you started it."

"You first. That's the rule."

I give in. But only because I'm finally tired. At least, a little bit. "Okay, but knock when you get in, okay?"

Rolls his eyes but nods just the same. "Jesus. Fine. Yes. Goodnight, kiddo."

I give a little wave. Our eyes meet one last time. I smile. Softly. He nods again. Gently this time. No more cocky, blustery bullshit. I nod back and quietly disappear. Shut the door behind me. Listen to my heart pounding in the dark stillness of my tidy little studio apartment. Leave the lights off as I drift down the hall toward the bedroom.

Lean against the wall until I hear his soft, tentative knock on the other side of the thin wall. Smile. Blush. Knock back. Linger, as if something else might happen.

But, of course, it never does.

SEVEN

BENJY

"You're home early."

I slide a greasy bag of takeout onto the kitchen counter and smirk. "You're up late."

Mom smirks back, smooth, ebony cheeks easing her fashionable glasses up her face until she looks like a mad librarian in the midst of a book buying binge. "Big contract tomorrow," she sighs, taking off her reading glasses and waving them at the laptop screen atop the kitchen counter. "Just dotting my 'i's' and crossing my 't's' before the closing, you know?"

I glance at the glowing digital numbers above the stainless-steel oven. "At one in the AM?"

She huffs, reaching for her "Boss Bitch" coffee mug and swilling a fresh swig of her favorite Caramel Mocha blend despite the late hour. "Hey, Junior Agent here. I gotta work twice as hard as the other agents in my office just to keep up."

I glance around the house, the living room still in the midst of a recent upgrade with hardwood floors replacing the old slate tile, a splurge after her last "big contract". The kitchen appliances, all sleek and new now, were another splurge. After another contract. Beyond the new living room furniture set, out past the hurricane proof sliding glass doors, the backyard is still torn up with the new pool being built.

Another upgrade, another big contract.

"Any more big contracts, Mom, and we're gonna have to move to a bigger house."

Mom snorts, her chiseled face a vague mask of pride despite the almost humble shrug. Then our eyes meet, and she delivers the inevitable zing. "Well, someone has to make an honest living around here. Not like your father's sending any child support checks this year."

I lean back against the kitchen counter across from her, despite wanting to be anywhere—literally, anywhere—else at that moment. Mom good. Dad bad. I get it, I get it. "I mean, I'll be 22 next month, Mom. Child support ended four years ago-ish?"

Mom waves her reading glasses, looking regal with her salt and pepper hair and cloaked in a rich burgundy robe that could double as a ball gown should she get a last-minute invite to Cinderella's castle. "Yeah, and I'm still waiting for the court to approve my request for back child support, so don't count it out just yet."

I shake my head and reach in the fridge for a can of flavored seltzer, no caffeine, no calories and just as much taste. Still, it will give me something to do with my hands other than clench and unclench my fists. "I'm not a kid anymore, Mom," I remind her for the umpteenth time. I mean, we've had this same discussion so many times by now, I could literally do this on autopilot. "And you haven't been married since I *was* a kid, so…"

She looks at me blankly over the laptop cover, wearing a leopard print skin, her favorite. "So? Your point is?"

I groan on the inside, wishing for all the world I'd followed Shay into her pool area after riding home together from work, even if it did mean being the third-wheel while she flirted with her lean, sexy, rugged silver fox of a neighbor. Better to be a third wheel in an awkward sex sandwich than stir up old memories with dear old mom.

Again.

"My point is, look at you now." I wave the bubbly pink seltzer can around the recently refurbished kitchen to the rest of the house, as stylish and sleek and modern as anything she was selling these days. "You divorced that philandering bum before it was too late, went to real-estate school, got your license, worked your way up in your new firm and now you're on the Sales Leader Board more times than not every month. What more do you want from him?"

"What he owes me, for starters," she huffs, slamming the laptop shut without even realizing she's doing it, probably. It's her version of a mic drop, I suppose, even though the audience she really wants to hear it, Dad, is half a world away by now. "Not just child support, but the years he insisted I stay at home, being a housewife instead of out there, in the real world, following my true passion."

"Selling other people's houses is your true passion?"

She smirks suddenly, just shy of laughing. Despite living together, Mom and I don't have the best of relationships. It doesn't help matters much that I vaguely, kinda sorta resemble my dad, save for his "lily white skin," of course. Her words, not mine. Or that my trying to support Mom often sounds, to her anyway, like I'm sticking up for him.

"Making money is my passion," she admits, hitting closer

to the truth. "Growing a big bankroll, is my passion. Retiring early, seeing you in your own career and then traveling the globe without a care in the world? *That's* my passion. And the years I sat at home, wasting my full potential while your father pursued his, have kept me from doing that."

"Until now," I remind her, almost on repeat. "And look at you now, making up for lost time, burning up that midnight oil while what? Dad's on his third marriage? Fourth?"

"Try fifth," she harumphs, waving her stylish purple glasses at the closed laptop as if perhaps Dad is in there somewhere, cozying up with his latest family. "He just announced it on Facebook."

"Gross," I chuckle, glancing wistfully at the rented post digger the workmen had left in the backyard after that day's labor. Beyond the sliding glass door and pale moonlight that hovers over the yard, I try to picture my father as best I can. Big, burly guy, from the pictures I've seen, that is. Curly blond hair, fond of pinky rings and big gold coins dangling from his neck. He split the scene when I was just a tyke, seven or eight years old. The details are murky, but that's about when the pictures of us together stopped being taken. Mom divorced him a year or so later, officially, though they'd been cold and distant for years before then thanks to his numerous affairs with coworkers and employees at his successful construction business.

Why she'd married him in the first place I have no clue, especially considering the way I see her now. Elegant and sassy and dignified and owning her future, with her hip, trendy glasses and funky laptop and can-do attitude.

Now, if only I'd inherited a little of that...

Mom sees my slack jaw and momentary trip down

Memory Lane and sighs over her coffee mug. "You're right, though. We're better off without him, anyway."

I nod. "Do you think, if you were still together, you'd be doing all this? Selling houses? Getting your realtors license? Making bank this way?"

Mom snorts, a deep and rich sound to match her growing bank account. "Hardly, I'd probably still be running around, barefoot and pregnant, the way he wanted me to be."

I snort, trying to picture it. Mom in a tiger print maternity dress, and me with yet another brother or sister on the way. "So, no regrets?"

She shakes her head right away, then looks me up and down. I follow her gaze, eyes scanning my faded Pig Out work shirt, lame khaki shorts, sagging tube socks and barbecue sauce-stained nonskid work shoes. "Well, I do wish you had a male role model around to help, uh, inspire you from time to time."

"What? I'm not manly enough for you?" I flex a muscle or two for emphasis, knowing exactly what she means—and where she's headed—and desperate to avoid it all costs.

"You know what I mean, Benjy. I just, you seem so aimless lately. Crashing here when all your friends are off at school. No plans or even ideas for the future. And that job? You know I want more for you than that, right?"

I groan, sipping my soda absently just so I won't throw it across the room. "Mom, I'm fine. It's just a gap year, that's all."

She snorts, adding a little "harumph" in for good measure as she wriggles impatiently atop her barstool, no doubt itching to be rid of her good for nothing son and back to banking a fresh, fat fee on her next house contract. "A gap year is one year, Benj. You're, what, three years graduated now? That's gap *years*, plural, and if you were at least taking a class or two, well…"

"I tried that, Mom, remember? When Cara first started at Crescent Community College. I just, it wasn't for me."

"But why not, Benjy? You're a smart boy, God knows you work hard, I just don't get it."

I sigh and toss my empty can in the trash by the sink. Stand up a little straighter and shrug. "I do work hard, Mom. I'm grinding, saving, doing what I'm doing. For now. When I'm ready, I'll move on. Or not. Or move up. Or not. I just…I'm off the streets, I don't drink too much or smoke, do drugs, I'm not hurting anyone, isn't that good enough?"

Mom sighs, opening her laptop back up as if she's wasted enough time on me for now. "For now, I suppose, but not forever, okay?"

I smirk, seeing my out. "Why not?" I chuckle, inching away from Mom's workstation and closer to the hallway that leads to my room and, for the first time since I started my night shift, blissed out peace and quiet. "When you close this contract out tomorrow, just add on another wing. Or a second story. That way, you'll never even know I'm here!"

I hear her laughing, a bittersweet, almost harsh sound, all the way down the back hallway. Wishing I could laugh as well. Wishing I was as ambitious as she was, with a purpose and a passion, even if it *was* just making money. But honestly? All I want to do is chill and hang. With Shay, in particular.

Is that so bad?

EIGHT

SHAY

"Hey girl!" I force a bright smile despite the late hour.

Cara waves from deep inside her dorm room. It's predictably chic, little strings of fairy lights softly glowing around the retro hip pastel rainbow tapestry hanging above her single bed. The single bed with throw pillows galore. Round ones and square ones and long ones and short ones. Some with tassels aplenty, some without any at all. Red ones and purple ones and orange ones and blue ones. Striped ones and solid colors and off-white ones with cringe-worthy sayings:

"No bad days."

"Totally blessed."

"You've got this."

"Boss bitch."

She beams at me. "What's up, Chica?"

Even at just past midnight she's still effortlessly beautiful with her straight black Cleopatra hair and soft green fluttery eyes with the smoky eyeliner to match. Radiant bronze skin glows even though I can tell she's already removed her makeup. She's in a forest green t-shirt two sizes two big, the kind that hits her right at mid-thigh and even then, will drift up to reveal the small boy-cut panties she favors. The words "Florida Southern University" spell out in gold block letters across her stylishly small cleavage. She could be a live cam girl if she'd just loosen up a bit.

She's sipping wine from a stemless glass she puts back on the desk under her window. There's a trio of books by her laptop. *Intro to Architecture. Architecture for Beginners. The Study of Design.* They're stacked and fanned out just so, like window dressing to match the rest of her Insta-worthy dorm room. She's got the smart girl chic, sexy librarian, bookworm aesthetic down pat. Then again, she always has. "Just getting home, Shay?"

"Yeah." I take a sip from the cheap can of beer I've just opened, the yin to her yang. Or is it, the yang to her yin? I'm not really thirsty, but it's habit when Face-Timing my bestie. I suppose it's my own carefully cultivated aesthetic: celibate, white trash, tomboy, waitress, nun.

She stretches. Lithe and limber and lean. The t-shirt inches up her thighs a bit. Shows a flash of tan lines and light blue cotton panties. I wonder if she owns any other color. Wonder, too, what she wears when she FaceTimes old Benjy. Scrub the thought away quickly. "How was work tonight?"

"Lonely without you there." Hub wasn't kidding about us being the *Three Musketeers*. Once upon a time, when Cara had worked with Benjy and me at Pig-Out, she'd been a hoot. Still flawless, still carefully manicured, still chilly and aloof, but funny and slick and sly in her own way. I thought it would always stay that way. That her promises of going off to a "real" school after getting her AA at the local community college would someday just evaporate like Benjy's and mine had. Instead, she'd made good on her promise and left us both stranded there, in our faded ball caps, dishing out pulled pork and vinegar slaw for the rest of our lives, probably. "I miss you."

Cara rolls her eyes predictably at the compliment. Loves to be flattered but doesn't like to *look* like she loves to be flattered. "You're sweet. You always say that."

I do always say it and it's mostly true. Time has been better to our friendship, I think, than it has to Cara and Benjy's relationship. For me, I can remember all the good times with Cara from back in the day: inside jokes and commiseration, switching shifts and the unsaid words about our classmates and, later, coworkers that always made us laugh. Distance has erased the catty way she could sometimes act, petty and jealous and vaguely conniving and low key diva-ish. In short, I don't mind being her long-distance friend.

In fact, in some ways, I even prefer it.

"I'm not sweet and I mean it. These other chicks are boring *AF*. Wouldn't know your personal brand of snark if it bit them in the ass. Anyway, how was *your* day?"

She yawns. "Long, girl. I just got back from study group."

"Really?" She must see my surprised face.

Frowns. Soft, maroon lips under a pert nose. Suddenly, irrationally defensive. "Yeah really. Why do you say it like that?"

Shrug. Sip. Give myself a chance to count to ten before responding. It's something I learned to do with irate tables at work. "Nothing, it's just...I don't remember you being this studious...in high school."

She lets down her guard a little. Even offers a wry, smoky little smile. "Cuz high school sucked, that's why. It's way different when you're actually interested in something you want to do for the rest of your life."

I nod diplomatically. Try not to bristle at her lecturing tone. She can sell that shit to some of her new college friends but I'm the one she cheated off every Algebra test senior year and we both know it.

Plus, there's always a dose of "not that you'd understand my enthusiasm for college being a head server at a barbecue joint for the rest of your miserable, pathetic life probably," layered on top of her responses like a coat of oil on old, stale water. So maybe I haven't figured out what I want to do with my life yet. Maybe I will finally give in to my manager's request to join the corporate team at some point. I'll decide when I decide, right? I mean, it's my business, not predictably perfect Cara's. "Yeah, I bet."

She brightens and turns on the charm. She always does that when she knows she's being a tad catty. "Anyway, how's my Benjy doing?"

My? Benjy? She's never quite put it like that before. I keep the smile fixed on good and tight to hide my own sudden flare of defensiveness. Like, what? Does she already know about me and Benjy? Is she hinting around at how much time we've been spending together lately? Does she know how long we stretch out those nightly bike rides home? Or am I just being paranoid? I keep it short, sweet and to the point, as if answering questions from a really good lawyer on the stand. "Good. We rode home together after work."

"That's sweet." She sounds distracted, suddenly. I can see the phone wiggle and blur as she stands abruptly and starts to pace around the room. It shifts downward slightly and comes back into focus just in time to give me a glimpse of the thin pink socks on her feet.

I keep going. I mean, she asked, right? "Yeah, he couldn't quite wrap his head around Treesgiving."

She pauses just enough to snort. "You're still on about that bullshit?"

"It's not bullshit."

"Of course he doesn't get it, Shay. No one gets that made up holiday of yours."

I chuckle at her vehemence and put down my beer to lean into this situation a little bit harder. She always *was* fun to piss off. "All holidays are made up, just so we're clear on the issue."

The phone cuts back to her face just in time for some major eye roll action. I smile and remember how much fun it was to work with her. "Okay, Buddha. I can tell you've been hanging out with that silver fox next door again."

I ignore the taunt, even as I realize the comment *did* sound vaguely Hub-like. "Anyway, you're still coming home, right? For Thanksgiving?"

She makes that face again. The impatient, noncommittal one she's been making all week. "I dunno, Shay. I'm trying, okay?"

"Well, I don't understand. Trying *how*, exactly? I mean, you've got the long weekend off, right?"

Gives me another one of her patented "God, you're such a dumb townie" faces. "From classes, yeah. But not my study group. Or my tutors. And I've got a big paper due the week I get back that I haven't even started, so... I'm just wondering if it's worth driving all the way there for a day or two just to turn around and come straight back to this giant pile of work that's waiting on me." She wiggles the phone to wave it at the stack of carefully curated Architecture books, as if I haven't already gotten the point.

I lean back against the kitchen counter. Sip my beer.

Scold her with my eyes, not that she'd notice. Cluck my tongue nice and loud before I reply with an icy tone. "Have you told Benjy yet?"

She out ices me, ten to one. Then again, she always could. "No, and don't you either. It's not definite. I'm still weighing my options. The pros and cons, you know?" She says it like she's pretty sure I don't even know what pros and cons mean.

I bite my lip and count to ten before I sound too pissy. Realize it doesn't help all that much. "Well, he's kind of counting on it."

She rolls her eyes. Her voice is unrepentant, to match her bristly body language and flat, dull shark eyes. "He's a big boy, Shay. He'll get over it." Her voice is suddenly cold, the way it always gets when she's made up her mind and expects the rest of us to just deal.

I take another sip. "Okay, well, you're a big girl and it's only right to communicate with *your* boy, right?"

Her sudden bark of laughter is humorless. "Oh, you're giving me relationship advice now?"

I give her a look. Because throw pillows not withstanding, she's not the only "boss bitch" in the conversation, if you know what I mean. "I mean, if it's gonna help you get home for Thanksgiving, yeah. I guess so."

"That's rich."

"What's rich?"

"When's the last time you even had a boyfriend, Shay? Prom? Junior year?"

"What does that have to do with anything?"

"Nothing, it's just...back off a little, okay? You have no idea the kind of pressure I'm under here."

I hold the phone low enough, so she doesn't see me roll my eyes. I mean, I get it, okay? It's college. But not quite

Harvard, you know? And architecture? Really? Get out of here with that fake diploma mill bullshit already. The only buildings Cara ever wanted to design were shopping malls, anyway.

"Okay, okay..." I mumble just to keep the peace. "Just think about it, okay?"

"Like I'm not already?"

I take a long sip from my beer. It's almost empty and I'm not having another one. Even if there was another one left in the fridge. Which there isn't. Even though it would be kind of nice. But no. Not tonight. "I said okay, Cara. We just miss you, okay?"

She pauses. Sips her wine. Lets me stew. "That's sweet. I miss you, too, boo."

There is a soft knocking at her door. I'm almost relieved. Cara makes a face. Not startled, exactly. Not annoyed, either. I can't quite put my finger on this particular face. It's new to me. Secretive? Guarded? Aloof? "Shit, my pizza's here. I gotta go, ho."

Hold up now. Cara? 'No Carbs' Cara? Eating pizza? After midnight? That must have been *some* study group. I tease her only because I know she's desperate to get rid of me and it's fun to dance right to the edge of her patience— and then stick around and swirl a little more, until she's really good and ticked off. "Yum. Stay on the call and I'll pretend to eat it with you."

Her smile is warm but vague. And fixed. And sticky and sweet and all kinds of insincere. "Naw, it's getting late. I've got class in the morning, so..."

I take the hint. Stifle a yawn myself. Even if I'm not all that tired. "No worries. Check in soon, okay?"

She's doubly impatient now. Drifting toward the door as the details of her room blur and come into focus, then blur again. A black and white poster of Manhattan's skyline here. More books stacked high on a desktop shelf. A dorm fridge with magnets from all over the world, even though she's a half-townie just like me and hasn't been anywhere except maybe to a concert in Orlando. She's still talking to me, but I can hear her voice already fading as she moves the phone away from her lips. "Sure will, babe. Ciao!"

She raises the phone one last time to blow an air kiss. Blurry and creamy and pink. Our customary sendoff. Goes to hang up but there's a pause first. Just a brief one. I can tell she's doing two things at once and just forgot to hit "end" on my thing before she started in on her new thing.

The phone's still in her hand. Pointed at the floor as she opens the door. Blurry as it shifts. Then clears up for just a second or two. I see light from the hallway outside invade the quiet, dimly lit space of her immaculately chic dorm room. Suddenly remember there's a whole ass university just outside her door.

See a pair of shoes inch from the hallway just inside. Guy's shoes. Clean deck shoes, not grungy sneakers with one lace untied, like a pizza guy's might be. Like mine are, frankly, by the end of most shifts. And…does the pizza guy need to come inside? Like, he doesn't just take one step forward to hand off the pizza. Oh no, he takes several, until the door is wide open and he's there, in her space, clean deck shoes and no socks?

I mean, I've never been to college, not even to visit, but are things really *that* different? Do the pizza guys run around in deck shoes and no socks, sauntering their frat boy asses into your domicile while you hold the door wide open for them? Has she never seen an episode of *Cold Case Files*? *Forensic Finds*? *Crime Diaries*? *The Killer at My Door*? I stand there, studying every frame of the scene in the left-on phone screen, like I'm staring at the opening scene of one of those cheesy scary found footage movies.

It all happens very quickly, like milliseconds. I keep hyper-studying each frame of the interaction like a fly on the wall. It's such a bizarre, quick, familiar, almost intimate exchange, like it's not the first time it's happened.

At all.

And then, just before the quick bleep of her phone finally disconnecting, Cara's syrupy, come-hither voice murmuring in the same way she always used to when seeing Benjy between classes at school. "Hey babe, what took you so long?"

NINE

SHAY

"You're up early."

"Am I?"

Hub makes a face. "And already ornery, I see."

I chuckle despite myself. Stupid Hub and his stupid observational expertise. I guess I am a little salty. Seeing your BFF greet the pizza guy like she's starring in soft core porn right before bed will do that to a person, I suppose.

I paddle closer, offering an apologetic half-smile along the way. The November water is cool but not cold on my mostly bare skin. Sit up on my surfboard when I reach him. He's wet and glistening in the early morning sun. I guess I am, too. Is that why he's looking at me that way?

Is he even really looking at me that way?

"I'm not ornery. I just didn't sleep well."

"Yeah, me either. Maybe Cool Beanz after for a little caffeine jolt?"

I grin. He couldn't have said anything sexier if he'd tried. "I could be enticed."

Then he goes and gets even sexier. "Black coffee? Iced?"

I sigh as if reminiscing about some big romantic blind

date or something. Literally lick my lips, already salty from the gentle sea breeze that bathes us in its unseasonably warm embrace. "Maybe share one of their big ass cinnamon buns?"

His grin tops mine. "Now you're talking. We could split an order of breakfast sliders, too. A little savory with our sweet?"

I slap the pebbly top of my waxy pink board, sending a smattering of saltwater droplets all over my thighs. "Shit, bro. Why even bother surfing?"

He chuckles. "Well, we're already out here, so…"

I sigh like maybe he just stood me up. "I guess you're right."

Still, neither of us makes a move to catch the next wave. Or the next. Or even the one after that. We just kind of bob there, straddling our boards, riding the gentle swells of another slow, breezy, easy morning in Crescent Beach.

"How come you didn't sleep well?" His voice is low, soft, understanding, and curious. Sincerely, organically curious. Like he actually gives a shit. And I wonder, not for the first time, why? Why does he care so much when, after all, we're just neighbors?

And why do I care that he cares so much? I mean, sure, my dad wasn't around much even before he left us, and could have cared less when he *was* around, but…still? Am I searching for a father figure in Hub? Is that why his counsel is so important to me? Is that why I listen so carefully to him, even when I'm pretending to really care less?

Or is that whole "daddy" thing too ick to think about? Yes, actually, it is.

I glance away from ogling the mermaid tat on his forearm. Blink saltwater out of my eyes. "Huh?"

He slows down his speech. Enunciates carefully. "Why didn't you sleep well last night, Shay?"

"I stupidly Face-Timed with my best friend last night and—"

"What's that?"

I frown. "What's what?"

"Face rhyme."

I snort a little. "Face Time?"

"Yeah. That."

"Seriously?"

He looks, in fact, quite serious. "Did I stutter?"

"It's just like using your phone as a video conference. You know? When you call someone? You can see them. They can see you."

"Gross." He makes a face like something wet and scaly just slithered along the bottom of his bare foot. "Why?"

"Why what?"

"Why do you need all that noise?"

"Just… I haven't seen her since last week. It's nice to see her face from time to time. We always call on Sundays, so…"

Shrugs. Broad, muscular shoulders. Tan and lean. "I guess. Still…"

"You've never done it?"

Another visible recoil. "God, no! Why would I?"

"Just…there's no one you want to catch up with? See in person?"

"Maybe. I just… I wouldn't know where to look."

I chuckle. For a smart guy, he says the dumbest things sometimes. "You look at their face. That's why it's called Face. Time. Get it?"

He splashes me gently. Big hands in the water. Water dappling on my bare thighs, warm and smooth, as if it's an extension of those big, manly hands. We both watch it dribble and drip back onto my board. "Yeah, I get it, smartass. I just…it seems awkward, you know?"

"No. I don't. More awkward than this dumbass conversation?"

He looks vaguely offended, even as he chuckles dryly at himself. "Well, this isn't awkward at all. We know each other."

"Well, you wouldn't do it with a stranger, you know? You'd have to have their number anyway…"

He shakes his head. "Can we talk about something else? This is making me anxious."

I can barely stop laughing, shaking to and fro, on my wobbly surfboard as my thighs clench to keep my balance. My belly hurts by the time I can catch my breath. "What? Why?"

"I dunno. It just is."

"Okay. Sorry." I wait. Splash him back. Wink. "I mean, you do have a cell phone, right?"

Splashes me back. "Very funny, smartass."

"Just sayin'. This isn't like science fiction. It's actually a simple piece of technology folks use every day, so…"

I watch him tense and lean into his board. Paddle and pop and catch the next wave. Effortlessly. Without a word or a grunt or so much as a glance back in my direction. I shrug and follow suit, not quite as effortlessly, but still managing to zoom by as he paddles back out.

We go on like that, surfing, and paddling, paddling, and surfing, until I've finally had enough and ride my last wave almost to the shore. Step off into the froth and stand, board in hand, watching him glide atop one last, choppy wave as if he made some kind of bargain with Neptune to be able to surf that well.

TEN

SHAY

I savor the first sip of black, cold, just bitter enough iced coffee. Let my eyes roll back into my skull and murmur through a vaguely erotic wave of shivers that echo all the way through my toes and back. "The. Best."

Hub nods, eyes vaguely fluttery like maybe he's making an O-face of his own. Even his voice is soft and low to respect the moment. "Right?"

I wriggle back into the soft cushion on the seat behind me. Glance out the window at the waves below our favorite corner booth. Nod. "Were they that small when we were down there?"

"How do you think you caught so many?"

I ignore his wheezy laughter at his own joke. Offer up a little sarcasm of my own. "I guess cuz I had such a great teacher?"

He nods. Follows my glance out the window at the cresting of a newly formed wave. We both watch it swell, riderless, before fizzling out on the shore.

Glance back at each other instinctively. "You've gotten really good, Shay."

My eyes bulge at the unprecedented, no BS compliment. "I have?"

He turns his soft, blue-eyed gaze at me. Frowns. "Yeah, really good at avoiding my question. So, I'll ask it again. Slower this time, for the folks in the back: Why? Didn't? You? Sleep? Well? Last? Night?"

I chuckle. I'd almost, *almost* forgotten all about that. Hub clearly hasn't. "You sure are persistent."

"Only with people I care about."

I cock my head. Give him puppy dog eyes. "Awwww…"

"Quit avoiding my question with your cuteness."

I slump a little. Wriggle deeper into my favorite beach hoodie. Glance around at the eccentric accents of our favorite cozy little bakery-slash-cafe-slash-coffee shack right next door to our beloved 9th Street beach access. The ancient surfboards hanging overhead. Hardwood floors shiny and scuffed down below. The whole retro rainbow and tie dye aesthetic writ large upon every available inch of wall space. The local artists' paintings of coconuts and sunglasses and waves and surfers and sunsets and surfers in sunsets and pineapples riding waves while wearing sunglasses.

Pick up one of the painted rocks on the windowsill. Look at it closely. It's a rainbow. With a face. Put it back on the sill next to the others. Sigh. Cross my arms. Stare back at him. He's still waiting. Watching me, curiously. "I'm not going anywhere, kid."

I chuckle. "Promise not to tell anyone?"

He glances around as if to signify his innately hermit nature. "Like who? The rocks on the windowsill?"

As if on cue, the comely waitress with the big jugs and creamy lipstick reappears with our giant cinnamon bun and buffalo breakfast sliders. "Here you go, Hub!"

He blushes like a teen on prom night. Thanks her with a

catch in his voice. She winks like it's a form of punctuation and sashays away in her super short shorts and pale, cheeky badonkadonk. We both watch her because, geez. How can you not? I nod at a particular region of her gluteus maximus. "Is that a butterfly tattoo on her left cheek?"

He frowns. Really mulls it over. Starts narrating it like a nature documentary. "It's a tiger, Shay. See? You're seeing its paw under the fringes of her short-shorts, and I could see how it might look like a butterfly at first glance, but there's more above that."

"Wow." I sit there, dumbfounded at his cluelessness.

"What?"

"I just... I mean...wow."

"Hey man, men have needs, you know?"

"Do they? I never knew..."

"Don't get distracted."

"By what? Our waitress, who you've clearly slept with. Or the six other servers in here you've probably also slept with."

"Who says I slept with her? Maybe I just ran into her on the beach one day and she was wearing a bikini."

"And what? You put your conversation on hold just long enough to bend her over your knee, whip the magnifying glass out of your baggies and do a real close-up study of the tiger tattoo on her left ass cheek?"

He chuckles. "Anyway, we didn't sleep together."

"You're right. Not a lot of sleeping went on, that's for sure." When he arches one eyebrow, I remind him. "Our walls are thin, remember? I'd recognize her husky voice anywhere. That, and the particular way she kind of oozes your name."

He rolls his eyes. But stops denying anything. Looks back out the window. Picks up the same rainbow rock absently. Sets it back down without really looking at it, the same way I had only moments earlier. "Christmas is coming, Shay. Remind me to get you some good headphones."

"Or just invest in a muzzle."

He winks and gives a little wriggle over there on his side of the booth. "Don't threaten me with a good time."

I tear off a wedge of the giant cinnamon bun. Nibble it to wash the taste of gag out of my throat. "Gross."

He looks surprised. Pinches off an edge for himself. Tastes it. Licks his fingers. "Really? I thought this was your favorite."

"The cinnamon bun is. Your frat boy behavior isn't."

He chuckles. Nibbles another wedge. "We can work on me some other time. Today is about you and why you're so tired and grumpy from lack of sleep!"

I glance away. Reach for the painted rock again. Hold it up to the light and savor the multi-colors of its painted rainbow. Wonder who painted it and brought it in to sit on the ledge for me to examine and why.

He interrupts my reverie once more. "And before you ask, no, I won't tell anyone. Not even tiger tattoo butt!"

ELEVEN

SHAY

I hold up my hands in surrender. "You win."

Hub nibbles a buffalo breakfast slider. Mini buffalo chicken breakfast patties between mini honey buttered biscuits. A miniature slice of cold, savory dill pickle on top of each. "So? Spill?"

"It's just, while I was talking to Cara last night, she was hanging up and, well, I think she's cheating on Benjy."

He frowns. Skeptical. "Think she's cheating? Or hope she's cheating?"

"Hub!"

"Just sayin'."

"What, exactly, are you just saying?"

"That if she were cheating, you wouldn't feel so bad about lusting over her boyfriend all day and all night."

I frown. Slump. Cross, then uncross my arms over the letters that spell out "B-E-A-C-H" on the front of my favorite cozy hoodie. "Lust still isn't the word I'd use."

He considers this. Nods. "True, he's more of a boy next door type."

ALEX WINTERS

I nod. A little too eagerly. A little too long. Then stop to make sure we're talking about the same thing. "Wait, what does that mean again?"

He frowns. "Shit, I dunno. You weren't supposed to ask me that. You were just supposed to go with it and think I'm all wise and stuff."

"I mean, I think I know, it's just…"

"It's kind of like a guy you hang out with, who should be Mr. Right. Looks good on paper, you know, but he's not the guy you want to leave the party with at the end of the night, you know?"

I grin. "I mean, you live next door and that doesn't sound like you, Hub. Not at all."

"It's not literally the guy next door, dope."

I frown. "That doesn't really describe Benjy, either."

He seems surprised. "No?"

"Not really, because I usually *do* want to leave the party with him."

He gives me a curious look, like maybe he wasn't expecting to hear that. Then he nudges my bare feet with his own underneath the table. His toes are sandy. So are mine. The friction is noticeable. "Okay, well, whatever Benjy is or isn't to you, let's quit beating around the bush. What, exactly, makes you think his girlfriend's cheating on him?"

I tell him. All of it. The fake pizza guy. The nice shoes. The no socks. The several entitled steps inside the door, like maybe he's been there before. The familiar greeting. The husky voiced, comely, even sultry "hey babe" there just at the end.

He frowns progressively until I finally wind down. "Hmmmmm…"

"Hmmmmm, what?"

"That's weird. I mean, why would the pizza guy come all the way in?"

"Right?" I nod. Shrug. Nibble. Listen.

"I mean, when I went to school, if we ordered a pizza from our dorm room, we had to meet the guy out in the lobby, you know, Shay?"

"You went to college?"

"Don't sound so surprised."

"Why? I mean, I am. Surprised, that is. Not because you're dumb, just because it seems like college would be too much time spent with *the man*, is all."

Hub shrugs. "It was, but I went anyway. For a spell."

"So how, exactly, did they deliver pizzas back then? By dinosaur? In stone boxes?"

He chortles despite himself. "Very funny. Did you call her on it?"

"No, she was hanging up, remember?"

"Okay, sure, but...today at all? Obviously, you lost sleep over it, right?"

"I don't want to get into it with her, you know? She'll just deny it and call me paranoid and she's a really good arguer. Like, I've never won an argument with her. Ever. Even when I knew 1,000% that I was right. She just wears you down with pure animosity until you finally just give up."

"I've known some folks like that." He nods thoughtfully, like maybe he's thinking of a few of them at the moment. Takes a thoughtful, almost pensive sip of his iced coffee. Glances back over at me. Arches one salt and pepper eyebrow. "What about Benjy?"

"What about him?"

"Are you gonna tell him?"

"Not if I can help it."

He looks genuinely surprised. "Really?"

"I want to. Don't get me wrong. But what if he thinks I'm just lying to make them break up?"

He nods, very sage like. "Good point."

"And what if she's not cheating? What if some pizza guys make really, really personal, familiar deliveries at Southern State University, you know?"

"Better point."

He nibbles a miniature pickle slice absently. Glances out the window, jaw vaguely clenched even after he's swallowed. I nudge his feet again, savoring the sandy scrape of skin on skin. He seems surprised I'm still there. "What's going on up there, Hub?"

"I'm just, I mean what if she...? Maybe I'm being dramatic, but she seems like a smart girl. From everything you've told me about her, anyway. And at least as good with technology as you are, right?"

"Yeah, so?"

He turns his full attention back to me for a change. "I mean, what if she didn't hang up on purpose? What if she *knew* the phone was still on and opened the door anyway? What if she let you see all that, hear all that, just to mess with you?"

I frown. Slump a little against the back of my booth. The lack of sleep is getting to me, all of a sudden. Or maybe it's just the sudden infusion of unwanted, unneeded drama in my life. This right here is half the reason I don't have a boyfriend in the first place. "I wish I could say I hadn't thought of that, too."

"Maybe she is slutting around and you weren't getting the hint fast enough, so she expedited things a little last night. Figures you'll give in to temptation and tell Benjy and he'll break up with her before she has to break up with him."

I frown, not that all of that hasn't already occurred to me at four in the morning last night. "Seems like a lot of work when she could just pick up the phone, you know?"

"Some people are just chickenshits, you know? It's more work to confront and do it herself than to choreograph some pizza guy stunt with her FaceRhyme app open and let you do the dirty work for her."

"I dunno, man. Cara's pretty slick, but that's pretty ambitious, even for her."

"People get real ambitious to get out of work, let me tell you what..."

Tiger Butt appears out of nowhere just then. I'm almost grateful for the interruption at this point. Even though, now all I can do is picture her in Hub's bed, sleek and sexy and frisky, tan lines and cheap lipstick writhing around in his clean white sheets. Her whole body oozes "I'm available" with every syllable as she purrs, "Anything else I can get you guys?"

I can't help but cluck my tongue. Oh, so now it's "guys" all of a sudden? The whole time she's been acting as if Hub's at the table all by his lonesome, and even as she says it her back's kind of to me. And while she's being rude with her rude ass, I can't help but glance down at her exposed left cheek. Sure enough, on closer inspection, I can just make out the tiger stripes. The hint of a tail. And a paw. I smirk as she flirts voraciously with Hub.

He says. "No, we're just fine. Thanks, Haley."

Even with her back to me I can sense her blushing. "You remembered!"

"Of course. How could I forget?" God. He's so cheesy

and syrupy and gross right now I want to kick his shin under the table.

She does a little thing where she crosses her ankles and juts out one hip. I see a little more of the tattoo than I want to. Realize that sometimes less really *is* more. "Well, it's been awhile..."

"Oh, not that long." I make a face. His flirty voice is so bad. Soft and low and I can tell he's on autopilot and since I know his real, non-flirty voice it just makes it that much worse. It's like when Benjy and I are out somewhere and I catch him using his fake server voice, this kind of cheesy falsetto choirboy thing he does while bending over slightly at the table, and all I can hear is needles on a chalkboard.

Tiger Butt Cheek Ho Bag scribbles something on her server pad. Tears it off. Slips it under Hub's empty plate like she's in some kind of black and white detective movie. If I could tear my eyes off the comely round nub of her exposed rump cheek I'd roll them at him, but I can't. I look away instead. Out the window, past the painted rocks on the dusty wooden sill to the gently crashing waves below.

"If you ever want a repeat performance, just gimme a call, K?"

He takes the paper in his thick fingers. Folds it up. Winks at her. "Will do."

Even though I still can't see her face, all her body language giggles. She spins gently around to finally acknowledge me. I quickly look up from her firm, round derriere. "Anyway, breakfast's on me guys. See you again soon!"

She disappears in a twirl, leaving behind only the scraps of our free meal and her perky drug store perfume. I nod. Impressed. "Wow, for once your scandalous, slutty ass ways paid off."

"You're welcome."

"That's not exactly a compliment."

He waves the number in my face as I try to drown the sudden sting of totally unreasonable jealousy with a fresh swig of cold back coffee. He winks. "Not from you, anyway."

TWELVE

BENJY

"You wore that to class?"

Cara giggles unexpectedly. Coyly. Thick. Deep. In a good mood for a change. She's got the phone propped up on some architecture books on her desk and flashes in front of it like a sultry little blur while grabbing some yogurt out of her dorm fridge in the corner of the screen. Of course, the bending down and rooting around for one in the back of the little black fridge part is just out of the camera range. Because me, obviously.

"It was a study group, remember?"

"No, I just got up. Remember?"

She snorts one of her "Gee, I wish I was a loser townie who gets to sleep in every morning" snorts. "Must be nice."

"Anyway..." I glance at the clock by my bed. It's still pretty darn early. And she was never really a morning person. "Isn't study group something you do *after* class?"

Her tone is vaguely patient. More the teacher addressing her pupil 'tude. "It's something you do in between class. Meaning I have class in a few, remember?"

I roll my eyes, propped up on my bed with a few pillows

behind me, chest bare above my extra baggy boxers. Just seeing her, hearing her, there alone in her dorm room, limber and lean and soft in the morning light through the window behind her, is making me frisky and thick in my shorts.

She's barely glanced my way but, in the old days, she would have gotten the hint and purred and licked her lips and wriggled her hips and leaned closer and, well, more. Now she just gulps yogurt out of the container like she hasn't eaten in a week and looks sexy as hell in her yoga pants and sports bra.

I say, "I mean, at least put a sweater on."

She looks personally offended. "It's hot as hell out there."

I grin. Finally, she's looking at me. I wriggle a little, tan lines and happy trail and bare nips and all. "It's hot as hell in here, babe."

She finally gets the hint. Glances back at the screen with a droll stare. Looks me up and down. Rolls her eyes some more. "Gross, Benj. I don't have time to pleasure you remotely this morning, boo. Sorry, not sorry."

I wriggle a little more in my powder blue sheets. Waistband of my baggy boxers shifting down just a little lower. Give her a chance to change her mind. "Once upon a time, *boo*, you'd have made time."

She growls, still vaguely playful. "This again? Swear to God you're worse than my mom, Benj."

I make a face. "You pleasure your mom remotely, too?"

I must catch her by surprise. Or maybe she wasn't really listening and just got clued in. Either way she snorts, big and bold, forgetting to cover her mouth the way she will in front of friends. She has a grey tooth on the upper left side, dead but not painful, and is usually sensitive about it. "Stop trying to charm me, Benj. I'm telling you I don't have time."

"Well, speaking of time—"

She waves a plastic spoon at me, the wall behind her covered in Paris and Eiffel tower prints and winking little fairy lights above the row of endless throw pillows that cover her single bed. "So, help me God if you use this phone sex thing to circle back around to Thanksgiving I will reach through this phone and choke you senseless."

I grin, suddenly excited at the prospect. "Thought you didn't have time to pleasure me remotely, babe."

Another surprised snort. Jesus, has she forgotten what this was all like? How much fun we used to have, once upon a time? "Benjy, honestly…" She sounds exasperated, but in a good way. It…it hasn't been like that in a while.

I switch course, but don't give up. "Well, if you can't make it in time for Thanksgiving, what about Treesgiving?"

"Please, that fake holiday Shay keeps pushing every time we talk? I'm gonna have to block both your numbers if you keep bringing this shit up. Has that girl ever heard the term 'chasing Christmas,' because she's doing it."

"Funny you should mention that," I murmur, before she cuts me off.

"I mean, aren't there enough holidays on the calendar without adding new ones willy-nilly?"

I feel myself growing vaguely defensive, the way I always do when Cara bristles at Shay's very name. "I mean, it could be fun," I try not to huff. "The three of us, back together again? Like old times?"

She tosses her empty yogurt cup away with a patented flourish and wriggles back in her desk chair. Arms over her chest, fixing me with a soft, gentle glare. "When did we ever sit around the day after Thanksgiving and decorate a tree together, bud?"

"So, like old new times then, huh?"

"Benjy, listen, I'm trying, okay?"

I hold my hands up, surrender style. Her favorite gesture of mine. "I'm not bugging you, Cara. I just miss you."

When she doesn't respond right away, either with her face or her words, I nudge a little more. "You get that, right? That I would miss you?"

I stifle a grin to see the irritation take full bloom in her suddenly rosy cheeks and pursed lips. "Yeah, Benjy, I get it. Honestly, I do, but this sudden neediness of yours? Every phone call? It's not a good look."

I flare up a bit myself because why not? Nothing I've been doing is working lately, why not at least swing my dick a little, you know? I'm certainly not using it for anything else these days. "How is it needy to want to see your girl? How is it clingy to ask you to check in once a day when you're on the other side of the state? I mean, I don't get that."

"You would if you were here, Benj."

"How would I know? You've never once asked me to come visit, Cara. In all this time, not once have you said, 'I miss you, boo, come surprise me.'"

Her voice is low and stiff to match her frozen brow. "Why should I have to ask, Benj?"

I ignore her not even close to an apology, apology. "Because every time I've even slightly, vaguely hinted that I might try and sneak up there, you know, just to feel you out a little, you give me a laundry list of excuses why it's never a good time and how that would be a really, really bad, very not so good idea, that's why."

"Right, well, this is going exactly as I expected."

She stands abruptly. Grabs the phone. I see blur. Face. Eiffel tower. Throw pillows. The Empire State Building. Blur.

Face. Door. Slow blur. Then…face! "I'm gonna be late for class if I don't bolt, so…"

"Take me with you, clown."

"What?"

"It's a. Mobile. Phone. Take me with you, Cara. That is, I mean, unless you don't want your precious college friends to know you have some townie boyfriend hidden away back in some shitty beach town you can't even be bothered to—"

"God, the projection is so thick right now I'd need a therapist to debunk all your insane conspiracy theories and, like I said, class awaits. So good luck with those therapy bills and maybe we can chat later after a few Xanax, k?"

"You can sass off all you want, Cara, but you know I'm right."

She pauses. Near the door. I know because the closet is right next to it and she's reaching inside for her backpack. I may have never been inside her room, physically, but we've had enough video calls for me to know every square inch of it. "Maybe we're both right, Benj. Did you ever think of that?"

"Only every day, dear."

She offers a fake smile. I know because it doesn't even reach halfway to her cold green eyes. She offers a little fake advice to go along. "Maybe…maybe that's the problem, boo. If you were a little busier, like I am at the moment, you might not have so much time to dwell on the fact that I'm not there."

"Good tip, boo. Maybe your next boyfriend won't give a shit about seeing you. Should make study groups a lot easier for you."

"Benjy, don't."

I huff a little more because I already sound like a big, fat, baby-man, bitch face. Too late to stop now, right? "Sorry, just did."

"Look, we'll talk later, okay?"

"Maybe we will. Or maybe I'll find a new hobby so I'm too busy to think about you."

"That's not what I meant, and you know it."

"It's what you said, and we both know it. I've got lunch shift today so I better bolt, but thanks for the chat." I lie. I work dinner but she wouldn't know that lately, either.

"Benjy, don't leave angry. We promised we wouldn't do that anymore."

"Only because your phone calls enrage me so damn much."

She giggles. Playful. Sexy. She's got the phone just so that I see her long, elegant throat bobbing with the sound. Dips just a little to show the taut pink material of her sports bra, stretched taut across her petite, perfect chest. I sigh. Think of the poofy pink nipples I know lurk just beneath, try to ignore the way they always felt under my trembling fingers, taut and tender to the touch. Relent. "Sorry, just... I miss you, okay?"

She doesn't say it back. I listen for it. Hasn't in our last few phone calls. Struggle to think what that might mean. I know if I pressed her on it, she'd just cluck her tongue and say, "That's understood, obviously. You know that, right?" But I don't know that. And I don't really understand. Anything. At all. Right now. "I know, Benj. Really, I get it. Okay? I just... Give me some time. This is all new to me too, you know?"

I try not to roll my eyes. It's college. It's two and a half hours away. Hardly a cross country trek. She's had three months to say she misses me. Still, I don't want any beef today. Not anymore. "I get it. Just check in after class, you know?"

Sighs. Glad I can't see the roll of her eyes as I stare at her rack instead. "You know I'll try."

I cluck my tongue like a damn girlfriend. "I know, babe. The struggle is real."

I hang up while she's still laughing because at least it's better than her still fuming. I sigh. Stand. Put on a tank top and glance around the room at the various pictures of us throughout the years. Proms, sports, concerts and more concerts and the beach and spring breaks and holidays.

I know I'm lucky to have her. Know she's out of my league. Know she could literally have any guy in high school and somehow, stupidly, chose me. I get that. I know even now in a campus swimming with hot college chicks she's a standout. I can't stop thinking about which guy she might be sitting next to in class or in the cafeteria or at some damn frat party. How handsome or smart or rich or funny or witty or clever or tall or strong he might be. How much better than me he surely is.

I wish I could stop. Really. I do. This isn't fun. For either of us. I get that, honestly, I do. It's not her fault she's out of my league. But she used to be kinder about it all. Friendlier, I suppose. Lately I can't shake the feeling that she's enjoying my uncertainty. And it makes me wonder what else she's enjoying while she's away and I'm stuck back here. At home.

I pause at the only non-Cara photo in my room. It's in a frame. A Halloween frame. Cheesy, like a haunted house. Think I got it at the dollar store way after Halloween. Closer to Thanksgiving, actually. There's still a red clearance sticker on the back, old and faded to a dull, rosy pink by now.

Inside is a picture of me. And Shay. Just us two. A rare

photo, perhaps even the only one of its kind, where it's just me and Shay and not me and Shay and Cara. Taken years ago. At a Halloween party. I smile and pick it up, like I will every few days or so. We look so young. So, awkward. So, confused. Coy and shy and excited and eager and hungry all at the same time. I'm wearing my baseball uniform and she looks casually breathtaking in black stockings and a long red cape. Her Little Red Riding Hood is down, brown ponytail casually resting on one shoulder of her frilly white tube top. Skin bronzed and radiant from surfing before school every day. Her smile is shy and reserved and almost unwilling.

I forget who took the picture of us. One of Cara's cheerleader besties at the time. It was supposed to be a group shot. The Three Amigos in action. But just out of frame Cara is turned, blurry and absent, talking to someone on the other side of us. You can just see the poofy shoulder of her sexy clown costume in the very far corner of the picture, swallowed up mostly by the cheesy haunted house frame and her eagerness to be the belle of the ball at any and every occasion.

So, it ended up being a picture of us after all. Me. And Shay. We are standing unnaturally close. For us, anyway. Being that close to Shay was always dangerous back then. Still is, I suppose. Maybe even more so lately, come to think of it. My hand is around her shoulder. Her hip rests on mine. Her smile is crooked. Curious. Coy. There's a vague side eye to her expression, like either she didn't like the girl taking the picture or is impatient with Cara for making her stand there, alone, with me for so long. Eventually the mystery photographer got tired of waiting and just snapped the damn pic. It's ironic, really, considering that was the night Cara and I finally hooked up for the first time.

Whoever it was sent the picture to Cara a few days later.

She snorted. Was about to delete it. I asked why. "I'm not even in it, duh!" I distracted her just long enough to grab her phone when she wasn't looking and sent the pic to myself. Got it printed later when I was doing a collage for Mom's Christmas present. Saw the clearance frame when I was getting wrapping paper and it's been on my bureau ever since.

I put it back and drift toward the shower, thinking how much has changed and how things are, in a way, absolutely the same. And wonder, not for the first time, why that thought makes me so stupid happy.

THIRTEEN

SHAY

"Back to this college thing…"

We're at the top of the stairs. Lingering in front of my apartment. Again. Hub seems distracted. Probably thinking about calling Tiger Butt the minute he gets back in his place and wishing I'd just. Shut. The hell. Up.

Hub makes an adorably frumpy face. "What college thing?"

"You? In college? Once upon a time?"

He waves a dismissive hand. "It was a long time ago in a galaxy far, far away…"

"Still. What was it for?"

He peers back at me. Uncertain. "You really want to know?"

"I'm asking, aren't I?"

"Yeah, but it seems like you're just killing time because you still have a few hours left before work and not much else to do."

I snort. I soooooo totally am. "Even so, I'm still curious."

He chuckles. Nods. "Graphic Design."

"You? Really?"

He pretends to look offended. "What's that supposed to mean?"

"I... I don't know. I didn't know what to expect."

"What'd you think I'd go to school for?"

"Retail management?"

"What? This was almost twenty years ago, kid. I don't even think Thrifty Dollar was in business back then. And if it was, I sure didn't want to work there."

"So, what happened?"

The reluctant dollar store manager glances just above my head as if struggling to find the answer there. "Life, little girl. Life happened."

"No, I mean, to Graphic Design School."

He shrugs. Broad shoulders in his soft blue tank top. Long legs in his clingy pink baggies. Neon green and yellow striped surfboard leaning on the walkway rail behind him. "They did everything on computers. I just wanted to paint."

"Paint? Really?"

Gets defensive again. "Yeah, why?"

I hold up my hands in surrender, so he doesn't keep getting offended every time I open my mouth. "Nothing, I just... Do you still do it?"

"Do what?"

I give a frustrated little sigh before replying. Why must the men in my life make every conversation like a tennis match? "Paint. Do you still do it?"

He scoffs like I should already know this about him. "Yeah. All the time. What? Why are you making that scrunchy face again?"

I chuckle to feel so seen. "Sorry, man. I just don't know where you'd find the time to paint between banging your servers every time you go out to eat, that's all."

His scowly face is vaguely paternal. "Shay, stop that."

I slip my key in the lock with a playful shrug. "Just sayin'."

"You should come by some time…"

I roll my eyes and pretend to be offended. "Hey, I may be a server, but…"

He makes a face that is vaguely grossed out. Half of me is offended, the other half is relieved? "I meant, to see my paintings."

I pause with my door half open. "You have some? Right now?"

"Yeah. I mean, sure…"

I see him hemming. Hawing. "What?"

"Nothing, I just have to be at work soon."

"Me too, Hub. Don't worry. I'm not going to take you up on your invitation. Even though you said it. Out loud. Just now. Remember?"

"I do. I want you to see them. Just… Not now."

I finally get it. Shove him backward with both hands. "Oh. My. God."

He looks surprised, and not just by the random act of violence. "What?"

"You have someone in there right now, don't you?"

"What?" He makes a startled face. Like I wouldn't figure it out. Like I'm that stupid. Then looks down at his feet. It means he's lying. Eleven months as his neighbor and I at least know that much about him. Not the college part. Not the painting stuff. But his tell? Oh, yeah, I got that one right away.

"No. Of course not."

"Then why can't I come over and see your paintings? Right now?" I bluff and pull my key back out of the lock. Wave it toward his place next door threateningly, thrilled to see the panicked look on his face. "Come on. Let's go."

"It's just..." He looks back up. Blushing slightly. Glances around the walkway as if searching for something. But his expression, his posture, his tone, make it clear he's not even trying to deny it anymore. "...the light's not good at the moment. I mean. Maybe later?"

"Screw you, man whore."

We're both giggling now. "Shay, honestly. I really want you to see them."

"So, bring one to me sometime. Or wear a chastity belt. And hopefully use a condom. Something. Jesus."

I still hear him giggling as he pads down the walkway toward his apartment.

FOURTEEN

SHAY

"I don't think Cara's coming home for Thanksgiving."

I glance over. Arch an eyebrow. Keep pedaling like I don't already know what he's talking about. "What makes you say that?"

He shrugs. Pedals slowly. Weaves a little closer to me. Then back away again. I like it when he does that. I mean, I figure that's the closest we'll ever get to dancing, so—

He pauses, then says, "She just keeps putting me off whenever I try to pin her down on a date."

The air is silken and warm on my skin. The sun soft in the pale blue sky. It helps to take the edge off my jealousy. If only slightly. "Putting you off how?"

His eyes are clear and brown as we pedal leisurely side by side. The day is young. It was slow. At work. Always is the week before Thanksgiving, though the week after is a whole other story. Either way, we got cut early. For some reason, I'm even less eager to get home than usual.

I don't know if it's the early cut or the unmistakable holiday vibe in the air or just Hub's casual horniness washing off on me, but at the moment I'm particularly rest-less and the thought of sitting home alone, hot, and half-dressed and avoiding the temptation of the "happy drawer" in the nightstand by my bed is a real turnoff.

Benjy shrugs. Hops back on the Cara train. I'd been so busy feeling the vibe and digging his eyes I'd almost forgot-ten. Clearly, he hasn't. "She does this thing where you back her in a corner and she's feeling guilty about whatever you're pinning her on, where she…"

"…insults you?" I finish the sentence for him.

He grins bashfully. "Something like that. Every time I ask about it, she calls me 'needy' or 'whiny,' so I'm done asking." He looks a little peeved. Not to the casual observer. It's just that his nostrils are gently flared. But I've been knowing him long enough by now to spot the signs.

I lie. "That doesn't sound like her."

He huffs. Glances away. "Lately it does."

I bite my lip. Wonder if he's gotten a few signs of Cara's wandering eye lately himself. Make that alleged wandering eye. "Maybe she just wants to surprise you?"

He glances over like maybe I'm right. Then frowns. "I wish I could say she was that spontaneous and romantic, but…" We both kind of chuckle. Cara's always been as predictable as they come, which is why her sultry "Hey babe" to the "pizza guy" from the other night still has me so rattled. It wasn't on accident. It wasn't random. She meant it, every throaty, sexy syllable, and knowing that has turned my already wobbly world straight upside down.

We cruise down alongside Ocean Drive until the Salty Seagull sign comes into view. I frown. It always looks so much better at night, with the blue and pink neon letters glossing over the truth. During the day they just look rusty and sad.

Instinctively, we both steer toward it. In tandem. Side by side, the rush of our wheels familiar and comforting on the clean white bike path. I hear Hub splashing gently in the pool. Glance up to see my front door, closed and quiet and dull. And just.

Keep.

Going.

"Hey, what the what?"

He's slightly behind me. I glance back over my shoulder as I turn right at the stop sign just past my parking lot. Apologize with my face. "I'm not ready to go home yet. Are you?"

He grins. Shakes his head. Hard, like maybe he's as restless as I am today. Then immediately looks doubtful. "So, where to then?"

"Feeling like a sushi date?"

Beams and picks up the pace, almost fast enough to overtake me. "Always. Duh."

"Cheers." A short time later, I hoist my tiny sake cup. Nod toward his. He gets the hint. Lifts it to meet mine. Then frowns. "To what?"

I roll my eyes. "Do I have to do everything around here?"

He looks slightly panicked. "What? You want me to make the toast?"

I look slightly annoyed. "Yeah. That would be nice for a change. But hurry, before the sake cools off."

He frowns. Purses his lips. Glances around at the geisha prints and old tin Kirin beer signs littering the walls. I'm about to crack wise when his eyes light up. Clinks my glass with his. A little too eagerly. Warm sake drizzles over my fingertips, soft and syrupy like the feeling in my trembling belly. "To us, of course."

Suddenly, my fingers aren't the only things warm and sticky. Our eyes meet in the dim, sushi bar lighting. Linger just a little longer than usual. Maybe, okay, a lot longer. They say deep, hidden things our mouths can't. Or shouldn't. Or won't.

"I like that." We glance away. Finally. Sip. The sake is warm. The beer chaser is cold. Crisp. The combination delightfully refreshing. We both sit back and "aaahhh" at the same time.

He glances around again. Arms down at his sides. Hands palms down on the cracked leather booth beneath him. He looks about ten years old under his faded Pig-Out ball cap. Glances at me from under the brim, brown eyes shiny and swimming in the shadows that so flatter his light brown skin. Smiles. "Nice."

"Right?" I grin. I left work before eating my shift meal, so the sake is hitting me like a warm, smooth freight train of sheer, sweet, sticky, inhibition-lowering bliss. "Good idea, huh?"

He nods again. Eyes bright and glassy. He probably didn't eat, either. And he's always been a bigger lightweight than me. Or Cara. By a mile. The times we lugged that boy back home from some keg party or another and dumped him into his bedroom window are too numerous to count by far, but always hilarious to remember. He licks his lips lazily, leaving them slick and wet and shiny. Jesus, that's hot. "Best. Idea. Ever."

I chuckle. Reach for my little sake cup. "You're welcome." Take a sip. Then some beer. Just a little. I have to be in control around him, always, just so I don't do something stupid or embarrassing or sappy or earth shatteringly frisky that I can never take back. I grin lazily at the hidden danger simmering at our little table for two and try to distract myself by focusing on the chirpy Asian string music above our heads.

Watch him follow suit. He puts down his beer. Grins. Pins me with those soft brown eyes and licks his lips absently as if he knows exactly what they do to me. "Why don't we do this more often?"

I pin him back. "You want the real reason?"

I watch his eyes drift away. Past my head. To something behind me. He raises a long finger. Like it's a real serious issue. "Hold that thought."

I glance to my side just as the server appears at our table. She's an older woman. Asian. Abrupt, but efficient. She's waited on us about a thousand times but always acts like she's just met us. She wears black polyester slacks and a silky smock that looks like a kimono but isn't quite. Smiles as she sets down our edamame on the table, swirls of steam rising from the cherry blossom covered bowl and smothered in glistening dots of rock salt.

"Anything else?" She's always in a hurry for us to order and we never really are and there's usually no one else ever in the place at the same time we are and for the life of me I just don't get it.

Benjy and I glance at each other. He shrugs. I smile at the server apologetically. Offer a little shoulder shrug as an explanation point. "Maybe after we finish this?"

She's already turned around before I can finish. Nothing to see here. Shuffles away on squeaky flip flops that would never pass muster at Pig-Out. I watch her drift all the way through the long, narrow restaurant until she disappears between the two flaps of an Asian curtain with an angry sumo wrestler on either side. We look back at each other and chuckle.

FIFTEEN
BENJY

Shay peers back at me from under the brim of her faded blue Pig-Out cap. She has a few of them. We both do. All of them faded and worn in. Distressed, is probably the best word, I guess you could say. I mean, if you give a shit about that kind of thing, that is.

Her red one is my favorite, by far, but the blue one's not bad, either. She always pulls her ponytail through the back and, whenever she's not looking, I like to watch it swish across her shoulders while she's carrying a tray full of pulled pork baskets through the crowded dining room.

She's a tomboy by nature, cocky and confident and physical and far from fussy, and it's the only time she's uniquely, quietly, supremely feminine. In those moments, busy and not self-conscious, she can't hide the sultry femininity of her walk. The swaying hips and ripe curve of her butt and the soft brown hair caressing her shoulders the way my fingers so often long to do themselves. Then again, I haven't gotten laid in months so I'm just really, really horny all the time. Day. Night. Morning. Even at work.

She gives me a look like she's just peeked into my

fevered brain pan and got a glimpse of my mental hard-on. I jut my chin back in reply. "What?"

"What, what? What are you looking at, weirdo?"

I snort. Vibing with the late afternoon sake and sushi aesthetic while getting a taste of Shay's trademark sarcasm. "You, kook."

I take a sip of sake while she rolls her eyes. Follow it with a cool swallow of beer. God, it's good. So. Good. She watches me carefully. "Did you even eat today?"

I shake my head, savoring the warm sake glow in my empty belly. Listening to the cheesy strings of the uniquely Asian soundtrack the restaurant is playing. It sounds like the same eight songs over and over again. Then I pause. This takes some actual effort. "No, wait. I had a strawberry toaster thing this morning, I think."

"You think?"

"I mean, all the days are kind of running together lately."

She huffs. Sips. Swallows. "Heard that."

I watch her put her beer glass down and notice her nails. She's never been a girly girl and her nails are predictably ratchet. "You gonna get special nails for Treesgiving or just do Halloween all year?"

She quickly hides her fingertips behind her glass. Even with the shadow of her brim across half her face I can see the blush rise to her cheeks. "I dunno, I hadn't thought of that."

"I mean, you still have your Halloween nails, so…"

She throws her balled up chopstick wrapper at me. We haven't eaten anything yet, but she's already unwrapped them and has them resting on top of her soy sauce bowl like she's in actual Asia or something. "Stop. I just haven't had time to get them done yet."

"I noticed."

"Bullshit."

I snort out some beer foam. Put my glass down. "Correct. That was some total bullshit. I just saw them now and it made me think you usually do something for the holidays, so…"

"Since when have you considered Treesgiving a holiday?"

"I don't, but you do, so…" I sip some more sake, struggling not to drain the little white cup every time I lift it to my lips. I'm usually pretty chill with my drinking but today I'm feeling good. We got off early. Took a nice, long bike ride after work in the midday sun and ended up at Chopstix, our favorite sushi bar. Mom won't be expecting me for hours, if at all, and the day is young. Plus, it's always a good time with Shay. Today seems particularly festive, for some reason.

I wash the sake down with beer and ease back even deeper into the booth behind me. I see Shay a lot. Most days, in fact. But sometimes I just glance and other times, like now, I really see, see her. Look at her closely. Drink it all in. Her chipped candy corn nails and crooked ball cap and creamy lip gloss and the rainbow tattoo on her left arm and the way she never wears earrings and the swell of her—

"Stop, Benjy."

I glance up from admiring the faded red logo on her white Pig-Out t-shirt and am too buzzed to blush. Or even look away. "What?"

"My eyes are up here, perv!"

"I'm just noticing you need a new shirt, is all."

"Oh, yeah?"

"Yeah, actually. And there's a stain on the sleeve of that one that's never come out. I see it every time you wear this one."

"Barbecue sauce, I know."

"Yeah, so, you're welcome?"

"Thanks. So much. But you weren't looking at my sleeve, pal."

I shrug. Sip. Quit trying to hide it. "Can you blame me?"

She wriggles playfully, jutting her chest out just so. She must be buzzed, too, because that's very un-Shay like behavior. Like, epically un-Shay.

"I mean, they are pretty nice, not gonna lie." She giggles, a little nervously. Self-consciously, as if to let me know she's joking. Which, of course, I already know. The most un-Shay thing in the world would be for her to brag about herself, even if we are day drinking on empty stomachs. Even if she is just acknowledging the plain and basic truth that her tits are, in fact, most dope.

I grin and remind her of our 'friends with no benefits' status. "I wouldn't know."

"That's right, and that's just how it's going to stay, too."

"I mean, I've pretty much seen most of them."

"What? The hell you have!" It's hard for her to talk between fits of adorably embarrassed giggles.

"Shay, please. We've known each other how long now?"

"Not long enough for you to see my zoombas."

I shrug. "That's debatable. I mean, given the amount of time we spend together, on and off the job, in and out of school, in various sporting and partying and beachy type activities over the years, the odds are actually quite good that I'd see some kind of slip at some point, you know?"

"Bullshit, perv. When?"

"You know. T-shirts with no bra. Wet t-shirts—"

"In what actual world would I ever wear a wet t-shirt in your presence? Or in anyone's, for that matter?"

I wave off her sputtering interruption with the force of sheer horniness. "And in bikinis, of course. Hundreds, maybe thousands, of bikinis. Like, really small bikinis. You know, the kind you like to wear. The kind that leave little to the imagination. The kind where tan lines from other, bigger bikinis poke out, all nice and pale and sexy like…"

"My bikinis are not small, Benjamin Bradley Houghton. I'm just not a twig like Cara so there's a little more to fill them with."

I cock one eyebrow the way she likes. She's never told me, specifically, she likes when I do that but she always kind of perks up when I do, so… I went ahead and put two and two together on my own. "You're not really disproving my point, you know?"

She takes a sip of sake, then another quick one like she's forgotten it was there and needs to catch up. Or maybe she's just suddenly nervous about me describing her breasts in such vivid detail. "Fine, Benjy, I admit we've spent a lot of time together over the years and, perhaps, you have seen a glimpse or two of side boob. Congrats. Maybe I'll give you a subscription to *National Geographic* for Treesgiving since you seem so obsessed with the ta-tas."

"Side boob? We're talking way more than that, sis."

She sighs like I've finally worn her down. "Fine, Benj, maybe you've seen a tan line or two over the years, but never the full Monty."

"You're telling me." She chuckles quietly at my pitiful-ness, probably. I reach over and fill our little white cups. She watches me curiously. Reaches for hers as I'm setting the white carafe back down on the table. I'm tempted to let our fingers graze in passing. I mean, they're close enough to without being too terribly obvious, but I chicken out at the last minute.

Like always.

"What's gotten into you, Benj?"

"Nothing. It's just, you would think I'd have seen your zoombas by now. Like, all of them. Nips and all."

She rolls her eyes. Sips her sake, licking her full, creamy lips afterward. "In what world would my BFF's boyfriend see my zoombas? Especially all of them."

"Not romantically, obvs. Just, in passing, you know? Scientifically speaking."

She chuckles and shakes her head. We're alone in the sushi bar, sitting in our favorite booth in the back of a long, slender restaurant in the middle of a cheap, rundown strip mall a few blocks from her cheap, rundown apartment.

While she's quiet, I savor my midday buzz and glance at the dented tin beer signs and geisha prints on the walls. It feels like we ordered an appetizer hours ago but in sake time it's probably only been a few minutes. I'm kinda glad for the privacy and the way the padded booth feels beneath me after another long week of the grind.

"I mean," she says, slowly, voice soft and feminine in a way it usually isn't, saying words she's probably going to regret. "It's not like I've ever seen your yazoo, you know?"

That...that was not the response I was expecting from her. At all. Not even a little. I frown, mulling it over. "Why would you?"

"I mean, I feel like I kind of have with the way you wear everything a size too big, and your drawers are always dragging down off your waist and such."

"I like comfort, you know. I like room down there."

"Gross."

"You're gross, thinking about your BFF's boyfriend's junk."

She literally gasps with disbelief. "Me? You just spent the better part of what felt like an hour talking about my ta-ta's and I dare to mention your yazoo once, and only once, and I'm the perv?"

I chuckle, belly full of sake and eyes full of Shay. Sweet, sexy Shay. "I did go on and on, didn't I? Still, zoombas and yazoos are different."

"How so?"

"Yours are just sitting out there, all day long." I wave across the table for effect. She glances down as if just noticing them. "Mine's tucked away for a reason."

She snorts. "Oh yeah, what reason?"

"So, you're not thinking about it 24/7, that's what reason."

"I'm not thinking about it ever, creep. You brought it up."

"I brought up your zoombas, not my yazoo."

"Where else was it gonna go after your eloquent discussion of the odds of seeing a flash of side boob in six long years? The weather?"

She chuckles. Then I do. She lifts her sake cup but doesn't drink. Pins me with her eyes instead. Pauses briefly before just spitting it out. "We both just need to get laid, that's all."

I snort and answer quickly. Too quickly. "No. Shit."

She chuckles. "No wonder you're so interested in getting Cara to come home and visit for Thanksgiving."

I shake off the side boob talk and focus. "It's not just that, Shay. You know that."

"I know that, bud. You're not actually a perv, but it'll be a nice fringe benefit."

"Yeah? What about your fringe benefits?"

Shay snorts. Glances away. More of the slight blush beneath her ball cap. "What about 'em?"

"I mean, you've got your pick at work, right?"

"Gross."

I think of the motley crew we work with. Most are either pimply high school kids or creepy older guys. Not a lot of in between there for a single gal who's not necessarily a big fan of Axe body spray and pierced, well, everything. "I guess. What about that neighbor of yours, the Silver Surfer guy? The one who's always swimming when I drop you off?"

She seems surprised I'd even notice. "Hub? He's a little old for me, don't you think?"

I shrug just for show, even though the thought of some other guy touching her makes me literally, absolutely insane. But I always like to suggest guys she'd never really go for in real life, so the likeliness of the scenario goes down considerably. "Not if you're into that kind of thing, I guess."

Shay seems to consider it for a moment. I grin, watching the waitress drift through the sumo wrestler curtains between the dining room and the kitchen behind her. "I mean, not that—"

She appears quickly and sets a steaming bowl of edamame down on our table. Asks if we want anything else. I just grin until Shay says, like usual, "Maybe after this?"

I sit back. Ooze back is more like it. My body, tense and taut and wired all week, molds itself to the back of the booth I'm sitting in. My brain follows. I watch her, aglow in the soft track lighting above our table, radiant and young and friendly and, at the moment, mine all mine.

"What? Why are you still looking at me that way? We've already talked about yazoos and zoombas. That's enough for one day."

I whine and wriggle a bit. "I can't help it."

She smiles despite herself. "Well, start helping it. We… we can't do this. You know that."

"Why?"

"You know why."

"I wanna hear you say it."

"I shouldn't have to by now, bud."

I roll my eyes. Deflate like someone just stuck a pin in me. "Bud."

"Yeah, bud. That's… that's what we are now, okay? So… quit giving me the googly eyes and eat something before you nod off over there and I have to drag your ass home like the good old days."

SIXTEEN

SHAY

He frowns at the steaming bowl of freshly salted soybean pods between us. Or maybe he's just frowning at me. At the way I shut down all his tits and ass talk in a hurry Well, not so much in a hurry, feels like we've been talking about body parts since we walked in!

Either way, he's acting so weird today, I can't really tell.

"What do we do with these again?" He literally scratches his head.

"God, you do this every time."

"Well, it's been awhile. Remember?"

"Jesus, not really. We were here just last week. And the week before that?"

"Well, I forget things, so..." He raises up his hands, big and boyish like the rest of him. For the life of me, the sake and all his booby talk has me wanting those hands all over me even more than usual. And that's... that's saying a lot because I never *not* want his hands on me.

I blink away the thought and pick one up. By the skinny end. With the little curly string attached. "You just..." I put the fatter end in my mouth and bite down gently on the first pod, then drag it through my teeth until it's empty. Hold it up, flat and deflated, little crumbs of rock salt stuck to my sake fingers and making me want to lick them all of a sudden. "See?"

He's grinning. I talk with my mouth full of fresh, crisp pea pods. "What?"

"I already know how to do it, Shay. I just really, really like watching you do that."

I blush and feel flattered and scold him and want him all at the same time. "God, you're gross."

He laughs and pours us more sake and then, surprisingly, sounds very, extremely thoughtful. Wise, even. "Not very often."

I nod begrudgingly. "That's true. You're pretty good, as far as guys go."

He raises his little white glass again. Waits for me to do the same. Taps it. More sticky warmth on my fingers. And, um, elsewhere. "You know, if you're going to make me cheers you every time, maybe fill the glass a little less."

He grins. Sips his sake. Follows it with beer. "You know, if you're going to invite someone out for sushi, you shouldn't harsh their buzz being so bossy about every little thing."

I laugh too hard. Feel too warm and soft and fuzzy in my belly. This is way too easy. So is his smile. Soft and warm to match his big brown eyes. He looks at ease. Comfortable. And I wish, for perhaps the millionth time, this could be us. In real time. All the time. Without—

"Cara."

I sit up. Is he a mind reader now? Jesus. I hope not because if he's been rooting around in my overheated noggin' for the last ten minutes or so, woof... I've got some explaining to do. Try to remain chill, just in case. Fail miserably. "W-w-what now?"

He grins. "We were talking about why we don't come here more often."

"We were? When?"

He chuckles. "Wow, no more sake for you."

"I'm fine, I just forgot for a second." I drink a little more, just to prove it. I nod. Make a little "go on" gesture. "And?"

"And...Cara. She's the reason we don't come here more often."

I chuckle. "Oh."

"Am I right?"

The waitress reappears. Picks up the empty beer bottle I've slid to the edge of the table, fellow server style. Wiggles the sake carafe beside it. Both are empty. Manages to look vaguely judgmental. Sighs. "More?"

I look to Benjy. So does she. He's already nodding. She looks back at me. Smiles for the first time in, like...ever. "Please?" I call out to her back, slightly hunched over as she shuffles away. "And thank you!"

Look around the empty restaurant. We're still the only ones here. Then again, it's only mid-afternoon. Turn back to Benjy. "What's gotten into you?"

He's leaning back in his booth again. Big and stretched out and rangy with those long, sinewy arms at his sides. T-shirt clinging to his taut, wiry torso. "Waddya mean?"

"You're not usually a big drinker."

He shrugs. Drains his empty sake cup even drier. "I guess I've had a lot on my mind lately."

"Yeah? Like what, for instance?"

"Just life, you know. Changes. Everything... keeps changing."

I know what the poor guy means, even if he's struggling

to put it into words at the moment. "It's just temporary, Benjy. All of this. You. Me. Cara. You'll see. She'll come home for Thanksgiving and… what? Why are you looking at me like that?"

He looks vaguely peeved. Nibbles on a soybean pod too long. Drops it in the empty bowl looking mangled. "Why do you assume I'm talking about her all the time? God, you always do that. Like, always."

"Are you serious?"

"Yeah."

I put my sake cup down a little harder than I intend to, backsplash making my fingers even stickier than before, the sound intended to warn him of the big moment about to come. When he looks up, surprised, I let him have it. "Cuz Benjy, she's all *you* talk about. Ever."

"Really?"

"Yeah, dude. Really. 'Cara's not coming home. Cara's coming home. Cara didn't call. Cara called. Cara and I are in a fight. Cara and I made up.' Since our junior year it's been like that, okay? So suddenly it's my fault I don't pick up on it the one time you're not in the mood to talk about her?"

But he's grinning. My nostrils are flaring. My chest is heaving. My fists are clenched.

And he's grinning. "Yeah, I do that, Shay. I talk about her a lot. I'm sorry. But I guess that's part of the change I'm talking about."

"What? You're not going to talk about her anymore?"

"Not as much."

"Well, that would be weird, too."

"So what?" He wriggles in his seat a little. Puffs out his chest like a big boy. "Life is weird. Right now. It's been weird. Ever since she left, I mean."

I frown. Fix him with my eyes. It's… I can't even

remember the last time I've heard him talk like this. If I ever have. He's not necessarily one for heart to hearts. I grow a little quieter, as if to better hear what he's really trying to say. "Like how?"

He pins me back. Soft brown eyes I've known so long, suddenly wiry, and alert and hungry in a way I've never known before, but always wanted to. "You know."

"I don't, actually. So, you're going to have to tell me. With actual words. That's why I asked."

He removes one of his big, flat hands from the booth beside him. I can hear it unstick from the vinyl material covering the bench. Waves it at me. A pointy finger. "You. Me. It's been… weird."

I'm surprised at his observation. Not that he's wrong. We've been weird since, literally, the day she left for college a few months back. I'm just surprised he noticed, that's all. "I thought we were doing pretty good, actually."

"We are good. That's what's so weird."

"What's weird about that, exactly?"

Shrugs. Big, broad shoulders. Firm and strong beneath his clingy grey Pig-Out t-shirt. "I thought I was over all that."

"All what?"

His eyes dance behind me again. I turn to see the waitress. She's smiling. Thinly. A mask barely containing her veiled impatience. Waitress pad and pen at the ready. I can tell she's not taking "no" for an answer this time. I mean, sure, legally, we could say "no." And get away with it. But then we'd never see her again and we should probably eat something, anything, before this whole conversation gets out of hand.

So, even though we're not really ready I order two bento boxes on the fly. Miso soup for me. Salad for the wimp, who thinks it tastes like dish water. Chunky dish water. She leaves. He grins. Pours us more sake.

"You can't avoid it forever, Shay."

"Avoid what?"

But, of course, I know.

I know exactly.

He rolls his eyes cause he does, too. "You know, Shay. Bridget Carlson's Halloween party. We were alone. Just you and me…"

I glance away. Bite my lip. He gently grazes my shoe with his beneath the table. Lets it linger there long enough that I draw mine away before I do something frisky and un-take-back-able. "I know you remember, Shay."

"Yeah, I remember, Benjy. You. Me. Alone in the back-yard while everyone else was inside for the costume contest. I remember, okay? Obviously. Obviously, I remember."

"And?"

"Don't make me say it, Benj."

"I want to know. Want to know if you remember it…"

"The kiss? Yeah. Of course, I do. Our first and last."

He wags a finger. "Our best. Don't forget."

I snort. Wag one back. "Our only, okay?"

He sits back. Pleased with himself. I remind him. "You were drunk, Benjy."

Sits back up. Wags the same finger. "Buzzed, Shay. Not drunk. We both were. And I remember everything. You wore those black tights, remember?"

"And the red cape. Yeah, I remember." I glance at him. Sake cup in hand. Beer at the ready. "You're buzzed now, Benjy. That's…that's…"

His keen eyes are challenging even if his hesitant smile is kind. "Maybe that's the only way I can talk to you like this, Shay. You ever think of that?"

"Like what?"

"Honestly. Openly. Tell you the way I think about you, all the time. The way I—"

"Just stop already."

He's not mad because I've interrupted him, exactly. Just curious. "Why?"

"Because you're forgetting what happened next. After…"

"After we kissed? I'm not forgetting, Shay. At all. I'm editing. It's different."

"How?"

"Because I'm choosing what to focus on."

"Well, I can't be so lucky. I can't forget that Cara won the costume contest, of course. And came looking for us, of course. And found us, of course. And you felt so guilty over what we'd done while she was MIA that you lost your shit and left with her and the next day, I found out you'd asked her to Homecoming and never looked back and I've… I've…"

"You've what?" He's sitting up now, literally on the edge of his seat. If I was a different girl, if this was a different world, I could kiss him by just leaning forward an inch or two.

Or slap the shit out of him. At the moment, I still can't decide which would feel better. But even that's a lie, too. Kissing him would feel better. Kissing him would always feel better than most anything, I suppose. Instead of doing either, of course, I sag back a little and finally come clean. "I've been left tasting that kiss ever since, Benj."

"Really? You still taste it?"

"Metaphorically, asshole!"

He chuckles. I chuckle. We chuckle. The waitress reappears. Looks at us funny. Sets the salad down in front of him. The soup in front of me. Backs away without another word.

He looks at my soup. "What?"

Shrugs. "That looks good today."

"Here. Take it. Maybe it'll sober you up."

"I'm not drunk, Shay. I'm just tired."

"Of what?"

"Of not saying what's on my mind all the time, even when I never stop feeling it. Not for one little second."

"Please. I'm only on your mind lately because you're pissed at Cara for not coming home for Thanksgiving."

He makes an "uggh" face. Empty spoon hovering over his just-tasted soup. "I was wrong. This is still crap."

"Why do you think I ordered you the salad, you big, fat baby? Gimme the soup back then."

He does. I'm grinning. When I look up, he's grinning back. "What's so funny, dick?"

"You called me baby."

"I meant like you're being a baby."

"That's not how it sounded to me."

"A big, fat baby, to be precise."

"I'll be your baby."

"God, you're so gross."

"That soup is gross."

I laugh some more. He grins. Ignores his salad. I wave my dripping soup spoon at it. "You're not going to eat that?"

"I told you. I don't want to harsh my buzz."

"Look man, you've got a whole box of sushi goodness coming your way, so you better be over that shit right quick."

"I'll eat it. I'll eat it, I just... I'm enjoying this moment."

I nod. Eat my soup. Finish it. Steal his salad. "What? You're not?"

I hold a ginger dressing slathered tomato between two chopsticks like an old pro. "Not what? I'm not wasting this."

He shakes his head gently. "Not the salad. You're not? Enjoying this moment?"

I sigh. Finish nibbling. Rest my chopsticks over the salad bowl. "Of course, I am, Benjy. I asked you here, remember? Anywhere we go. Anything we do. Whatever happens between us, I make happen. Why? Because I enjoy your company and I'm not afraid to admit it."

Nudges out his chin in defiance. "Me either."

I pick up my chopsticks again. Nab a cucumber and nibble it. Enjoy the way he always looks impressed whenever I do that. "You are, Benjy. You're a chicken shit. That's fine. I enjoy your company anyway."

"I'm not chicken."

"You are. Like I said, it's fine."

He crosses his arms over his chest. "Clearly it isn't if you're resorting to name calling."

I snort. Eat some more salad. "Look, I've made peace with all this…" Wave my chopsticks around to encompass our booth. Our table. Our spilled sake mixed with edamame salt. Our shared, weird, cozy goodness.

"You chose her," I remind him. "I get it. I've gotten it, ever since that night. So, you can't just sit there with your sake buzz and big brown eyes and long, tempting fingers and start shit up again just because your girl's been gone since August and now it's mid-November and you've probably got big balls by now and…"

His adorable face is placidly startled. "I've got what now?"

I wave my chopsticks some more. "You know? Big balls. When a guy hasn't gotten any for a while and he's—"

He schools me. When he's done laughing, that is.

Laughing so hard I'm afraid the server is going to come and kick us out of our favorite sushi bar. "Blue balls, Shay. *Blue. Balls.* I believe that's the term you're looking for."

I blush. He laughs. "Big. Blue. Whatever. You're just horny, so it's making you brave enough to flirt with me harmlessly because you know nothing's ever going to happen and—Don't. Don't do that to me. It's just confusing and messy and I'm trying to have a good time here, okay?"

"Why?"

I finish my salad. Move it away. It was small, okay? "What? Why what?"

"Why do I know nothing's going to happen?"

SEVENTEEN

SHAY

The waitress appears just then. Slides a bento box in front of each of us. Does the empty beer bottle, sake carafe wiggle thing again. Disappears without a word.

He watches her breeze through the sumo wrestler curtains. "Does that mean we're getting more?"

I frown. "I'm not sure. Probably best if we don't."

He whines. Adorably. "But I *want* more."

"Yeah, me too Benj. Doesn't mean we should have more."

He makes a face. Sits up like a big boy wearing a big boy grin. "Why? I think things are going very well."

I snort. He sounds so formal. "How so?"

"We're really breaking down some walls here, I think."

"Do you?" I pour reduced sodium soy sauce into the empty space in our bento boxes.

He watches me carefully. "Yeah, I do. Don't you?"

"I do. I'm just not sure it's such a good thing, you know?"

He grins. Fiddles with his chopstick wrapper with big, clumsy fingers. I wonder, not for the first time, if they'd be clumsy with me. Like on my bra strap, per se. Or the top button of my khaki work shorts. Or maybe, even, the waistband of my embarrassing blue workaday panties. *Jesus, Shay, slow down.* I guess he's not the only one with blue balls.

"Well, you haven't gotten up and stormed out on me yet, Shay. I consider that a good thing."

"I told you I'm hungry, right?"

He chuckles. Watches me smear a dot of wasabi on a piece of vibrant red tuna. I pick it up. Drag it gently through the soy sauce. Savor it with the last of my sake and beer chaser.

Sure enough, the waitress reappears with a fresh round. Sets them down on the table. "Last one, okay?"

I chuckle. "Good idea."

She smiles. Relieved. Like maybe she was thinking of kicking us out for being too rowdy. Sets down the check. I nab it before he can even think about reaching for it. Slide it under my hip for later. He drops his wasabi. Then his tuna. Then the small, tidy rectangle of rice beneath it. "Shit." Puts down his chopstick and picks up his fork. Goes to town.

Winces. Swallows it down with a sake beer combo. "Is it all raw?"

I nod at his box. "The salmon teriyaki isn't. There's a tempura roll in there, too. The shrimp inside is fried."

He shrugs and pushes some of it around. Watches me nibble a salmon nigiri like I'm some kind of superhero. "Back to this whole nothing happening thing."

"Come on, Blue Balls. I'm trying to eat here."

He chuckles. "You can eat. Just hear me out."

"I can't, Benjy. Don't you get it? I can't entertain that notion and still be friends with you. Not the way we are now. Not the way we've been since that night. It doesn't work like that."

"It has for years."

"Yeah, because I've worn a mental chastity belt where you're concerned. Now you're asking me to unlock it just because… because you have…" I wave my chopsticks like punctuation. To finish the sentence.

He sits back. Watches me eat. "Big balls."

I point my chopsticks at him like a baton. "That's a fallacy, by the way."

He leans forward a bit to spear a piece of tempura roll with his fork. No wasabi. No ginger. No soy sauce. Just plucks it in. Nibbles. Doesn't frown. Polishes off the rest of the roll in three more quick bites. Sits back again. "What is?"

"They don't get bigger just because you're horny."

He shrugs. "They sure feel bigger."

"Stop."

"Just sayin'."

I finish my sushi. Move on to the spicy tuna roll. He watches me take my time with the wasabi and ginger. The soy sauce. The sake and beer chaser. I glance over between bites. "What?"

"You're telling me you don't have blue balls?"

Try not to laugh. Fail. "Not literally. No."

"You know what I mean, Shay."

I put down my chopsticks. Look around. No one else has come in yet. Still. The waitress is leaning on the sushi bar near the front entrance, talking to the chef as he sharpens a knife with expert precision. I lean forward. "Listen, Benjy. The size, or color, of my non-existent balls is none of your business."

He grins. "That's code for yes you do have big, ginormous balls right now, Shay."

I groan. "So what if I do, Benj? You're not going to do anything about it."

"Why not?"

"Because I'm not helping you cheat on Cara, dude. No. No way."

"You kind of already have."

"When?"

"Technically, I mean."

My waving chopsticks are coming dangerously close to his eyeballs. "I said… when?"

"When I kissed you that Halloween."

"How?"

"I was already gonna ask Cara to Homecoming, and then you kissed me and—"

I don't just wave my chopsticks. I point them. Menacingly. I'm not sure they're strong enough to pierce human flesh, but it's worth a shot right about now. "You. Benjy. You. Kissed. Me."

"Anyway, so technically we've already cheated."

"And technically, you're an asshole for not asking me instead."

"What? You would have said 'no,' for sure."

He's kind of right. I'd been hoping for Preston Wilcox to ask me all semester long. He never did. "Of course, I would have."

He rolls his eyes. Knows better.

I eat a little more, but my heart's just not in it. It takes a lot to put me off my sushi, but he's gone and managed even that. He's stopped eating, too, ignoring his sake cup and sipping his beer slowly.

We're quiet for a moment, digesting more than just the rice and raw fish. "Anyway… I could never talk to Cara like this."

"Waddya mean?"

"Blue balls? She's probably never even seen my balls."

I snort hopefully. "You're not saving it for marriage, are you?"

"No, she just prefers it in the dark, you know?"

"Ewwwwwww. Stop." I make a face. Then, tentatively, because of course I've always been curious. "Every time?"

He kind of seems glad I asked. Like maybe he's been waiting for someone to talk about this with for a good long time. "Every time."

I wave my chopsticks toward the wall next to our booth, indicating the outside world where, presumably, it's still light out. "What about afternoon delight?"

Shakes his head. I press a little more, even though I'm not sure I really want to know, because he only talks about sexy times when he's buzzed like this. "Morning wood sex?"

"Ha. Not likely. Sex is to be performed between 8 and 10 p.m. or not at all. Weekends only."

"With the lights off. Heard." I snort and unstick the bill from beneath my thigh. "No wonder you've got blue balls, Big Guy."

EIGHTEEN

SHAY

"I f you want me to come home with you, just say so. Gheez."

I grunt. Trying to hold him up on his bike as the tinny, stringy Asian music strings tinnily overhead. I managed to get him out of Chopstix without knocking over the host stand or the gumball machine by the door, just barely, mind you, but now we're struggling in the strip mall walkway just outside. "I just don't want to hear about this from your mom for the rest of my life, okay?"

He leans against the brick wall under a swaying Asian lantern. Waves his big, stupid, gentle hands. "I'm fine. It's like a block away."

"Uh, it's more like three blocks and you can't even sit on your bike, Dude. Come on. Get off. We'll walk it back to my place. Maybe that will sober you up."

He nods. Sits there anyway. I roll my eyes as another stringy bit of Asian music plays from the rusty speaker over our heads. Part of me just wants to give up and pour him back into a booth inside. The other knows that only time, and lots of it, will help his useless ass.

He nods again. Harder this time. Like he's made some decision up there where the sake and beer are still swimming around in his useless noggin. Sighs big time. "Okay." I prop him up as he unfolds his long, gangly legs over the top of the bike. It's not easy. But somehow, he manages.

I nod. Impressed that he hasn't fallen ass over teakettle into the parking lot and skinned both knees by now.

He grins. Pleased with himself, too. "See? No bigs!" Then he turns, slightly, bumps the bike and it falls to the ground with a cacophonous crash. I'm pretty sure our already judgmental waitress hears it as well. Good luck getting a third round of drinks next time we come in. He chuckles. Stares at it helplessly, like it's just crash landed there from another planet.

I roll my eyes and help him pick it up. "We good now?"

He grips the handlebars carefully. Nods very seriously. "We're great. Where are we going for dinner?"

I grunt and finally get him into the street. "My place, remember?"

He nods. Winks. Nudges my shoulder with his. Not too buzzed to forget his big blue balls. "Mmmmmm…."

I roll my eyes. "Gross."

He chuckles at something inside his own warped head. I steer him onto the sidewalk along Ocean Drive. It's still bright out. Hot Florida November heat. His body is warm and sticky alongside mine as I walk beside him, my own bike in my hands.

He uses his like a walker. A hand on either handlebar. Focusing intently on putting one foot in front of the other. He does pretty well. The fresh air must help. The sunshine. The movement. At least he ate, so in a few hours he should be good to go. Still, it's gonna feel like babysitting until then.

He perks up in a few feet. Interjects a random comment. "Thanks for lunch."

"You're welcome, Benj. My pleasure."

Nothing. Then, a few feet later. "Hope business picks up again soon. Then I'll take you to lunch."

"It will, Benj. It always does right after the holiday when folks are back in town visiting family. Everyone's grocery shopping this week."

He nudges me again. "Not us." Winks.

I chuckle. Nudge him back. He smiles. A big, soft, goofy grin. We walk in silence a little more. In the waning sunlight, shadows playing across his boyish face, it's easy to picture him as he was that night. So many years ago.

He'd worn a baseball costume that night. To Bridget's party. Which was lame because he just put on his baseball uniform from school, duh. Kleets and jersey and ball cap and all. He didn't care about the costume contest anyway. I really didn't, either.

Halloween was always more Cara's thing than ours. We just went to the party for free beer. Okay, and because I'd wanted Preston Wilcox to notice me in my sexy sheer stockings and black leotard and glowing red cape. Newsflash: he never did.

Benjy had been buzzed that night, too. Well, we both were, I suppose. It was Halloween, after all. A weeknight, but still. Free beer. And lots of it. He'd looked even more boyish back then in his baseball cap and soft, tight jersey and even tighter baseball pants. They'd announced the costume contest and everyone else had cleared off the back porch in a hurry.

Neither of us had moved. I can't remember what the prize was that year, or if there even was one. People just love contests, I guess. Either way we suddenly had the whole deck to ourselves. All of it. We'd been crowded into a corner when it was full, heads leaning in close to be able to hear each other above the bad house music and millions of people talking all at once, but now it felt weird, awkward, to still be so close with all that space to ourselves.

And still, neither of us had moved. It was like we were frozen in time. I was leaning back against the corner of the porch railing. There was a railing on either side of me. I had a red plastic cup full of lukewarm beer I wasn't really drinking anymore in one hand. A cigarette I was even less interested in smoldering in the other.

We'd been talking. About what, I couldn't remember now if you put a gun to my head. Something stupid, I'm sure. A song lyric neither of us could remember but suddenly wanted to for some unknown reason. A movie we both wanted to see but never would because we knew Cara wouldn't be into it and we couldn't exactly go together and neither of us would be caught dead in a movie theater alone. Some chemistry test neither of us wanted to take the next day. Either way, the emptiness made us quiet.

Our eyes met in the silence. We'd laughed. Nervously, I guess. There was laughter inside, too, from the living room where everyone else had gathered. Applause. We'd glanced over to see what was happening through the slats. Commotion. Cheering. Hooting. Hollering. All eyes were definitely not on us. When we glanced back at each other, he kissed me. Just, he didn't have to go far. He just leaned in a little farther than he already had been when we were talking nonsense. Cocked his head gently sideways and our lips met. It was soft. Gentle. Warm. Smooth.

Almost… chaste.

Then I realized what was happening. Leaned back. He paused. Licked his lips and looked uncertain. Not hurt, just uncertain. Cocked his head like… WTF? I grinned. Leaned back in. The kiss was harder this time. Breathless. Exotic. New. Unexpected. He inched closer. His body against mine. Hard. Taut. Lean. Big hands and long fingers around my waist. The crowd inside cheered some more and we thought it was for us and we stopped, looking inside. But it was only another stupid skeleton trophy being handed out.

By then the spell was broken. He looked embarrassed. Wiped his lips with the back of his hand. I made a face. "Rude." My voice was husky and vague and confused. He smiled anyway. Was about to say something when the sliding glass door slid open. He took a step back. Cara took a step forward. Holding the trophy high. Beaming in her sexy clown costume because of course. "I won!"

We golf clapped. Excited for her. Truly. Because we knew how much it meant to her. Benjy took a step closer to her. Or, maybe, just a step further away from me. They shared a glance. It was only for a moment, but unmistakable. She was wary. Suddenly. Glancing from Benjy to me and back to him again. She arched one severe, smoky black eyebrow beneath her curly red clown wig and that was that. He seemed embarrassed. Flustered. Apologetic. All in a glance and a brush of his long, trembling fingers along the brim of his crooked ball cap.

Either way, I was forgotten.

Or so it felt. And then the crowd returned. Festive. Gay. Festooned as pirates and wenches and kings and queens and monsters and skeletons and lazy asses in generic pumpkin t-shirts from Bargain Barn that said, "This is my costume". The moment passed and, in the chaos, Cara and Beny drifted away with each other, disappearing to parts unknown in the festive, frolicking crowd.

They never came back.

I left shortly afterward. Not through the house, where I might have seen them whispering, or necking or worse. I just kind of drifted toward the back steps of the porch, took them down to the pool deck, drifted past the lawn furniture and flickering pumpkins and off through the bushes and out into the next street. Got my bearings and headed home.

On foot.

Alone.

I was still living at home back then. Dad was long gone at that point. Mom had been through half a dozen boyfriends after him. We were still living in the doublewide then, the one Mom had rented after some bozo had dragged her and, by association, me down to Florida in the first place and then dumped her two weeks later. She was working in some warehouse, off and on, mostly off and had barely noticed my Little Red Riding Hood costume when I'd stumbled in, mascara running and out of breath from the long walk back from the party. I'd grabbed something from the fridge for dinner, mumbled goodnight and gone back to my room to cry myself to sleep. Another ho hum night at Chez Witherspoon.

The next day at school Benjy and Cara were a couple. Just like that. "We're going to homecoming, Shay!" I remember her waiting out in front of the school to tell me. She could have texted me. I guess in all the hubbub she forgot. Or maybe she wanted everyone else around us to hear. That was more her style.

Still is, I suppose.

And now here we are. Over six years later. Walking alongside Ocean Drive. The sun in our faces. Benjy in a ball cap. Long fingers gripping his handlebars. He catches me looking. Winks. Sounds twice as sober as he was, say, five minutes ago. "Thanks for giving me some place to crash for a while, Shay."

I'm surprised by the sudden lump in my throat. Croak out the first thing that comes to mind, hoping he'll forget it by tomorrow. "I'll always have room for you, Benjy."

His grin is gently interrupted. He stops walking his bike long enough to stay steady on his feet. "Hey, why are you crying?"

"Am I?"

I definitely am. "Yeah, you definitely are. What…what's wrong, Shay?"

"I have no idea, Benj."

He looks doubtful. The sake and the sun have clearly made him more insightful than usual. That is when he's not nodding off or swerving gently into the road. "None at all?"

I shake my head. Hot tears streaming down my face at four in the afternoon on a sunny November day. He lets the bike fall against his waist. Opens his arms wide. "You need a hug."

"I do. I totally do. But…"

He makes a face. "No funny stuff. I know, Shay. Honest. Come on. Just a hug. Between friends."

I put my kickstand down. Leave my bike in the middle of the path like it's no big deal that I'm a big, quivering, slobbering mess in the middle of the afternoon on the city's main drag. Hug him. Tight and warm and hard and long, not caring who might see or what they'd think if they did.

NINETEEN

SHAY

"We should totally go swimming, Shay."

We're at the foot of the stairs. I finally got him to lock up his bike. It took ten minutes. "We'll swim later, buddy."

"Come on. Can't we swim now? I'm. Soooooo. Hot."

He is pretty sweaty. Glistening, is more like it. From head to toe and back again, making his copper-toned physique even sexier than usual. I just... all I need now is for Hub to hear us futzing around down here and come out with a beer or something to get Benjy started all over again.

I grin, suddenly inspired. "Yup, but we gotta get a swimsuit first, right, Benj?"

He takes a step. Now at least he's more motivated. Even if it is by a lie. "Duh."

"Anyway, let's get a move on there, buddy."

He turns around. Winks. "It'd be faster if you gave me a boost."

I wink back. "You just want me to grab your butt, perv."

He wriggles it. Jesus, this kid. And damn. That ass, tho! "If you insist."

I join him on the same step. He is warm and sweaty and smells like tempura shrimp and beer and sunshine and summer even though it's only a few days until Thanksgiving. Then take one step past him. "Hey."

I reach back for him. "Let's try this instead."

He shrugs. Grabs my hand. I help tug him up another step. Then another. We reach the top and almost fall into each other. He leans casually against the wall while I open the door. Watches me with soft, sleepy eyes that maybe aren't as buzzed as they seem. The door swings open.

He glances inside. "Nice!" Wanders in. "I love what you've done with the place." Heads straight for the couch and sinks right down without so much as a glance at my carefully choreographed wall art and interior staging.

"Very funny."

He finally starts looking around as I shut the door behind me. Lock it. Put my keys in the little bowl on the bureau under the picture window. Hang my backpack on the hook behind the door.

He shakes his head. "No, I'm serious. I can't remember the last time I've been up here."

"Come on, Benj. Really?"

He thinks. "I mean, not since Cara left."

I shrug. Do a little mental math and calculate some of the recent upgrades. "You could be right, actually."

He grins. Self-satisfied. Snuggles into the comfy couch. "I know I am."

I shrug. Drift toward the closet in the hallway. "It's not my fault you dump me off here every time we ride home together."

"No, but it is your fault for not inviting me up."

I keep up the running patter while I rummage through the closet. "You're not shy."

I turn back to him with a stack of stuff in my hand. He shrugs. "Too shy to invite myself up, I suppose."

I grin. Set the stack on the kitchen counter. Pour us glasses of water. Listen to the ice cubes clink as I put one in front of him. "So, it took you three carafes of sake to invite yourself over?"

He chuckles. Ignores the water. "I guess I'm chicken, huh?"

I turn and grab the stack. "I guess."

Put it in front of him. "What's all this?"

"Just stuff you'll need. You know. For when you fall asleep."

"I'm not sleepy."

His eyes are literally at half-mast. "Okay, big guy."

"I'm not." He yawns as if to prove how right I am. Looks through the stack. Sees the boxer shorts on top. Perks right the hell up. "Hey, these aren't mine."

I chuckle. "No shit?"

Narrows his eyes. They're wide open now. Shit, he was almost asleep. I should have put the boxers on the bottom of the stack. Rookie mistake. Then again, it has been awhile since I've had a guy sleep over, so...

He taps the superhero boxers pointedly. "Whose are they, anyway?"

"Just a friend of mine left them behind awhile back. They should fit."

His nostrils flare. "What friend?"

"What do you care?" They're not actually a friend's. I won them out of the claw machine at work when it was brutally slow one day and nobody else wanted them, so I brought them home and stowed them away in case some random guy ever came over and needed them. Who knew that rando would be Benjy?

"I care."

"What? You're jealous?"

"Slightly. Maybe even more than slightly."

I smirk and let him squirm for a moment. We've never talked about my sexual past, not that there's much of one, mind you, but what little there is I've always managed to keep lowkey and off the radar. Why? Not a clue. I suppose to avoid moments like this one, with Benjy mildly hurt and overly curious and who needs it? No matter who I've slept with in the past, it was never Benjy and, so to me anyway? It never felt like it officially counted.

All the same, he doesn't need to know that.

"Benjy. You're dating my best friend. Who you talk about constantly. God knows how many times you two have had sex since you started hooking up. I have one pair of men's boxer shorts in my house and suddenly you're the jealous one?"

He chuckles. Picks them up finally. Waves them around. They're colorful. Some super-hero I don't recognize. "Pretty big. I hope they don't fall off."

I sigh. Glance around the apartment. I'm hot and sticky and restless but don't want to leave him alone while I take a dip in the pool. Plus, I'm not up for Hub's teasing tonight. I'm too hungry and vulnerable and receptive. I reach for the bathroom door. "Look, I'm going to hop in the shower. You okay putting those on by yourself, or…?"

He grins. "I think I can manage. Want some company?"

I make a face. "Gross. Drink your water, Benjy. Get some rest."

But I don't lock the bathroom door when I shut it, just the same. And I take my time turning on the water. Hanging my clothes, piece after piece, on the row of hooks hanging over the back of the bathroom door. Waiting for his footsteps to pad across the hardwood floor, unsteady but persistent. Waiting for the knob to jiggle.

Playfully, at first. Then more earnestly when he finally gets the courage up to walk inside. Waiting to hear what I'll say when he opens the door to find me, naked and limber and hungry and aching and reaching for the nozzle as if him showing up was the very last thing I expected.

Instead, I hear him snoring before I even turn on the water. Sigh and step into the shower. Still naked. Still. So. Very. Hungry...

TWENTY

BENJY

I blink my eyes open. Suddenly, and slowly, at the same time. Stare at the ceiling for a minute. It's not my ceiling. I glance around, trying to ignore the pounding in my head, the crick in my neck and butterflies in my gut.

Struggle to get a lay of the land as I remain, fixed in place. Fluttering curtains. Gauzy and light and tan. The tang of saltwater on the gentle breeze seeping inside between them. A flickering jar candle sputtering out some kind of fall scent, heavy on the nutmeg and cinnamon. Thick fashion magazines fanned out on the edge of a strange wicker coffee table that's not mine, either.

I'm straddling the couch like it's an easy chair, arms, and legs at extreme, uncomfortable angles. I sit up, wincing from the odd angle and a wicked middle of the night hangover. Groan softly as I put my feet on the hardwood floor beneath me. They come to rest by a rumpled pile of clothes. My clothes. Work clothes, from earlier in the day. Brush them to one side with my feet as I try to get my bearings.

There's a glass of water on the coffee table. Tall and sweating all over a coaster shaped like a pumpkin. I grin, despite the throbbing in my head. Reach for it and gulp half of it down at a clip. Realize suddenly that I need to pee. Desperately. I stand on wobbly legs and see a nightlight on in a small bathroom just down the hall from the living room. Pee so long I almost fall back asleep, then root through a medicine cabinet full of nail polish and vitamins and tampons until I find a bottle of aspirin. Grab a handful and drift back to the kitchen.

Open the fridge and find a bevy of iced coffee drinks in tall, fancy looking, tall brown cans and not much else. I grab one, crack it open and down the aspirin with a big, bold, sweet, black swallow that revives my soul in ways church never could. Burp and grin and drink some more until I feel halfway human again. Press the cold, tall can against my forehead and literally shiver with relief as my eyes begin to scan the small but stylish apartment with slightly more clarity this time around.

The couch is small. More like a love seat. No wonder I was flailing all over it and woke up with a sore neck. I grin to see Shay has folded up a blanket and pillow on one of the two cushions. Surprised I didn't kick it off while I was tossing and turning.

Next to it is a wicker chair. Old. Stylish. Retro. Filled with throw pillows in a variety of pastel colors to match the washed out pink and blue surfer prints and woven tapestries hanging from the walls. There are plants on little tables clustered here and there, filling the room with green-ery, a record player on an end table against the wall, every-thing spaced just so to make the small room look bigger than it actually is. Her surfboard leans next to the front door, green and pink striped and matching the cool, retro vibe of the living room as if it's part of the furniture.

I hear gentle breathing from the master bedroom and

inch in the opposite direction, to a small guest bedroom off to the right of the living room. It feels vaguely thrilling, and slightly larcenous, to be snooping around Shay's apartment while she sleeps but I'm just spaced out enough after the long, weird day to give it a shot.

There's no bed inside the little room, just a big papa-san chair full of more pastel throw pillows, wicker hats and scarves hanging from the walls like fancy paintings and a round, super fuzzy pink rug in the middle of the floor. Like the living room, she's taken a less is more approach in here to make the small room look big or, at least, bigger. The only other furniture in the room is a round wicker table by the chair stacked high with thick, dog-eared books. A jar candle, brown and fancy with an old-timey apothecary type label, rests on top of the stack.

I smile, imagining Shay sitting in here, comfy in a pair of knee-high socks and an oversized t-shirt and not much else, nestled deep in the throw pillows and reading a big, fat romance novel between sips of chamomile tea. The candle flickers, late afternoon sunlight drifts through the half-closed blinds, bathing her in sexy shadows as she licks her full, plump lips after every sip. Crossing and uncrossing her long, coltish legs and wriggling deeper into the pillows when her racy romance book heats up every so often.

Then I realize I don't even know what type of books she's into. Or if she drinks tea. Or wears knee-high socks. Or has ever used this room at all. Who knows? Maybe she's just really into the boho aesthetic and bought the books at a thrift store for props while looking at a sample room from a page ripped out of one of those dream design house magazines.

I shut the door and stand in the hallway. Feel a slight chill as I drift back into the living room to stand in front of the fluttering curtains on either side of the picture window.

Glance out at the walkway outside the open window and, beyond, to the shimmering pool downstairs. Think a swim might be nice. Scratch my belly while I think about how much work that might entail. Realize it's bare. My belly, that is. Hell, I'm bare. Well, for the most part. Glance down to find a ridiculous pair of Spiderman boxer shorts clinging loosely to my hips and not much else.

I grin. Turn from the window. Wide awake now. Glimpses from the sushi bar dancing through my head. Sake. Too much sake. Edamame and sushi and pad thai and beer. Snatches of a sun-drenched bike ride home, more like a walk, intermingle with the Asian string music and judge-y server and Shay's voice, exasperated and, vaguely, amused. It's been awhile since I've gotten that gronked in the middle of the day.

And now, it's the middle of a strange, weird night.

Inevitably, slowly, carefully, I find myself standing at Shay's bedroom door. It's ajar, more than half open. Even wider with a little push. A soft glow from the hallway outside her window bathes her in a most flattering light. Not that she needs it, but damn. Hot. Holy. Damn. She's in a t-shirt. Loose but clinging to her ripe, young curves. It's ridden up in her sleep, the hem coming to rest just above her belly button. Her belly is soft and tempting above a pair of even softer blue panties. They're small, but not bikini. Her legs are long and copper in the hazy orange glow and I've never wanted her more than at that very moment. And I've wanted her. A lot and often.

She snores gently, pert nostrils flaring between eyes lightly shut. I know if I make a noise, any noise—clear my throat, squeak my foot on the floor, burp again, crumple the empty iced coffee can in my hand – she'll wake and rise and find me there, standing in her doorway, half-naked in baggy boxers and a semi-chub about to poke out the little flap in front and wink at her with its skinny little eye. I'm tempted to do just that, but I've been creepy enough tonight. Sigh just quietly enough not to rouse her and pad the few steps back to the couch.

I sink down on the love seat next to the carefully folded sheets and pillow, too wired to even think of sleep. I should probably go home. Just slink back into my clothes and grab my bike and head on home. Pull my pud in the shower like a good boy and try to get some rest before another chaste day as Cara's dutiful boyfriend begins. That's what I should do, but... I don't really want to. Not even a little.

I want Shay to wake up. Want her to read my mind and feel the same, antsy, horny. Want her to get up, stir and rise and slither to the door on those long, endless legs and scratch at the hip of her blue panties as her t-shirt clings to her ripe, full breasts and she blinks her big green eyes and asks me, "What's up, Benj?"

It'll never happen but I'd still rather sit here swimming in my baggy boxer shorts, semi-hard and wishing it so, than ride home on my creaky ten-speed and try to navigate the squeaky floor mat and avoid Mom on the way to the shower. So, I sit, and I wait and give myself another few minutes before I finally tell myself to do the old heave-ho and hit the road.

I mean, what's the worst that could happen if I stay?

TWENTY-ONE

SHAY

"**B**enjy?"

"Yeah." He sounds surprised. No, that's not it. Relieved, is more like it.

It's dark, clearly still nighttime. But not too dark. A gentle breeze rustles the curtains on either side of the picture window. There's a candle glowing on the coffee table. Flickering gently in the breeze. Casting his lean, bare torso in a most flattering light. I'd lit it earlier so he wouldn't wake up in total darkness. Now I'm kind of regretting it. If it was dark, I couldn't see how much I still want him.

I'm standing in my bedroom doorway. Wearing a t-shirt. Big and flouncy over soft blue panties. Nothing else. He's wearing the Spiderman boxers. And only the boxers. He's right. They are big. Loose and baggy around his lean, narrow, bare waist. Sagging low over his bony hips. "What are you doing?"

He's sitting up straight on the couch, is what he's doing. Rigid and stiff and quiet and frozen in place. The sheets and blanket I gave him are carefully folded on the cushion next to him. The pillow rests on top of that. "I dunno. Waiting for you I guess?"

"For how long?"

Shrugs those big, broad, smooth bare shoulders. "A little while, I suppose."

I cock my head. Try not to stammer or stutter over the pounding of my suddenly frantic heart. "What were you gonna do if I didn't wake up?"

Shrugs. "Leave, I guess."

"Without saying goodbye?"

We're whispering. It feels only right in the deep, still darkness of the middle of the night. Neither of us have slept much. The glowing numbers on the digital clock on the oven read just after 3 AM. I'm suddenly, thoroughly, epically wide awake. Hungry and desperate and raw with thunder and fire in my veins. It might as well be midday.

Or a certain Halloween party six long years ago...

I drift closer. From leaning against my bedroom door to leaning against the kitchen counter halfway across the room. I hear my bare feet slap against the wooden floor beneath them. My panties feel suddenly too tight.

His eyes are alive and liquid in the flickering candlelight as they follow my progress. He shrugs. "I guess so. I wouldn't want to wake you up just for that."

I nod. Wait a bit until the sounds of fluttering curtains and flickering candle and my own heartbeat pounding are deafening. "Are you okay?"

He answers quickly. Certainly. "Not at all. Are you?"

I grin. Soft and warm where I shouldn't be. Stiff and tender where my thin shirt drifts across my bare breasts. Mapping the weak spots of my naked desire. My voice is soft and low and flat. Almost confessional. "Not really. No."

He pats the cushion next to him. All I can see are his

knees and thighs and bare, flat quivering belly. I shake my head. Bite my lip. Will myself to stand in place despite every fiber of my being wanting me to literally pole vault across the room and land next to him.

His smile is soft but threatening. The uncertain boy from the sushi bar suddenly replaced with someone more determined to get what he wants. "If you don't come over here, Shay, I'm just gonna have to come over there."

I shiver. His voice is low. Deep in a way I've never heard it before. Insistent, too. Not a question, not an answer, more like a command. I don't say anything back. I don't do anything. He nods. Like he's decided. Stands from the couch, long arms and legs unfolding as the hardwood floor finally creaks beneath his big bare feet.

Stops midway. "You're so beautiful, Shay."

"You're just drunk, Benjy. It's called beer goggles. You'll know better when you sober up."

Shakes his head. Keeps walking. Bare feet slapping against the floor, boxers swimming around his waist, the heft of his thickness swaying to and fro against the fly with every step. I swallow. Hard. Wait for what he might say, or do, next.

"I was drunk before, Shay. I'm not anymore. I know exactly what I see."

My voice is low. Breathless. Almost unrecognizable, like the frenzied beating of my pounding heart. "Stop, Benjy. Don't."

Shakes his head. "I won't, Shay. Not if you don't want me to."

I bite my lip. He takes another step. "I don't know..."

He's in front of me. All of him. Lean and bare and hard. He stops just shy of bowling me over. His hand rests near mine on the kitchen counter. I look slightly up, his lean, handsome face still dancing in the flickering shadows of the candle flame.

I can't stop trembling. When he moves his hand, slightly, closer to mine, I see he is, too. Somehow that makes me feel somewhat better. I can still barely breathe. Somehow manage to stammer out a reply. "What...what are you doing?"

"I just want you to know what, whatever happens next, I'm not buzzed anymore."

"Nothing's going to happen—"

He kisses me then. Gently at first, like he did so many years ago. Back on Bridget Carlson's porch. Soft lips. Full. Pressed against mine. I murmur something. Lips gently open. He kisses me harder. Or maybe that's just me. We tangle, bodies and limbs until he's somehow turned, his back to the countertop.

My hands are all over his body. Soft skin and lean muscle and quivering, yielding flesh. He's trembling even more now. A soft whimper escapes those full, wet lips as I slide my hands down his hips and drag the boxers, already sagging, with them. They fall to his feet, puddling around his ankles as I take him gently in hand.

He shivers. Bites his lower lip. His eyes flicker until they shut, tight. He stands, powerless, frozen, as I stroke his silken skin between trembling, willing fingers that map out every vein and inch of long, thrusting flesh. Already epically hard, he murmurs and gently thrusts in and out of my tentative grasp. Both of us are acting involuntarily. I couldn't stop if I tried, and he's not even trying. In moments he is damp and sticky and trembling, the motion making slick, sultry sounds in the stillness of the flickering night.

I watch him, all of him, taking in every moment as if to sear it into my brain, knowing it shouldn't happen in the first place and never will again. His eyelids flutter. His throat blushes. He grits his teeth. Bites his lip. Winces, murmurs, hunches over at the waist as if trying to resist the inevitable with every fiber of his being. Our foreheads gently touch as I glance down to admire the approaching finale. Already thick and throbbing he seems to swell to bursting until, suddenly, he erupts with a gasp and a gush, my hands sticky and drizzled as I murmur and kiss and reassure his breathless cries away.

Gasping, he pushes me away. He's sweaty and panting like he just ran over from his house. Grins and blushes and apologizes with embarrassed eyes. "I...I told you I had blue balls."

For a moment, I think that's it. We're done. It's over. I drink in his body, long and lean, quivering and flushed, sweaty and sticky and trembling in the afterglow. Savor every inch of soft, steaming, naked skin. Freeze it in my brain as the memory. It would have been enough. Honestly and sincerely, so help me God, that moment, frozen in time, would have been enough for me. And I'm grateful, in a way, that I haven't done anything worse.

Then he wraps me in his arms and buries his head in my hair. Sniffs long and hard, like he's memorizing this moment, too. Moves his face and gently whispers in my ear, husky and low and deep and rumbling like it was his plan all along. "Your turn."

I murmur something between a nervous chuckle and a confused sob and a hopeful choke as his fingers, long and limber, drift down my sides and beneath my shirt. The fabric rasps against flushed skin and stiff, tender breasts. I murmur and moan and quake with every fiber of my helpless, quivering being. His fingertips dance across my swollen nipples as if they know exactly what I want, and where and when and how and how long.

I gasp and know I'm done for. Right or wrong, good, or bad idea, I couldn't, I wouldn't, stop even if the roof caved in just then.

I sag back against the wall just outside my bedroom, as if needing someplace to rest before I float up and out and away from my seismically quaking body. He drags the shirt over my head like he's peeling me open. Tosses it to the floor where it merges with his baggy boxers. Tilts his head down to kiss me just as I tilt mine up to do the same. Our lips entwine as his fingertips drizzle down my rib cage, tug at my panties and make quick work of dragging them to my knees.

I wriggle and gasp as his left-hand drifts around to cup me from behind, gently, firmly, as the other hand makes me whimper and moan and gush between my trembling legs. The warmth fills my whole body. My skin is on fire. He suffocates me with his lips even as he skillfully presses and glances and dances his sticky fingertips along my swollen, desperate bud.

I'm ripe and hungry and easy, gasping and writhing against his long, thick fingers until I buck and bite down on his shoulder to stifle a long-buried squeal that makes me hoarse from the effort. I sag against him, sticky, feverish skin clinging to his stiff, rigid torso.

Once more I think we're done. Once more I couldn't be more wrong. He patiently waits out the first wave, thick and sticky and passionate. Then thrills me to another, and then three more before I'm conscious enough to feel the stiffness against my thigh and recognize it as his own.

I push him away. Watch it rise even stiffer still. "How…"

He chuckles. Blushes. Grabs my hand and whisks me

into the bedroom. We collapse onto the bed, clammy and sweaty in the soft white sheets. A gentle breeze from the window dances along our glistening bodies. Soft moonlight streams in through the open window as I peer up into his warm brown eyes.

"I've waited years for this, Shay. I'm not wasting a single minute..."

I writhe beneath him as he pins me to the mattress with a kiss so intense it brings me back to life even as it threatens to smother me with the same fervent intensity. I feel him on top of me, then easily and deeply inside me, the pleasure so intense I bite down onto the sheets to stifle another whimpering, pathetic climax.

And he wasn't wrong. It's just the beginning...

TWENTY-TWO

SHAY

"Benj?"

This time? Nothing.

"Are you out there?" My voice, husky and ragged even as I sense the stillness in reply.

I lie in bed. Spent. Sticky. Alone.

It's still dark out. The moonlight casting my naked, splayed body in shadows and peaks and valleys. How? How is it not three days later? In full, vivid sunshine? I feel like I've lived a week in one night and it's not even over yet!

I sit up, naked and twisted in the damp, sticky bed sheets. Glance around the room for signs of life. See my t-shirt, desperate and wanton in a puddle on the living room floor just outside my door. Panties next to it, soft and blue and staring back at me with shame and regret written all over them. Blush at the memory of being pinned to the wall, gasping for release even as he gave it to me, over and over again. Calling out his name, screaming and crying out in bittersweet joy and ecstasy, silenced only by his smothering kisses, leaving me breathless and spent.

Blush and shiver and shake the thought away. Listen

more closely for the sounds of brewing coffee or the shower running or even snoring from the couch. But I can tell from the dead silence hovering around the empty apartment that he's gone.

Just like he said he'd be.

I drift from bed, the mattress squeaking with my departure. Look back down at the moonlit sheets to see his outline, still fresh on his side of the bed.

Drift into the hall and pick up my panties. Slip them on over sore, sticky thighs. Then my t-shirt, soft and silken on my tender, bruised nips. See the sheets still folded on the empty couch cushion. Feel the darkness and regret closing in as I realize he's really, truly gone.

I hear stirring outside the window. The familiar scraping of a well-worn chair leg on pink concrete. The unmistakable flick of an old Bic lighter, the same one he always uses. Then the soft, acrid waft of a puff of cheap cigarette smoke. Sag against the kitchen counter.

It's just Hub.

I glance around the empty apartment. See the numbers, still and stark on the microwave oven in the dark, quiet kitchen. Jesus. It's not even 5 a.m. yet.

What the fuck is that stoner doing up at this hour?

I drift closer to the door. Then another smell wafts in through the window. Coffee. Hot and fresh and black and strong. My very soul aches for it. I open the door. See him sitting there, soft and smirking in the dim light of an overhead bulb.

See two cups of coffee on the table in front of him. One full to the brim and softly steaming in front of the empty chair closest to my door. I smile for some reason.

Want to cry for another.

My voice is an almost unrecognizable croak, surprising

to us both. "You can't sleep, either?"

He coughs out a cloud or two of cheap cigarette smoke, chuckling in smoke signals at some secret, inside joke. Or maybe just my desperate, smutty appearance. Or the sound of my choky, croaky voice. "Yeah. No."

I nod toward the coffee. Struggle not to lick my lips. "That for me?"

Nods and slides the cheap black ashtray closer to his side of the table so I won't smell the smoke. He does that sometimes when he's feeling extra gentlemanly. Doesn't happen often, just enough so that he's not a complete and utter Neanderthal. I melt into the chair like I'm being dribbled off the end of a spoon. Nod at the pack of cigarettes, cheap and crumpled, between us. "Can I have one of those, too?"

He smirks. Pushes the pack closer. I reach for one. He lights it for me with the hula girl lighter. Still grinning as I soak the intense heat into my lungs and expel it with a deep, soulful sigh. "What's so funny, old man?"

Chuckles to himself again. "Oh, not a thing… Neighbor."

I inhale. Puff. Just my chin out in his general direction. Wince once more at my burly trucker voice. "Then what's with the shit-eating grin at five in the am?"

Glances away for a moment. "No particular reason."

I look away, too. For once, I actually have a pretty good reason to grin. As if on cue, Benjy flashes before my eyes. Naked and writhing and sweaty between my legs. I blush and inhale another whiff of cheap, flaky tobacco. Glance at my coffee mug through the smoky haze left behind. I've never felt more white trash trampy in my life, but am not particularly worried about it, either. Wonder if that makes me even trampier and don't particularly care.

I reach for the coffee with my free hand. Take a warm,

sweet, savory sip that literally fills my soul with glee. "Jesus, that's good."

He chuckles dryly from his seat across from me, little rumbles that send a vaguely jolly tremor through the cheap patio furniture set between our apartment doors. I feel it all the way to my bare feet. "What? The hell? Is wrong with you?"

Holds his hands up in surrender. Grins amidst his ever-present three-day stubble, salty and peppery and casually sexy. Little laugh lines around his washed-out blue eyes. "Just enjoying your company, is all."

I glance at him suspiciously over my coffee cup. My voice is as hoarse and husky as Benjy's last night. "Bullshit. What's up?"

He looks uncomfortable. A first. Fidgets in his chair. "Okay, well…uh…are we gonna talk about what happened last night?" Then shakes his head. Pretends to glance at an imaginary watch on his naked wrist. "Ehhr, I mean, this morning?"

I freeze, the coffee cup halfway to my lips. "Come again?"

Literally snorts. Holds up his hand in surrender like I'm the funniest comedienne in the world and he can't take another wave of belly laughs. "You sure did, little lady."

He can't have. There's no way. I wasn't, I mean, we weren't *that* loud were we? "What? Are? You? On? About?"

"What? How about those animal sex noises you made, for starters?"

I groan, stomach leaden and stiff. The last thing I ever wanted to become was him. "Jesus. You heard that?"

He tamps out his cigarette in the overflowing ashtray with a flourish. Waves a hand toward the walkway railing and beyond. "Honey, half the town probably heard it."

I set the mug down on the table with a too loud clatter. I'm surprised it didn't just fall from my hand. "Bull. Shit."

"What do you think I'm doing out here at this ungodly hour, Shay? I even put my headphones on and still heard your live sex show."

"Get out of here!"

Hub gives me another playful grin. "I'll have to if this shit keeps up on the nightly."

He sees the look on my face, desperate and defeated. My hands trembling on a fresh drag from the cigarette. Nudges my bare, skanky foot under the table with his. "Shay, I'm just kidding."

"Just kidding you heard me have sex? Or just kidding the whole town heard it?"

He lights another cigarette. Narrows his eyes at me through the curling shivers of soft, white smoke. "Which answer is going to make your hands stop shaking?"

"Hub!"

"Shay, it's okay. You're a young girl in the prime of your life. When you first moved in, I honestly thought I'd be hearing that kind of shit every night. I'm surprised it took so long."

I finally chuckle. Well, a little. "You and me both."

He sees an opening. Crosses his legs like a good girlfriend. Inches closer atop the small, fake wood table. "So, who was it?"

I groan. Reach for another sip of coffee. Wonder idly what he used to flavor it with and where I can get some and how soon. "You don't want to know."

"Someone from work?"

I bite my lower lip. Wonder why I'm being so coy. "You could say that?"

He nods. Leans back. Grins. "The tall skinny kid who rides you home during the week?"

I cluck knowingly. "He's not skinny!"

Hub claps his hands. "I knew it!"

"Stop, Hub. It's not funny."

He ignores me. "I mean, it kind of is."

It totally is. "Doesn't feel too funny at the moment."

He shrugs. "Would it be funnier if I tell you I already knew who it was before I asked?"

"How?"

"I mean, you only called his name 50 times before the headboard quit pounding against my—"

"Hub! So, help me God if you don't stop teasing me, I will literally toss you into that pool down there."

He chuckles. Nods. Puts his hands up. Grins and begins anew. "But isn't he that other girl's boyfriend?"

"Don't remind me."

"The one who calls the pizza gay 'babe' when he steps into her dorm room?"

"Hub."

He gets my tone. Sits back. Sips his coffee thoughtfully. I watch him consider the pack of cigarettes between us before apparently deciding against another one so soon. "So, all that passion I heard was from the forbidden lust you felt for your best friend's boyfriend all these years?"

I'm about to correct him. Sit up. Raise a finger. Open my mouth. Then I realize he's factually correct. There is literally not a single incorrect assumption in his statement. Slump back in my deck chair like someone's just cut my strings. "Yeah, basically."

"So, it wasn't wrong then."

"It was completely wrong. On every level."

"Shay, take it from me. Sex that good can never be

wrong."

I want to believe him. "Stop reminding me."

His eyes, soft and faded blue, pin me with real talk. "Shay, I'm not kidding anymore. This is a verbal gift, from me to you. Give. Yourself. A. Break. It happened. You enjoyed it. Benjy clearly did, too. You can't take it back and regretting it will only waste precious time and mental energy. Move on in that direction or you're gonna ruin whatever good thing you two shared last night."

My hands shake on the coffee mug. I put it back down. Look at him desperately. "I cheated, Hub. I broke a promise to myself that I would never, ever sleep with another girl's man. Especially Cara's. It's not just personally wrong. I'm not just imagining how wrong it is. It's...it's objectively, historically, factually wrong. There's no grey area here. I did a genuinely shitty thing."

He doesn't deny it. But doesn't look away, either. Nods soberly, just like an adult would. Looks back at me, clear-eyed and somber. "So did he, Shay. It takes two to, uh... make that much noise. Over and over again. For so very, very long."

I snort humorlessly. "That doesn't make it right."

"Didn't you say she was cheating, too?"

I start to bite my nail, then think better of it. "I don't know that for sure." Wait for him to say something comforting. When he doesn't, I harrumph. "And even if she is, how am I any better?"

"It's not about being better or worse, kid. Honestly, it's just about living your best life."

"By dicking around with someone else's man?"

He makes a face. "Do you have a side hustle as a long-haul trucker, because where are you getting this language all of a sudden?"

I laugh despite myself, grateful again for Hub's playful presence. Despite the icky embarrassment factor, I'd be having these same thoughts anyway. Him being here, fatherly and understanding, is perhaps the best tonic. Besides coffee and nicotine, that is. "We're both up because of a late-night booty call and my language is what you're worried about?"

He grabs another cigarette after all. Makes a big deal about crinkling the plastic wrapper and flicking the lighter and inhaling crisply and fully. "Fair point. I'm just saying you're not breaking anybody up by having loud sex at 3 in the morning, that's all. And once more at 3:30. And then again at 4…"

I ignore his good-natured jabs. "What if I am, though? What if this confuses Benjy and he gets all weird and…" My words drift away. My mind wanders to the very last thing I was thinking about in the middle of the night, Benjy naked and sprawled out next to me in my bed. What happens *now*?

Part of me wants to believe Hub. That it was all natural. Two young people giving in to temptation. No harm, no foul. The other part knows what a piece of shit friend I am and how the echoes of this transgression will haunt me for the rest of my natural life.

He seems to sense the war going on in my head. Reaches out with a gentle hand to cover my own. Squeezes it gently, rough skin on my trembling fingers. "Relax, Shay. Take a breath. It's five in the morning. You had a big night. It's honestly not the end of the—"

His thoughtful gesture crumbles in the wake of my mounting stress bomb. "No, dude, you don't understand. My anxiety is going to be through the roof until I sort this shit out."

He takes his hand away. Nods. Sits back thoughtfully.

"Yeah, probably. Want some St. John's Wort?"

"You already gave me some. Remember?"

He thinks back. Nods with a wry grin. "When you ran that guy's credit card on the wrong check at work and he threatened to sue you in a Yelp review?"

My stomach knots just thinking about it. Trigger warning much? Even though it was literally months ago. I'm... I'm surprised he even remembers that. Maybe he does listen to my immature nonsense ramblings while we eat greasy to go food together after all. "Right."

"Probably gonna be hard to sleep for awhile, too. Want some Valerian root?"

I smile through bruised, puffy lips. "You gave me some when I first moved in, remember?"

He grins so gently it makes me see him in a whole new light. "You had a hard time sleeping in a new place."

I nod, warmed by the breadth of our shared history. He beams. "Damn, I'm a pretty good neighbor, dude."

I chuckle. Grateful for the company. For the diversion. But most of all, for the coffee. "Speaking of good, this coffee is lit."

He chuckles knowingly again. "It ain't just the coffee that's lit, little girl."

I sniff gently. Smell the hint of something sweet and vaguely medicinal. How have I not noticed it before? "Is this shit spiked?"

He glances away. "Possibly."

I groan. But not too convincingly. "Hub. I have to work later."

"Yeah, later. Not at five in the damn morning."

I shrug. He's not wrong. "What's in it?"

"Just a little hair of the dog, that's all."

I take a sip. Strong, hot, and spiked. "Khalua?"

"Sure. I mean, knockoff Khalua from the liquor store around the corner, but what's the diff?"

I pick my cigarette back up. Tap the ashes off in the tray like a pro. Inhale deeply. Exhale extravagantly. Wash down the warm, acrid smoke with a swig of spiked coffee like I'm some kind of pro at all this or something. "Thanks, Hub."

"For what?"

I feel my throat tightening again, sore, and raw from the screaming and the trying not to scream and the giving up on trying not to scream. More sore now from choking back a tear. I don't think about fatherhood much, if ever. Sometimes I'll see a nice family in the restaurant, all together. A nuclear family? That's what it's called, right? Father, mother, two kids, that kind of thing. A happy family, all together, talking, laughing, and I get a little emotional thinking of what I've missed over the years and how it's probably, most definitely, affected me on some level I'm not tapping in on yet.

I don't miss my own father, per se. Never knew him enough to miss him, I suppose. And the occasional things Mom still says about him from time to time, though less and less often these days, makes me miss him even less. But mornings like this, anxious and wistful, make me wish for that fantasy family I never had. Never was going to have. Instead, I have to rely on my found family, mostly from work: Benjy. Glenda. And, now, Hub. I glance over at him, quiet and stubbly, still waiting for my reply as my fevered brain takes its time winding through memories new and old.

"Thank you for…this? I guess? Just everything."

He stands. "Don't thank me until you've had a pool shower."

"Now?"

He holds out a hand. Helps me up from my chair. "Sure. You don't wanna smell like sex all day, do you?"

TWENTY-THREE

SHAY

"So, what are you gonna do now?"

I shrug my shoulders, clad only in a soft pink bikini top. "Put on my big girl panties and deal with it, I guess."

Hub bobs gently up and down in the pool, face soft in the approaching glow of daybreak. "You're not gonna tell her, are you?"

I wipe chlorine out of my eyes. We're treading water in the deep end. It feels good to have the water, cool and soft on my blistering skin. Shrug. "I don't know yet. Benjy might have already. He's a wimp that way."

Hub's stubbly hair is damp. Skin taut and tan over his handsome face. Shoulders broad just beneath the water's rippling surface. His eyes are wet and understanding. "No matter what happens, Shay, you're a good person. Remember that."

"A good person who sleeps with her best friend's boyfriend?"

"Yeah, it happens."

"To you, maybe. I'm not a pothead surfer slut, remember?"

He chuckles. Splashes me. I splash him back. "You sure sounded like one last night, kid."

"Screw you."

Arches one eyebrow. "Don't threaten me with a good time."

I sigh and drift gently a few inches away. "Jesus, forget I said that, surfer slut."

"At least I don't beat myself up about it, Shay. You need to stand on a desk somewhere. Look around from a new viewpoint. Get a new perspective. Realize it's not the end of the world."

I sigh. Drift toward the shallow end. Reluctantly. "I will, one day. Right now, it feels like the worst thing I've ever done."

He grunts. Following me. "If having good sex with someone you care about after waiting years and years to do it is the worst thing you've ever done, Shay, then you're an even better person than I thought."

I chuckle. We drift in the shallow end. Closer to getting out but not quite ready yet. My buzz has worn off. So has the caffeine. I don't work until tonight and I'm ready for some actual sleep.

"You do care about him, right?"

I nod. Sleepily, but insistently. "Very much so, Hub."

He leans with his back against the wet floor tiles that surround the pool. "You weren't, like a virgin were you?"

I chuckle dryly. "Not exactly."

His face crumples. "What does that mean? Either you are or you aren't."

"I mean, not that it's any of your business, but I've had sex, just not like that before."

He chuckles. Blushes slightly. Or maybe it's just the

approaching sun. Nods. "So, you've had sex but never made an 'O' face before?"

I grin. "Oh, I've made the face before, just never without faking it."

He grins. "Well, congratulations. No wonder you were so, uh, verbal last night."

I splash him one last time. Float toward the pool stairs and slowly climb up them. I feel his eyes on me as I pass by, dripping wet and in my skimpy two-piece. Wonder what he's thinking. Wonder what he thought, last night, one wall away while I screamed and squealed and moaned and wailed, thinking it was all in my head or just not caring enough to bite into a damn pillow like a good neighbor. Wonder what he thought this morning, quiet and contemplative at the little table between our doors. Before I walked outside, that is. My spiked cup of coffee cooling in front of my empty chair.

I blink the thoughts away under the splash of gentle rain at the pool shower. Aware of his thick, muscled, masculine presence just nearby as he waits his turn. Hold the chain for him as he takes it from my hand. Gently pass by him to reach for my towel. Watch the water drizzle down his lean, compact body. Trace his patchwork landscape of oddly random tattoos with my eyes as his close under the splattering spray. Hear it stop and find him standing there, head cocked gently, watching me watching him.

Hand him the towel and reach for my white linen cover up. Gather it loosely over myself as if he hasn't seen most of me already, hundreds of times before. He dries himself. Tosses the threadbare beach towel over one shoulder. I hold the gate open for him. He drifts past. Waits for me at the bottom of the stairs. I pause next to him. Glance behind us one last time.

Incredibly, it's still dark out.

Jesus. H. Christ.

He senses my weariness. Takes my hand. I flinch. Just a little. Then relax. He never lets go. Drags me up each step, one by one, as my weariness grows with every step. I've never been so tired. Or, simply, relaxed.

Or maybe even helpless.

We arrive at my doorstep. It's still got my candy corn covered welcome mat from Halloween. I only notice because it's scratchy beneath my bare feet. He chuckles at my zone out. Squeezes my hand as his gently drifts away. Turns the knob. Presses the door open.

The apartment is dark save for the still flickering jar candle on the coffee table. The one I set out for Benjy. I smirk. Silently. Secretly. He sees it anyway. I blush. "Thanks, Hub. For this morning. For everything."

He blushes a little, too. Or maybe it's just the sun finally starting to rise. Leans in gently to plant a chaste, dry, gentle kiss on my forehead, still damp from the pool shower. "Thank you, Shay, for an entertaining night."

I chuckle. He gently nudges me inside. I swear I'm half asleep. I reach for the door. He pauses it with one hand. "Just remember, Shay, this too, will pass. Get some rest. You'll feel better in the morning."

"It is the morning."

"You'll feel better in the afternoon."

I chuckle. "What are you going to do?"

He grins. No longer subtle. "Me? I guess I'll try to grab a few hours of sleep before work."

"And then?"

He winks. Starts to drift away. "I guess I'll try to find me a girl who's as loud as you are in bed."

"Gross."

He gives me a wriggly wink. "Not from my side of the wall it wasn't, hot pants."

TWENTY-FOUR

BENJY

"You're up early." Cara's voice is low and husky and tight. She doesn't sound particularly surprised. Or, for that matter, tired. Or even all that glad to hear from me. Well, no surprise there.

I chuckle on autopilot. Nervously. Run my fingers through my wet hair. I'm still running on adrenaline and sake and spunk and whatever the hell was in that hopped up can of supercharged iced coffee I chugged back at Shay's in the middle of the night.

"Or late." I say, distracted as hell and even more nervous. "I can't tell which."

"Me either." Cara yawns and stretches like a cat. I can almost hear her purr through the phone screen. She's got a soft pink towel wrapped around her hair, a thin flannel robe hanging loosely from around her long, silky torso, like she's gearing up to star in a lady's razor commercial or a bubble bath ad.

"I can't believe you answered."

"I can't believe you called."

"I always call, Cara." That's true. A little melodramatic,

perhaps, but true. I can count on my fingers the number of times she's called me since she went away to school that fall, and it's usually to say she'll be busy so not to bother to call.

"Yeah, but you never call this early."

Well, she's got me there, I suppose. I hem a little. If she asks why, I'll tell her. About Shay and me. If she asks anything about why I'm calling, or why so early, or why I'm acting so weird, or taking a shower at this hour or sitting around half-naked, I'll spill the beans. All of them, every last single sexy bean. I've already decided. I mean, I pretty much decided on the way home from Shay's.

I won't be happy about it, but I feel the words lodged in my throat already and have to trust my instincts. "I can't sleep," I murmur noncommittally, pacing the room like a caged panther. That much, at least, is true.

You'd think after work and sake and a nonstop sex fest I'd be sacked out for days, but the opposite is true. I've never felt so wired. So very, very energetic, robust and alive.

Cara's voice, low and thoughtful, interrupts my reverie. Every time I close my eyes, every time my thoughts aren't entirely laser focused on some menial task, all I see are flashes of Shay in all her damp, sweaty, swollen, writhing glory.

Suddenly, Cara is there instead. Soft, sultry, and somber on the other end of another FaceTime call. "Me either."

I cock my head. "Why not?"

She glances back at me, as if surprised by the question. Or maybe just surprised that I'd ask. "I dunno. Lots going on, I guess. I can't turn my mind off."

I snort with relatability. "Tell me about it." I pause, giving her the chance to reciprocate. To ask, "Hey bud, what's going on in your mind that's got you ringing me up before dawn on a random weekday morning?" Instead, she turns back to painting her nails. Business as usual, I suppose.

I sigh. "Anything I can do to help?"

She grins, still looking down at her feet. It's almost better this way, with her not looking at me so curiously. I see the soft, rosy glow of her knee, shiny with some fancy special mail order lotion she uses.

Normally I'd be hungry to reach out and touch it, glide my fingers over her quivering thigh and toy with the soft, silken tuft of wispy fur between her legs. Make her forget what a cold, crafty B she's been lately and tap into the moaning, feverish, frantic Cara who always kept me on my toes, laughing and hungry for more.

But Shay drained me to the point where I'm no longer thirsty. I wonder if Cara will notice. Doubt, frankly, that she will. Wonder, maybe, if that's why I sat there on Shay's couch for so long in the first place last night. Not that I'm victim blaming, but...

Cara snorts. Widens her eyes a little so that I think she's finally noticed my damp, bare skin, and the loose knot of the towel around my waist, tempting to sag down or even fall off at a moment's notice. She never explains the mysterious sound, so I ask about it. "What?"

Looks up from her nails. Eyes piercing and smile tentatively as she nods at something behind me. Not my body. Not my belly. Not my towel, just a spot on the wall over my shoulder. "Nothing, I guess." She gives a sly little wink, face a mask of superior housekeeping skills as she murmurs, "Good to see you're keeping the room all nice and polished while I'm away."

I pause. Blush. Smirk. Glance around, trying to see my childhood bedroom the way she is now. The trophies on the shelves. The ribbons and medals and team photos hanging from the walls. Awards from sports I thought I should play to get girls. The surfing posters and magazine covers I tacked up on the wall when Mom and I first moved in after the divorce and never took down. The single bed, sheets ruffled, the same scarred bureau with the skater stickers to hide where it got bruised and scratched over the years. So far, this room is untouched from Mom's various Home Makeover plans, but who knows for how long? A few more "big contracts" and all of my well-worn memorabilia might be gone, traded out in favor of a real, actual matching bedroom set like the big boys have.

Cara's phone is propped up against a stack of her Architecture books, revealing not just her but her spotless, tidy, Pinterest worthy dorm room, full of all the hip, trendy, girly things that make up her oh so modern coed aesthetic. "Sorry we can't all be neat freaks like you, Cara."

I hold my breath. That was a little harsh. Even by our standards. But she doesn't freak out, huff or even sigh. "Yeah, well, I like to think my room is a reflection of my inner mind."

I roll my eyes, glance around my frat-inspired bedroom, frozen in time from mid-high school and huff, "So what does my room say about my mind?"

She narrows those big, sexy eyes back at me. "You really want to know, Benj?"

"I asked, didn't I?" I mean, I was expecting a throw away comment, something silly and quick, but I guess I forgot who I was talking to.

She shifts position, the robe shifting with her, little glints of her sexy body, the cool, almost austere expression making us feel like strangers. Then again, sleeping with our mutual friend last night probably didn't help matters much. Glancing past me at the room in her own phone screen, she clucks a tongue. "I see someone who refuses to move on," she insists, almost making me laugh.

Move on? That's putting it mildly. After last night, after the last few months, I'm not sure I can ever go back to the way things were. I'm not sure, honestly, if I even want to anymore. If that isn't moving on...

"Someone who stays put, stuck in place, I mean all that stuff is from three years ago."

Cara squints at the trophies and ribbons before correcting herself. "Four, five even."

"And?" I'm trying not to get huffy. "We can't all start fresh at college like you did, Cara."

"Uh, yes, we can. You've been to college, Benjy. Remember? We started together and then, I dunno. You pulled back. Dropped out of our first semester before you even gave it a chance."

I nod. Shrug. Wince a little at the memory. "The timing wasn't right," I murmur, using the same old excuse. "I'm just not where you are, Cara."

"Obviously," she huffs.

"No, I mean, literally I'm not where you are but I'm just not as motivated as you are right now. To be there. To be away. At college."

"Why not, though?"

"I'm not sure," I confess, peering back at her phone screen, past her, to the dorm room and the life I suppose I should be living now. I mean, after all, all my friends are. The bros I used to hang with in school, all gone away to school the summer we graduated. Cara's friends, too. And now she's gone, where she's supposed to be, I suppose, and I'm still here. In my old room. Trophies on the shelves. Posters on the wall, closet half-empty, dirty clothes in an overflowing hamper, like I'm still a teenager, breaking curfew and sneaking in the window.

"Is it me?" Cara asks, apropos of nothing. Or everything.

I sit up, out of my reverie. "What? No? Why...why would you say that?"

"I dunno, I just... You seem like you're marinating back home. Sitting in your own juices, stuck in the same rut and I thought, maybe if I stirred the pot a little, got out of there once and for all, it might motivate you to get off your butt."

I snort. "You sound like my mom right now."

"Yeah, and? At least she's doing something with her life, Benjy."

I nod. There it is. The old Cara. The real Cara. The "can't you do anything right, Benjy" Cara. "I'm doing my life, Cara. My way. On my own terms and, I suppose at my own pace. Just because it's not your life, doesn't make it...worthless."

"I never said worthless, Benjy. Just... You're so much better than...than...what you're doing now."

I shrug and wriggle in my towel. "People keep saying that, but I'm happy. No stress to speak of, no deadlines or assignments or due dates, just... it's working for me for now. Doesn't that count for something?"

"Happy? Living in your old bedroom? Waiting tables? Smelling like barbecue sauce every day after work? Hauling all your cash tips to the bank every week? I just don't get it." Her face may not be sneering, but there's more than enough sneer in her voice to make up for it.

"You don't *have* to get it, Cara. You just have to not make me feel like shit about it every time we talk. Is that so hard?"

"Is *what* so hard? Trying to snap you out of it? Are you..." Cara closes her eyes. Breathes heavily, possibly even counting to ten like you might with an overgrown toddler so you won't use four-letter words on them. Opens them back up. Fixes a smile, saccharine and slick. "Is this…is this why you called me this morning? To tug on my last nerve? Dredge up old shit you know was gonna get my goat right out of the box?"

I tense a little. I mean, she could be right. She usually is. Maybe I wanted to start a fight all along, just to avoid those beady, knowing eyes and what they might pry out of me if I gave her half a chance. Maybe I knew the towel wouldn't distract her and, frankly, half-naked and wet on my old bed, maybe I'm showing off just a little bit. Maybe I deserve all the huffing and puffing.

"No, not at all." Okay, okay, that's still technically not a lie. If I did call just to bait her into a fight, it was only subconsciously. Mostly. "Literally the last reason I called you this morning was to talk about my stupid bedroom, of all things."

Cara rolls her eyes, as if eager to NEVER talk about my room, ever again. "I get that, trust. So why did you call? When it's still dark out? And you're all tense and pacing and coiled up like you're ready to pounce on something?"

More with the tensing. "I couldn't sleep, remember?"

She makes her concerned face. It's not much different from her impatient face. Or her happy face, for that matter. "Didn't you get that book I sent you last month? That history book always puts me to sleep when I was trying to do a recap of it for class. Just try reading it when you get like this."

I grin. "But I'd rather talk to you, babe. Especially in that robe."

"Stop, Benj." She covers up as if I might see something I haven't seen four million times before. "So, what? You're saying I put you to sleep now?"

I pretend to growl because she'd definitely know something was up if I didn't act like a total horndog when we're both half-naked on the phone together. "Just the opposite, boo. You know that." She rolls her eyes, and it feels like we're both on autopilot. I've never felt so fake or unauthentic around her. I don't like it. Not even a bit. And I wonder, perhaps for the first time, if this is how she feels when she talks to me.

If, maybe, it's how she's always felt around me.

My phone is propped up, as always, on the bureau by my door. I'm standing in front of it, mid-pace, bare-chested, still damp from my shower, towel about to fall off my waist at any moment. I'm not bragging but she's never complained about seeing me like this before. Now? Nothing. Nada. Zip. Zed. Zero.

I sigh and give up on the frisky portion of our call. Shift toward the sentimental instead. "Anyway, Happy Thanksgiving Eve, boo."

She sits up with a start. "Oh shit, that's right." Looks vaguely guilty, then unsettlingly defiant. Two sides of the same, shitty coin. "Happy... happy Thanksgiving Eve, Benj. You working tomorrow?"

"You know it."

I hem. I haw. Don't ask what I really want to. She's quick to change the subject so I won't. "Well, give everybody my best, okay? I'll... I'll call you when you're done, okay?"

"Sure. That'd be nice."

Jesus, this feels like a damn funeral. But at least she hasn't pressed me. About the early hour. The shower damp hair. The pacing and frantic energy. Then, just before I sign off, she does.

Because of course she does. "Are you okay?"

"Sure. Why wouldn't I be?" I mean, there are only 4 million reasons, but whatevs.

"I just, everything about this phone call feels weird."

"How so?" She's not the only one who's good at deflecting. I mean, who do you think taught me the tricks of the trade?

"Well, for one, you haven't gotten up this early since we took our SATs. You're pacing around half-naked and haven't even asked me to remotely pleasure you for, like, the first time ever. You're picking fights about your stupid bedroom, and you haven't even asked about me coming home."

"I gave up on that, remember?"

"Yeah, well, something feels off."

I shrug, almost hoping the towel will fall off for a little more distraction. Magically, it doesn't, though I suspect it will the minute she hangs up.

The awkward pause stretches like summer taffy, just nowhere near as sweet. She puts the cap on her nail polish. Rests her chin on her knee like a damn puppy dog. Fixes me with a curious gaze and grins. Naked. Raw. Honest. "So, are you gonna tell me what's the what or am I going to have to beat it out of you?"

I snort. Almost relieved. Relieved to have the weight off my shoulders. The guilt and the shame and the pleasure and the pain and the sheer thrill of what Shay and I did and how eager I am to do it all again but know I can't. And... I'm about to do it. About to fess the fuck up. I have to. I mean, not only did I promise myself I would before I dialed her number but, hell, it's the right thing to do. Right? I mean, she's still my girl, after all. No matter what happened last night. Or this morning, or how many times. "Listen..."

Then, suddenly, a glitch in the Matrix. A ghost in the machine. A wrinkle in time. There's the telltale beep of another call coming in, the screen freezes for a tic and she sits up. Straight. Fast. So fast I see some boob flash behind her baggy silken robe, the ruby blur of her thick, puffy nips and the vague glow of a fading tan line. "Listen, babe, hold that thought. My, uh, study group partner is calling, and I've got to... I'll call you back later, okay?"

Relief gives way to surprise and, just as quickly, suspicion. "This early? I mean—"

She huffs, "It's for half my grade, okay?" It's like her mantra every time I press her on something.

I don't even have the chance to back off before she blows a meaningless air kiss at the screen a millisecond before it goes blank. I literally sag with relief, falling back onto the corner of my bed to find myself panting, lathered in a layer of flop sweat so thick and shiny it's like I just took another shower.

My heart is racing. I'm practically panting with relief. Or disappointment. Or both. Probably both. Definitely both. I sag, the energy quickly draining like I'm about to run out of charge. I scroll through my phone until I find Dexter's number.

He's this newish server at work who's not very good, at all, but who will pick up any shift, under any circumstance, any time anyone asks because he's always saving up for a new surfboard or camping tent or motorcycle or tattoo or trip to Fiji or some random hippie type bullshit.

I hit him up with a quick, "Hey, would you mind picking up my shift tonight" text, hoping he'll pick up for me and, drift back onto my pillows, hoping I won't sack out before he writes back. The minute he does, with a long string of thumbs up emojis like he always sends, I set the phone on my nightstand, curl into a ball, and cry myself to sleep.

TWENTY-FIVE

SHAY

"This one?"

At this point, I just have to laugh. "Glenda. Jesus. No. This is the damn Painted Pelican."

She looks legitimately shocked. "Isn't this where you live?"

"I said the Salty Seagull like, five apartment buildings ago. Remember?"

"Well, wasn't that the last one we stopped at?"

"No, that was the dang Flying Frigate."

She rolls her eyes. Leans forward in the driver's seat. Clutches the steering wheel a little harder with her chubby, ring-bejeweled fingers as if it might help her drive better. "The hell are all these cute bird name apartment complexes for?"

"It's a block from the ocean. What would you call them?"

"Basic white girl boxes?"

I chuckle. She's not entirely wrong. The wipers scrape another sheet of soft, drizzling rain from her ginormous windshield. "This is fine. It's close enough if you want to let me out."

Clucks her tongue that way only she does. "No, I came this far. I want to see what makes the Sandy Seagull different from the Party Pelican and the Frickin' Frigate and the Tasty Toucan and whatever else we just passed."

"Just the name is different, Glenda. Just the name…"

At last, a block away from the Painted Pelican and one street over from the Happy Heron and two blocks past the Flying Frigate, we arrive at my place. The neon sign looks even brighter, actually almost kind of inviting, in the light mist that's been falling ever since we closed the restaurant an hour or two ago.

Glenda clucks her tongue again. Rolls her eyes. Again. "Oh, I see the difference now. Totally different from those last three places I tried to drop your ungrateful ass. Whatever was I thinking?"

I nudge her playfully from the passenger seat. "Thanks for the ride home, Glenda. You didn't have to do that."

She softens, suddenly motherly. Chosen family, remember? My favorite kind. "No worries. It was on the way home."

"No, it isn't. You live literally and completely in the opposite direction."

She shrugs. "Well, I've always wanted a tour of Crazy Sounding Seabird Name Street. Now I can cross that off my bucket list."

The mist is only light. It was only ever light. I could have easily fast-tracked it home wearing a trash bag with holes cut out for my arms and gotten only mildly soaked. But she'd seen me heading to my bike as we were both leaving and wouldn't have it. I take off my seatbelt. Reach down between my legs for my backpack.

Her voice is soft and low. Hardly above a whisper. "Don't you want to wait for the rain to let up?"

The wipers swipe another swath of clear windshield before the mist fills it back up again. "It's just a few steps until I'm under cover. Honestly, it's fine."

Usually restless and always on the go, Glenda seems surprisingly chill for someone who's just gone out of her way to give an employee a ride home she didn't really need. "Just wait a sec."

I sigh and slump back into the passenger seat. It's plush and thick and leathery and roomy. I wriggle deeper into the buttery comfort and admit, "I don't think I've ever been in a Cadillac before."

She seems surprisingly blasé about it. "No? I've never driven anything else."

"Oh, sorry, Ms. Kardashian."

She snorts playfully, the way she always does when I catch her by surprise. "Shit. You think I pay for this?"

"Who then? Your Sugar Daddy?"

"Please. Pig-Out does."

"Really?"

"If your store does over a certain percent in profit every month, for however months straight then, bam, instant Cadillac."

"Wow."

"Maybe now you'll consider it when I bring up the subject of you joining the management team during your annual review every year."

"Please. You think I want to drive little waifs home after a long night shift every time it rains?"

She chuckles like she's surprised, round face soft and thoughtful in the pink and blue neon from the Salty Seagull sign. "True, true…"

The rain fizzles out to match the vibe of her aborted response. Clouds shift. Moonlight beckons. Still, she doesn't seem to be in much of a hurry. I guess I'm not really, either. The thought of walking into my dark apartment alone, just to see Benjy's sheets still folded on the couch, is vaguely bumming me out. "So, what's with you and Benjy?" As usual, it's as if the woman can read my mind.

I avoid her always probing eyes. "Waddya mean?"

"You know how many times he's called off a shift before tonight?"

"Dozens."

"How about nozens?"

"What's that?" Although I know. Of course, I know.

She gives me a withering, disappointed look. "Practically none, girl. Ever. Never. That's how many times he's called out. And you're standing around all night, mooning about with your face all spacey and your t-shirt half-tucked and your belt on backward, forgetting barbecue sauce for Table 11, ringing Table 14's desserts up on Table 18's check. That's not like you two."

I shrug. Bite my lip. Tempted to spill it all. Just unload the whole sordid affair. Drop it on her lap and see what she says. Will her advice be chill and accepting, like Hub's? Or shrill and motherly and all responsible-like? Instead, I lie. Just a little. Well, not really. Cuz he totally kind of is. "He's just upset about Cara not coming home for Thanksgiving, that's all."

She taps the steering wheel thoughtfully. Glances up at something on the second floor. Squints. "That why he volunteered to work Thanksgiving?"

I glance away. Mutter another little white lie. Okay, maybe not so little. "Uh huh."

She gives me another look. "With you?"

"At least we can make each other laugh."

"Not if you keep mooning about stumbling into tables

with your shirt half-tucked and wearing mismatched socks, you can't."

I pretend to reach for my backpack again. Glance at my socks. Grin. She's right. One's pink and the other's blue. One of them may even be inside the hell out. Jesus. "Anyway…"

She doesn't stop me this time. Points to where she's been staring for the last few minutes. "Who's that silver fox pacing around up there?"

Even though I already know who she's talking about, I mean, who else could it be, I squint through the latest squeak of the unnecessary windshield wipers as if I don't have the faintest clue.

Grin with a sly little secret shimmer. "That's my neighbor."

"What's his problem?"

"Problem?"

Gives a little nod in his general direction, chubby hands still clenched protectively on either side of the steering wheel like maybe she's going to rip it off its hinges and toss it up there at him if I don't give her the right answer. A smattering of gold rings glisten in the pool lights. "Why's he pacing around up there like that?"

"He always worries when I don't get home from work on time."

Gives me a curly question mark eyebrow. "He knows when you get home from work?"

"We're neighbors. The walls are thin. Plus, usually I share my shift meal with him."

"Sounds cozy." She waits a beat. Leans in a little closer like someone might hear. Someone in the backseat maybe? "You two, uh… you know?"

I make a face. "Gross. No."

She glances up through the squeaking wipers at him.

Gets frustrated, like maybe she forgot they were still on. Turns them off. "Is he single?"

I make a clucking sound. "Very."

"So, what's the problem?"

"Weren't you the one who told me not to shit where I eat?"

"Yeah, at work."

"So, I should hook-up with my surfer slut neighbor?"

She sighs. Grips the steering wheel harder. "I don't know what you should do anymore, Shay. If your choices are being tempted by your best friend's boyfriend or banging the guy next door, maybe you need to consider widening your horizons a tad."

"How do I do that? I'm only ever at work or at home."

She nods with the weariness of supreme mutual under-standing. "Good point."

I nudge her elbow with mine. "Well?"

"Well, what?"

"What's the answer?"

"What answer?"

"You're supposed to be helping me, remember?"

"I drove you home in the rain, didn't I?"

I grab my backpack. "And now you're sending me into the arms of... What'd you call him?"

"Who?"

"Hub. My neighbor."

She glances up at the second floor again. Smiles merrily to herself. "Silver fox?"

"Yeah, that." I grin. Has she heard Benjy call Hub the Silver Surfer? Or is her nickname just a slight variation? Either way, I feel attacked and vaguely flattered, for some weird reason.

"Maybe you can invite him to Treesgiving and get to know him a little better, huh?"

I glance down at my shoes. "Who says I haven't already?"

"That's good," she teased. "Now you two can rush the season together. Who knows, maybe you can fit New Year's Eve in while you're at it?"

"Not you too?" I pretend to be insulted, but at this point I'm just convinced all the Treesgiving haters are just jealous. Yeah, that's it!

Glenda winks at me in the glow of the dome light as I open the heavy Cadillac door. "Good luck, honey."

I turn back before standing up out of her gleaming, shimmering car. "With what?"

She looks as tired as I feel. "With everything, I guess."

I nod and, somehow, know exactly what she means.

TWENTY-SIX

SHAY

"Finally."

I drift up the last step. Slowly. See the rarely lit jar candle on the table between our apartments. The bottle of wine. The two glasses. Struggle not to smile. "Sorry, it sprinkled ever so lightly, and my boss insisted on driving me home."

"That was nice of her." He leans back against the rail that runs the length of the upstairs walkway. Looks spiffy in a soft, tan Hawaiian shirt over powder blue cargo shorts.

I slide my backpack down onto my still Halloween welcome mat, wondering if I'll ever be motivated enough to get one for Thanksgiving. I guess if I wait another day or two, they'll all be half-off. "Speaking of nice, what's all this?"

He grins. Bashful. Blushes a little. Very un-Hub-like. "I just thought, after your very long, very rainy day, you might need a little treat."

I reach down and unzip my backpack. Grab the crinkly, greasy Pig-Out paper sack from inside and set it down between the flickering candle and the open bottle of wine.

"Yeah? And what if I was dead tired and just wanted to fall face down onto the throw rug inside the foyer the minute I got home?"

His eyes are soft and vaguely wise. He waits a few long, heavy seconds before responding. So long I think he might not answer at all. "Then we would have both missed a great opportunity, I suppose."

I sink into the chair, weary and bruised from the long, emotional, clumsy, sideways shift. He grins. Inches closer—he's far too cool to hurry—and pours the wine with a slow, steady hand. "Good, because I really wanted to try this wine."

"You didn't have to wait on me to do that."

He sits down as I tear open the bag of takeout. "I kinda did. I mean, when you weren't home by midnight, I..."

"That's sweet."

He looks surprised. A little hurt. "You think I hang out every night just for the free food?"

"Some nights, sure."

He grins. "Okay, it's a nice bonus but someone has to look out for you, kid."

I reach for my glass. I'm just tired enough to be cocky. Coy. Clever, or at least my clumsy versions of those. "That the only reason you do it?"

He shrugs, noncommittal. Sips the wine instead of answering. Savors it. I follow suit. It is pretty good. So good I take a second, longer sip right away. Glance back over at him after closing my eyes to savor the dry, red, tart goodness.

He's staring back. Nods at me. "What is this?"

I look at the glass. He bought it, what the hell's he asking me for? I make a human question mark with my tired shoulders. "Cabernet?"

He chuckles. Waves his hand. Big, strong fingers. Tan, hairy knuckles. "No, this. Suddenly you're questioning why I'm a good neighbor?"

I cluck my tongue again. I must have caught that from Glenda on the ride home tonight. "I guess, lately, I'm questioning everything."

"I don't blame you. You've had a loud 24-hours."

I snort with laughter. I think I needed that more than the wine. The only good thing about work, I realized when he didn't show up tonight, is Benjy. The way he makes me smile. And laugh. Almost every time I see him. The way he commiserates and comments on every moment of every shift, as if he's voicing the very words inside my head. Narrating our time together in a live feed of constant, wry, clever sarcasm, absurdity and nonstop one-liners that come so naturally I suppose I've taken them for granted all these years. I don't feel that connection with anyone else. Never have.

Except maybe with Hub. If only he didn't remind me of our age difference with every fatherly jab or scritch and scratch of his thick, manly fingers along his salt and pepper stubble.

I nod back at him, jutting out my chin defensively. "I like how I have one verbal night and you're gonna give me shit about it like, literally, forever when there's a virtual gang-bang going on at your place every other afternoon and I've never said shit."

"Cuz I'm discreet, that's why."

"Either that, or you've invested in some extra insulation for your walls."

"We're not talking about me."

I wave my wine glass. "We actually were."

He frowns. Reaches for a chicken tender tossed in savory

sweet barbecue sauce from the eco-friendly to-go box between us. "Okay, look. I'm a good neighbor because I care about you, all right?"

"And?"

"And what?"

I nibble a fry. Dip it in the tangy honey mustard sauce container he opened. "And that's it?"

"Yup. Sure is."

"You just light candles and open bottles of wine and pace the walkway waiting for Mrs. Johnson in Unit 2-C to get home, huh?"

"No, because she never leaves her house."

"You know what I mean."

"I know what you're asking, Shay. I'm not stupid and neither are you. We're both adults here."

"And?"

He sighs. "And yes, I care about you. Obviously. Naturally. You, personally. Okay?"

I pour more wine. "Was that so hard?"

"Have I ever hidden my feelings for you?"

"Please. You have feelings for every woman under the age of thirty."

He chuckles. "That's not true. But I do have a type."

"And?"

He looks genuinely surprised. Grins broadly, the echoes of a chuckle in his slow as honey mustard reply. "Shay, are you asking if...if you're my type?"

"I guess so."

"Do you really have to?"

I wave my wine glass, suddenly so mature and sophisticated. "Humor me."

Rolls his eyes. "Sure, Shay. You're my type. With your ankle bracelets and your smiley face nail polish and your little striped surfboard and your rainbow tattoo and—"

"How the hell have you seen my tattoo?"

"What? I can see it every time you wear that blue bikini bottom."

"It's on my butt, Hub!"

"It's a small bikini bottom, Shay!"

We chuckle. Pour more wine. "So how come you've never tried anything before?"

He answers fairly quickly, like maybe he's thought about it before. "Because you *look* like you'd be my type, but you're also not."

"Wow."

His tone, his expression, are both analytical. Clinical, even. Like he's studying a bug under glass in some laboratory somewhere. "I mean that in the best way possible, trust me."

"Such as?"

"Just trust me." He pauses. Nibbles. Sips. I wait. Then: "Where's all this coming from, anyway?"

I glance at him. He looks away. Downstairs. At the bike rack. Back to me. Putting two and two together with every careful, clinical glance. "Where's your little buddy today, anyway?"

"Which one?"

Frowns. Harumphs. "Don't be cute."

I give him a look. Flutter my eyelids and grin falsely. "I can't help it, remember? With my faded ankle bracelets and tattoo and plucky attitude?"

He nibbles on a fry. "I don't recall saying anything about a plucky attitude, but I'll give you that one."

I shrug. "It fit the aesthetic you were describing, I guess."

He waits a beat then gets back to Benjy. "He didn't come

to work tonight, did he?"

"What if he wasn't scheduled to?"

"But he was, right?"

"Yeah, so?"

"He texted you yet?"

"Maybe."

Hub grins knowingly, if not triumphantly. "Which means no."

"Maybe."

"So, let's see. You share a night of wild passion the likes of which romance novels are written about. Then... you wake up alone. He ghosts you. Bails on you at work. So now you're feeling vulnerable and needy, and you probably haven't eaten all day so the wine's gone straight to your head and I'm sitting here all gussied up, flattering you and..."

I golf clap for emphasis. "Wow, you're a real gumshoe, Hub. Good work."

"And this is why you're not my type, Shay."

"Why? Too much of a smartass?"

"Too smart. For your own good. And before you get even more flattered, that's not a compliment."

"I'm pretty stupid, obviously."

"Why? Because guys don't respond to intimacy the same way as girls do?"

"Maybe."

"You think I'd respond any better?"

"No. But I wouldn't expect you to."

He pretends to look offended. "Why? Cuz I'm a surfer slut?"

"Kinda."

"So, you don't know me at all."

"Like you know me?"

He chuckles. I sit back, realize I've bowed up slightly, leaning forward as the convo got more and more heated. Grin. "Sorry, it's just… I am feeling a little more than vulnerable, I guess."

"Yeah, and if I was a real slut, I'd hop on that. But I'm not."

I wave my wineglass his way. "So, you're a good slut? Half a slut? Slut with a heart of gold?"

"I try not to hurt anyone, yeah."

I glance over at him. Nod. Smile. "I believe that."

"But I don't want to hurt you, Shay."

"Maybe I want to be hurt."

He scoffs. Openly. "No, you don't. You just want to forget about what's-his-name for a little while and I'm making it really, really easy for you to imagine doing that, is all."

"What's so bad about that? We're two consenting adults, right? No one's paying attention to us. No one will judge us, no one will ever even know. That is, if you put your hand over my mouth."

He smirks. Then makes his serious face. "I'll know, Shay."

"So, it'll be our dirty little secret then, Hub."

"Because you *will* feel dirty about it, Shay. And then you'll hate me. And things would get awkward. And you'd quit bringing me food. And hanging out with me at the pool. And you'd never sit here at this table with me. Or share a bottle of wine. Or make me laugh again, and I care about you, like you too much for that to happen."

I frown, secretly relieved. Shrug. Sag in my chair just a little.

Then he winks, waves his wineglass and, as usual, has to have the last word. "Even if you are totally my type."

TWENTY-SEVEN

BENJY

I smell the grease wafting greasily from the crinkly Burrito Barn bag in my basket. I'm too nervous to be hungry right now but I'm hoping that, when I finally see Shay and apologize and she gives me her trademark crooked grin, bashful and defiant and defensive and coy all at the same time, my stomach muscles will unwind themselves from the massive knot they've been in all day and then I'll immediately want to wolf down half the bag.

That's the plan, anyway. We shall see…

It's late now. Well after midnight. Closer to one, actually. The whole town is asleep, quiet, and desolate and bathed in its usual neon glow as I swerve from one side to the other in the middle of the street, avoiding puddles from a recent shower. It's still a little misty off and on, sticky and humid, but I'd ride through a Cat 5 hurricane right now just to make sure Shay and I are still okay.

I'm wide awake all over again. Then again, why wouldn't I be? I just woke up a few hours ago, dazed and confused and wondering why it was already dark out. Between being up all night and knocked out all day, my sleep schedule is going to be so jacked for the next few days. I just know it.

I grin anyway, like a kid playing hooky. Free and safe and alone and aloof and wired and weirded out in the middle of the street, neon lights reflected in a puddle as I pass by in a blur. Cara is safely holed up in her dorm room for Thanksgiving weekend, all the way across the state, and instead of feeling guilty about finally sleeping with Shay I can feel vaguely wounded and victim-atic over my girl-friend not coming home to see me.

I mean, it won't last forever. She'll be bitchy and indig-nant and self-righteous again come Monday morning and I'll have to deal with the Shay incident at some point, but for now I've bought myself a whole miraculous weekend of work, Shay, work, and more Shay. I don't even mind the work as long as Shay is there with me.

I guess I never have.

I'm smiling when I finally see the winking neon of the Salty Seagull sign. Just one more wave of shimmering blue and pink in a sea of colored lights that stretch from one end of Ocean Drive to the other. Then smile just a little more. Just the thought of seeing Shay again, wired, antsy and angsty after work, crooked ball cap and tight shorts and long, tanned legs and pink hi-tops and I'm breathless.

It's like when I gawked at her in class after she moved to Crescent Beach during sophomore year. A fresh face in a sea of kids I'd been staring at since we all started school together back in kindergarten.

And here I am, however, many years later, nervous, and anxious and uncertain about what to do next. And still doing it anyway because what other choice do I have?

I cruise to a stop just shy of the bike rack. Frown for the first time since I woke up. Her bike's not there. The fuck? No way, she's still at work at this hour. I mean, it's not like it's inventory night or anything. Then I inch a little forward, through a puddle reflecting the glow of the orange street-light above and remember the rain. Someone, probably Glenda, definitely Glenda, gave her a ride home.

Right? I mean, that has to be it.

My heart rate gradually returns to normal, but my instantly juvenile reaction makes me wonder if I shouldn't have just stayed home in bed. I mean, it's just Shay, right? This shouldn't be so hard. That's always the best thing about Shay. She makes everything easy.

Talking to her, laughing with her, nudging her hip, sneaking a glimpse of the little rainbow tattoo on her left cheek, snorting, and giggling and eating and burping and drinking and it all came so naturally. Now, suddenly, it's like she's a… she's a girl or something.

I wait to hear the trickling in the pool. The one her silver surfer neighbor's always lounging in, shirtless and tatted up and hunky, just out of range while I'm saying goodbye after another long shift together. But tonight, the pool is empty. Quiet. Serene. The only ripples, gentle and small, come from the slight offshore breeze at my back.

Then I hear the sharp bark of laughter, quick and breezy and unmistakably Shay's. I glance upstairs, still hidden behind the skinny cluster of dried out palm trees at the far end of the pool. There, bathed in the glow of a flickering candle, Shay laughs her sexy laugh. Across from her sits her surfer neighbor, wagging a playful finger next to the bottle of wine on the table between them.

My stomach knots in ways I never knew it could before. I grip the handlebars tighter, straddling the bike I never got off as blood races through my ears like a train through a tunnel. Stare like a stalker as I drink in the scene, cozy and warm and chummy and even vaguely romantic. Literally, the aesthetic couldn't scream "date" any louder if they were sitting in a corner booth at some fancy restaurant, holding fucking hands.

Shay is as expected. She's lithe and lean and coppery in her work outfit, effortlessly sexy and comfortable in her skin. Her long legs are crossed, her shoe taps merrily up and down as the two share another slight tremor of laughter, lower this time. Huskier. Deeper. Almost secretive.

She's being what I call Flirty Shay. I see it at work sometimes, when she's waiting on a cute guy and slips into this flirtatious persona that drives me crazy, even if only from afar. The way she leans forward, tucking stray tufts of chestnut brown hair behind her blushing pink ear. Her tone of voice changes. It gets slightly deeper, huskier and when she laughs, it sounds nervous, mechanical, not like her real laugh at all. She'll stand a little closer each time she visits the table, tugging on her tip apron self-consciously as if wishing it wasn't there.

She's doing that now. All of it, just dialed up to Eleven. Flirty Shay Squared, if you will. The wisps of hair behind her ear. The husky laugh, rich and mechanical as if she's saving all her mental energy for witty comebacks and coy one-liners. She'll lean forward, murmur something, chuckle coyly, then sit back like she's just scored a point. Linger over her wine glass, full lips caressing the rim before taking a long, luxurious sip.

She has to lean forward a little to put it back on the patio table and even that movement, slow and casual, sends ripples of flirtatiousness toward the Silver Surfer. I mean, they're so strong, so unmistakable, I can feel them all the way downstairs, past the pool deck and on into the parking lot.

I watch them like that for a while. The back and forth, the low, steady murmurs of a quiet, late-night conversation. The chuckles, the snorts, the occasional giggle, the foot shifting and leg crossing and then uncrossing and then crossing again. I glance away, find myself white-knuckling my handlebars and wonder, maybe even for the first time, if this is the way Shay feels when she sees Cara and I together. And how long she's been feeling that way.

I turn away before I can chicken out. Sulk away in the night, walking my bike awkwardly, flat footing it on either side of the pedals, as if they might hear the creak of my bike seat if I just rode away like a normal person.

Then again, would a normal person stand there in the parking lot, the smell of taco meat and cheese sauce wafting up toward his nose on the ocean breeze, watching the girl he'd just slept with flirt with her next-door neighbor for half an hour?

No, I think not.

The beach beckons from across the street. The crashing waves. The moonlit froth, foamy and bright. The soft, warm sand under my bare feet. The calming lull of the ocean to wash away the sight of Flirty Shay and leave me with just my Shay. The one who wanted me, and only me, from the minute she stood in her bedroom door the night before, eyes sleepy and smoky and beckoning all at the same time.

It doesn't take long to reach my zen spot. The Salty Seagull is across the street from a row of oceanfront condos and, between the blue one and the white one is the 8th Street Beach Access. I lean my bike against the wooden boardwalk, no fear of pawn shop robbers in the middle of the night, and drift along down the sandy wooden planks until the warm sand rises to greet the last few steps and welcome me to a place far from the flirty, sexy walkway between Shay and her neighbor's doors.

The tide is high. The moon beckons and after a few long strides I plunk down in the sand like an overgrown toddler, the bag of Burrito Barn goodies and a crisp, sweaty soda between my legs. I am, inexplicably, undeniably, starving.

Instead of quiet, moonlit reflection I dive into the bag of burritos like a stoner after a giant bong rip. And tacos. And chips. And queso. Devouring them all with sandy, trembling fingers and washing them all down with bursts of watered-down soda until I lean back, sated, stuffed, foil wrappers balled up in the sand like turtle eggs at my feet.

I belch openly. Proudly. Savoring the aftertaste of onions and spices and fizzy soda and shaking my head at the surreal landscape of my dysfunctional, twisted, sexy, sad little life. Honestly, even if I hadn't just slept with Shay twenty-four-hours earlier, I would have still been pissed to find her sitting there, drinking wine, and sharing knowing, giggly sips with the Silver Surfer with their stupid toes mere inches away from each other's.

Fact is, I've loved her for as long as I can remember. Since the day I first saw her, I guess, walking into homeroom that first day of spring semester our sophomore year at Crescent Beach High. Her mom had followed some guy all the way to Florida from Ohio or one of those random middle America states. Broke up with him just before Christmas. Found a cheap place in town and Shay had started school halfway through the year. They'd moved into a faded green double wide at the Twisted Palm Trailer Park, but you never would have known it. She showed up that first day, preppy and frisky and lean and tan like she'd just stepped off the beach and out of an Instagram post.

The teacher introduced her, and she nodded, smiled

shyly, before grabbing the last empty seat at the back of the room. I was back there, too. In the far corner, three or four seats away, watching her every move at a safe distance. The retro denim of her thrift shop backpack as she hung it off the back of her chair. The new notebook, the freshly sharpened pencil, the way she clung to her little yellow schedule slip even after she'd found the class and sat down and settled in.

She'd dressed down for the occasion. Later she'd settled into her daily uniform of jean shorts with frayed hems, faded concert t-shirts, black high tops and ankle bracelets. But that first day she'd worn a plaid skirt, not too short, not too long. Scuffed brown loafers and a wheat-colored turtle-neck a size too big. For all I know it could have been a man's sweater, it was that big and ill-fitting. It was like she wanted to disappear into her clothes, be as anonymous and unas-suming and quiet and reserved as possible.

But even bundled up on a cold, January day I could tell she wasn't wearing a bra and I never stopped wondering, up until just a few short hours ago, in fact, what she would look like without that big, dowdy sweater on.

It wasn't just the way you could see the unmistakable outline of her soft, puffy nipples when she moved a certain way. It was that she'd worn such a dowdy outfit to her first day of school and then said, at the last minute, "Screw it, let 'em see my full-on nips if they want!"

It said something about her. I wasn't sure what, yet. I didn't know, not until later, not until we'd become friends, how screwed up her home life was. How broken she was, deep down inside where no one else could see. How lost and alone and outsider-y she felt, that first day and, really, every day after.

How much, really, we had in common.

How she was pretty much orphaned, in a way. No dad to

speak of. Not for years, anyway. Her mom out all hours of the night, with this guy or that guy. The fridge was always empty. The lights turned off, sometimes. Never knowing if they'd make the rent that month or where they'd go next if they didn't.

That's why she'd gotten the job at Pig-Out in the first place. To help her mom out with money. Not because they shared a ton of affection for each other but to make sure the bills were paid on time and there was always at least something in the fridge when she came home from school. Or work.

Later, after we graduated, her mom quit pretending to work entirely and Shay became the sole breadwinner of their fractured little family. Not that her mom was around much by then, thankfully. Shay had the trailer to herself most days. She didn't have much time to enjoy it between working every possible shift she could get, banking none of the cash for herself and merely paying long overdue bills until she'd gotten her mom caught up. Again. But still, life was easier, less dramatic, when her mother was shacking up with some guy for a month or two.

But I didn't know any of that, that first day back in sophomore year. Didn't know the drama or the history or the back story or the resentment or the pain or the scars. Just knew there was something punk about her that I wanted to get to know better.

And, you know...nipples. Big poofy nipples I couldn't keep my eyes off until the bell rang, and homeroom ended, and she sprang for the door, the crowd in the bustling halls outside swallowing her whole until I lost sight of her completely. And now, here I am, as broken and confused and lonely and outsider-y as I was back then. Sure, I've seen her nipples, up close and personal. Felt them, even, soft, and slippery and trembling between my fingers, taut and tangy beneath my tongue.

But what now? It was always and ever about more than just nipples and hi-tops and a rainbow butt tattoo. That first day, I knew we'd become friends. And then we did, and clicked so hard and fast and suddenly I never wanted it to end.

It didn't end. At least, not until last night and now I'm left here, sitting on the beach trying to keep little tinfoil burrito balls from flying away in the not so gentle breeze as the ocean froth threatens to drown my flip flops and the night wears on and the tide inevitably rises.

I do, too. Finally. Gather up my little tinfoil balls before they scatter away, toss them in the Burrito Barn bag with the empty cup and dump it all in the plastic bin at the top of the boardwalk. My bike is still there. The street still empty, Shay's apartment sign still glowing as I pedal past in the opposite direction. Back home. Home, where I don't belong any more than I do at Shay's apartment. Or Cara's dorm room. Or anyplace at all, really, in the crazy, mixed-up world.

TWENTY-EIGHT

SHAY

I stand abruptly, more hurt by the sting of Hub's rejection than I thought I'd be. I should feel relieved, actually. Relieved that my mouth didn't write a check my body couldn't cash. Grateful, he pulled the 'friends' card. Instead, I just feel stung. Like the only two men in my life I vaguely care about have ghosted me in the same 24-hour period. One to my phone and one to my face.

My voice is husky again, smoky even, but for all the wrong reasons. "That sounds like my cue to leave, neighbor."

He stands, too. The fold-up wooden chair he's been sitting in scrapes a little. He winces. Glances back at his apartment like a teenager who's just snuck out for the night.

I push the pause button on my dramatic exit. Cock my head instead. "What's wrong?"

He flushes. Waves a hand. "Nothing. Why?"

I'm vaguely buzzed off half a bottle of mid-priced red. Cocky and flirtatious and wounded and personal and close in a way we've never been before. Like somehow him listening to me have sex through the wall has made us almost intimate as well. "Are you afraid your apartment will hear you?"

He's oddly defensive. In a very odd but also kinda familiar way. "No. What? Why?"

Suddenly, it hits me like a tiger tattoo on the butt. "Oh, my Gawd!" My hand literally flies to cover my mouth like some shocked, indignant Victorian school marm. "You have another girl in there, don't you?"

"Who says it's not the same girl?"

So, he does. This. Damn. Slut. "I do. Because it's not, is it?"

He chuckles. Is predictably charming even in his blatant trampiness. "Shay, listen…"

I creep closer to his door. The closest to going inside his apartment I've gotten for the better part of a year. He stays one step in front of me like he's suddenly built for speed. As if I might barge in or something. "How does this even work?"

He starts talking lower. Inches a little closer so suddenly I smell his vaguely musky cologne over the scent of greasy takeout food and dry red wine. Barely above a whisper now. "What? How does what work?"

I find myself whispering, too. Point to the door. Then the table. Then me. "This? Us? Her? How do all the dysfunctional pieces of tonight's particular sex puzzle fit in your warped little slutty mind?"

He doesn't get the joke, for once. Instead takes me quite seriously. "I just…she was asleep."

I'm too impressed by his stamina and stealth to even be all that offended. "So what? You just decided to kill some time yakking with me before she woke back up?"

"No. Actually. You were my plan for tonight. My only plan. Then she showed up."

I blink several times in disbelief. My body can react in no other way. "You're literally unbelievable. As in, I can't even believe you."

"It's true, though. I was settling in for a nice night. Slow. Waiting for you. To check on you, see how your anxiety level was going after this morning. Then...then she showed up when her friends ditched her at some bar. In a little black dress and...and not much else. High heels, maybe. And legs for days. Days, Shay." He holds his hand up like he's measuring a little kid for an amusement park ride. To show me how long her legs are, I guess? "I'm supposed to just turn that away?"

I find my arms crossed over my chest like some wounded girlfriend. "How long ago?"

"Around ten?"

I do the mental math, both queasy and impressed at the same time. "So, you've already...you know?"

He looks vaguely down at my barbecue sauce splattered work sneakers. Shrugs to avoid answering, even though his evasive body language and shit eating grin give him away. I shove him playfully. "You really are a slut, Hub. I mean, I feel bad even calling you that anymore because now it's like a medical condition or something and I'm being politically incorrect. Like, you seriously have an actual problem."

He grabs my hand. Firmly. Not romantically. Tugs me gently back to my door. "My only problem, Shay, is I'm not enough of a slut to sleep with my neighbor. Okay? That's, like my biggest problem in life right now."

I reach down for my backpack. Grab my keys. Slide them in the door. Turn to him with a wry, trembling grin. "Aw, that's the nicest thing you've ever said to me."

He pushes the door open. "Good. Now get inside before I change my mind."

"Don't flatter yourself, slut."

He chuckles. I shut the door. Hear him drift away in his fancy sandals. Flip. Flop. Flip. And I wonder, for the first time, if he wore them for me or whoever he's got snoring in his bed.

I'm in bed. Staring up at the ceiling. Lying in the dark alone. The alarm on my phone goes off, a quietly jangly ringtone I chose months ago, making me chuckle. I'd already set it for way earlier than usual but have been up for a good hour or more before it finally goes off officially. I swing my legs over the bed. Tap the phone on the nightstand to quiet the jaunty jangles. Grateful for the silence.

Stand and finally greet Thanksgiving properly. I stumble through making coffee. Shower while it's sputtering and brewing and making a big, splattery racket I can hear even through the warm, soapy spray.

Smell the pumpkin spice goodness as it drifts through the tiny apartment. I dry my hair and dress for the day, rolling up the sleeves on my Special Edition Pig-Out holiday t-shirt. It's got the usual pig face in the middle but in honor of Thanksgiving he's wearing a Pilgrim hat. Har dee har. Underneath are the words "Gobble. Oink. Gobble!"

God, I love my job.

I tuck it in and roll my eyes. Will eventually add it to my growing collection of Valentine's Day and St. Patrick's Day and Halloween Pig-Out t-shirts. Wonder what I'll ever do with them once I leave.

That is, if I ever leave.

Stand in the kitchen and sip the coffee. It's good and hot and strong and spicy and sweet, even black. I'm not really tired. Just numb. Weary, is more like it. I mean, it's been a week. Plus, Thanksgiving always sucks. It gets busy the minute we open the doors and never quite stops until we close them for the night about twelve hours later. I know it'll be a long one, too. I wouldn't mind it if Benjy and I were chuckling and rolling our eyes and giggling the whole time, but who knows if he'll even show up after yesterday.

Let alone to Treesgiving tomorrow.

I sigh and clean up the coffee. It's not hard when you're only making it for one. Root around in the fridge past the cookie dough and schnapps and peppermint mocha creamer for a cheese stick. Pair it with an apple and a few Triscuits and call it a morning.

I fix my cap while I brush my teeth. Give everything one last look and turn out the bathroom light. Grab the envelope on my way out the door. It's still dark out, but I can see the fringes of morning on the horizon from the second-floor walkway. I'm about to turn left and squeeze the envelope in the crack between Hub's door and the door jamb when I hear splashing downstairs. Smile.

Even better. I'll give it to him in person. Maybe even flash a little leg and wriggle my butt for good measure. Drink in his lean, glistening torso and those random tats for a little pre-dawn nourishment.

Then I hear laughter. Not his laughter. I glance down just in time to see bare feet disappear under water. Hub leaning against the pool tiles. Distracted by the rippling pool. Smiling. A head pops up. Shaggy blonde hair. Big red lips. A coarse, barking laughter born from a thousand bad decisions and an equal amount of cheap cigarettes.

A girl drifts closer to him. Big and busty, her black bikini top barely holding in a rack to die for. There is an ashtray on the pool deck next to him. How did I not notice that trashy little detail before? Smoke curls from two cigarettes set just inside. She grabs one with long, wet fingers. Puffs. Chuckles. Reaches for a beer. A big blue tall boy. Cheap looking. Sips long and hard like she's finding salvation inside.

I glance across the pool at the purple-blue horizon with a mix of revulsion and awe. I mean, damn girl, it's barely sunup. Wonder idly if that's the same girl who was in his bed last night when he wined and dined me. Or if it's someone new. Neither, frankly, would surprise me at this point. Then she sets the can down, loud, and hard on the pool tile like maybe it's not her first sip, let alone her first can, of the day. Winks luridly and takes another limber dive into the water. There's a moment, just so, when her rump, ripe derriere is poised to slip beneath the surface, and I see the flash of a tattoo.

A tiger tattoo.

Tiger Butt!

I smile and feel a door closing firmly shut on what did Hub call it last night? Oh yeah, a great opportunity. I drift down the stairs. Quietly, slowly, glad for the worn treads on my seasonally red hi-tops that no longer squeak. Not that they'd notice, between the frolicking and the drinking and the smoking and the cavorting and the canoodling. Toss the invitation on top of the trash can at the foot of the stairs because sca-rew that noise. I mean, I may be desperate for Treesgiving guests but the last thing I need is Hub showing up with his tramp-of-the-day on one arm and a build-it-yourself gingerbread house in the other. Although, come to think of it, building a cookie house with him would be actually kind of cool.

I take the long way around the pool, past a line of cars, to find myself at the bike bike rack, grateful that in her usual motherly way, Glenda had thought to drop my bike off so I could get to work.

Maybe she'll be as verbal as me and he'll get his Thanksgiving miracle after all.

TWENTY-NINE

SHAY

"Hey."

Benjy stands next to the row of recycling bins just past the bike rack. Looking tall and lean and spiffy in his own version of the Pig-Out Special Edition "Gobble Oink Gobble" Thanksgiving shirt. His is rust colored, the flying pig silhouette is white, and I know he's gonna get about a hundred compliments on it today. "Hey yourself."

He's shy, suddenly. Bashful. Cute with the way he's kind of nervously curled all into himself, glancing down at his feet and then up at me and then back down again like he's watching a tennis match only he can see.

Whatever. I'm still vaguely pissed no matter how cute he is in his clingy new t-shirt with the rising sun casting sexy shadows on his lean, embarrassed, stupid face. "You're up early."

I loop the lock back around my handlebars, taking my time until it sits. Just. Right. Wheel myself over to him with long, leisurely steps. I can see why he's standing there instead of next to my bike. You can't see the pool from here.

I suppose I'm grateful for that small favor, at least.

He follows my eyes to the sound of splashing in the just out of sight pool. "Looks like your neighbor's getting an early start on the holiday."

I get on my bike with a vague "harrumph" sound. "Glad someone's having fun today."

His eyes meet mine. Stay there. A smile follows, just below. Soft and gentle and crooked and kind. The old Benjy smile.

My Benjy smile. "We can have fun today, Shay."

I nod. Too tired, or maybe still just too numb, to fight anymore. "Maybe, if you were the old Benjy and not the new one."

He climbs on his bike, and we push off into the street together, both of us glad to be free of the sexy, smoky, splashy frolicking. "New Benjy?"

"Yeah, the one who fucks me and then ghosts me. Calls out of work the next day for the first time in, I dunno…ever? Without a word. A call. A text. Nothing. Lets me wonder what I did wrong for a whole day and sleepless night. That new Benjy."

"Oh, yeah. That." We ride for a little while, not very far, slowly, like usual. Then, he says, "I'm sorry about that."

"Too late."

He shrugs. "Yeah, I know. I fucked up, okay?"

"Whatever. It happens."

The road is emptier than usual at this hour. I forget for a moment that the rest of the world is still in bed, turkey and stuffing and cranberry and pumpkin spice candle smells wafting through the quiet, darkened houses all around us. We drift from side to side in the middle of the street like kids playing hooky. Mad or hurt or wounded or grateful or sad, I could do this all day.

I wanted to be over him. To believe all the promises I told

myself lying awake last night. The ones that said I could quit him. That said what was done was done but no more. Never, ever, ever, never again.

But even now, the moody pink sunrise on his soft, light skin, makes my heart race. Watching his long fingers grip the handlebars of his ratty bike just makes me remember how many times they danced along my swollen, tender bud to bring me to one. More. Climax.

"Shay! Car! Jesus!"

I look up just before the horn honks. Flick the driver off irrationally as he passes innocently by. Benjy chuckles. Shakes his head. Waves me over with those long, dexterous fingers. "Get up here on the sidewalk, kook."

"Fine. Yes. Okay." My heart is still pounding, for more reasons than one.

"What's gotten into you?"

"Besides you, you mean?"

He frowns. "Okay. Gross."

I shrug. Mutter, "Wasn't gross to me." He either doesn't hear or chooses to ignore me. I don't blame him. I'm being kind of a witch. I shrug some more, indifferent even with myself. Even on the wide sidewalk running alongside Ocean Drive, we still have room to swerve from side to side as we take the slow road to Restaurant Row.

His voice is mildly curious between lips that are both frowning and grinning. "Is this the new Shay I have to look forward to now?"

"Yeah. Maybe. What of it?"

"I dunno. I feel responsible, somehow."

"You should."

His sigh is louder than his rickety bike seat as he shifts uncomfortably from side to side. "I didn't know what to do, Shay."

"Which time?"

"Both. Either. I'm all fucked up."

I snort ironically. "Yeah, you are."

"Oh, it's just me then?"

I shrug with the weight of a hundred unspoken apologies. "Sorry, *we* are."

His grin, momentarily, outweighs his frown. "That's more like it."

We cruise along together. The sun is too pretty for my shitty mood. It's so quiet I hear waves crash on the beach behind the colorful condos we pass. I look over at him. Glad he's looking back. "So, what now?"

"No idea, Shay."

I nod. "Fair enough. You're here today. That's a start."

He nods. Looks away. Then down. Starts to say something, then stops. Then we ride in silence the rest of the way to work.

Another first in a long day or two full of them.

The parking lot is already littered with cars. Cheap ones. Ratty ones. Littered with rust stains and primer paint and bent antennas and fading Pig-Out bumper stickers. Employee cars. Parked on the far edges of the lot, to leave more room for the paying customers.

We drift along the open spaces, cutting a wide swath, taking the last of our free time before we walk into an hour or two of extra stupid holiday-related prep work before our usual side work and then a long, grinding day of waiting on happy, smiling, nuclear families that look, act and sound nothing like our own.

We drift up to the bike rack. Smell the pork butts smoking and the bacon sizzling and the beans baking and the fryers frying. Lock up our bikes. Stand beside them as if we know we're not quite done yet.

He reaches over. Confidently, not cautiously. Long fingers nestle in mine. I smile despite myself. Shiver with a thousand different feelings, the best two being relief and then more relief on top of that relief. Can't look up at him for fear of crying.

He squeezes my fingers. Tugs me a little closer. Voice deep and low and daringly intimate. "Hey."

He makes me look up anyway. "What?"

"I may be an asshole. I may be a chicken shit. You may hate me. Right now. This, whatever this is, may not work. But I don't regret a single moment we spent together, okay?"

I nod. Cry anyway. His free hand wipes away the two soft, single tears before they can completely ruin my makeup. In a lifetime of kind things, it's maybe the kindest thing he's ever done for me. "Me either, Benjy."

Squeezes my hand again. "No matter what happens. Remember that."

That sounds a little ominous. I look up, a little started. "Why? What's gonna happen?"

He shrugs, releases my hand. I miss his touch already. Stop myself from grabbing his back just narrowly. "No idea. Just sayin'."

Glenda appears suddenly from the entrance to the side deck. She's halfway through a smoldering cigarette and already in a mood. "And I'm just sayin', if you two lovebirds don't get your skinny little asses inside pronto, I'm reneging on my promise to give you tomorrow off!"

THIRTY

BENJY

"What's gotten into you?"

I snort. "Besides seven orders of cornbread stuffing, you mean?"

Glenda chuckles. Sighs. Lets out a puff of smoke with a low, lazy chuckle. The midday sun shines off her dark, sweaty skin. Even in late November, it's hot as balls out here in Smoker's Alley. Her voice is husky and low, the way it always gets when she wants to talk about SOMETHING SERIOUS. "That shit is pretty good, huh?"

"I can't get enough. Was it always this good? I mean, I only had six helpings last year so I can't really be sure. I may need to have one more."

She rolls her eyes. "Quit avoiding the question, pretty boy."

"I'm not."

"Sure, you are. When's the last time we talked about cornbread stuffing out here, you and me?"

"When's the last time we talked about anything?"

She arches a thick black eyebrow, softly growing gray to match her close-cropped salt and pepper stubble. "I guess you're right. Still, you're even weirder than usual today. And trust me, that's saying something, Benj."

I chuckle and light a second cigarette. I won't have time to finish it, neither of us will, but it's my first smoke break of the day and damn if I'm going to waste it having just one. "I'm always weird. Remember? That's why you love me so much."

"Weirder. Than. Usual." She punctuates each syllable with a stab of her cigarette in my general direction.

It doesn't sound like a question, but I know it is. "I dunno, I just... Lots going on, you know?" I want to spill the tea, but she's super extra chummy with Shay and I know it'll get back to her if I say too much.

She knows I'm still avoiding it. "With which girl, Benjy? Cara or Shay?"

I chuckle and snort smoke through all three holes. "Both?"

"I told you not to shit where you eat, didn't I? Told you that years ago when Cara was still working here, and I could see the drama waiting to happen between the three of you."

"Like I could help myself?"

She snorts and lets some smoke slip through a few extra orifices as well. "You got me there, player. I just... Now it's affecting your work, you know?"

I make a face. "What? How?"

"You've had your head in the clouds all day, kid, and I need you extra focused today, not half-assed. Feel me?"

"Yes, yes. Fine, I just...it's a weird holiday, you know?"

"You're telling me? I got three kids at home waiting for me to bring dinner, but *you* think working on Thanksgiving's weird? With your childish, no responsibility ass and no one waiting up for you when you get home from work."

I snort more smoke. Keep it light. "Please, your kids are

older than me! They can make their own dinner by now, surely."

She chuckles as more smoke oozes. "I know, I was just hoping for some sympathy, so you'd whip your ass into shape before we go back in there for the dinner rush."

"Gross, don't remind me."

She glances left and right. Looks vaguely anxious. Then again, she always looks like that. Lights up a second cigarette anyway. Maybe I *will* have time to finish mine after all. "You're really not gonna tell me what you're mooning about?"

"What's to tell? You can't do anything about it anyway."

"Sometimes listening is the best help you can get. Plus, I'm pretty wise. Have I ever steered you wrong in the past?"

"Only every damn time you give me advice."

"Like when?"

"When? How about that hot stock tip you gave me last year?"

She rolls her eyes. "Look, I lost money on that deal, too. Okay?"

"And the time you started selling vitamins as a side hustle and I bought a hundred dollars' worth just to shut you up and broke out in hives two days after I started taking them?"

She's laughing too hard to argue. "Need I go on?"

"Those were money advice issues, Benjy. I'm talking life advice issues."

"Have you ever given me any?"

"No, cuz you won't let me. But if I may?"

"I'm all ears, boss lady."

She snubs out her cigarette even though it's only half-smoked. Mine is long gone. She inches a little closer, as if the alley between Pig-Out and Salsa Sally's Mexican Cantina next door isn't already small enough. "The longer Cara stays away, the closer you get to Shay. And, if I may, the happier you seem. Maybe, maybe it's a good thing Cara's not coming home for Thanksgiving, you know?"

I nod because, yes, I do know. I'm almost relieved. "But doesn't that make me a bad person?"

"Which part, kid? Being happy? Or being happy with the wrong person?"

"Both?"

She nudges me with her hip before turning, slightly, toward the back kitchen door. "If I knew the answer to that one, kid, I wouldn't be divorced with three kids from two different fathers, you know what I mean?"

"So, why exactly am I taking your life advice again?"

"You're not, remember?"

"This…this wasn't very helpful."

She turns just before opening the kitchen door. Inside is a beehive of activity waiting for us to rejoin it, and we both know it. She breathes deep and forces an encouraging smile. I realize, maybe for the first time, that it doesn't come naturally for her.

"Look, Benjy, we both know you're going to do what you want to do. Maybe, from the looks of things lately, you already have. And not a damn thing I can say will change your mind. All I can tell you is that you're a good kid. And so is Shay."

"And? I feel an 'and' coming somewhere."

Her hand reaches for the door latch, but she doesn't quite pull on it. Yet. "And, if you make each other happy being good kids together, well, that's not the worst thing in the world now, is it?"

"But what if I'm already with someone else? What then?"

"Then maybe you're with the wrong person, is all I'm

saying."

I stand next to her. She has to look up to meet my eyes. I frown. "This is still less than helpful, boss."

She winks. Pulls open the door. "Now you know why I don't give out too much life advice around here. Nobody ever takes it—"

It seems like she has more to say, but someone sees her, calls out to her with some urgent issue and, in moments, she is swallowed up by the task of managing a busy restaurant on a $40,000 holiday. I stand, hand on the door she just opened, and sigh.

A busboy washing his hands in the dish pit sink sees me. Shouts, "Benj, Table 7 just sat. Where you been?"

I shake my head and grumble, "Oh, just reevaluating my whole life, kid. Where you been?"

He juts out a chin. All of 17 and already full of piss and vinegar. "Telling your table you'd be there in a second, so... don't make a liar out of me, okay bud?"

I start to school him on the chain of command and then just sag. It's not worth it. I've got a table waiting and if I play my cards right, I'll make more tips on this one table than he will all night, so I let him have his moment and fix my smile as he holds the door open for me.

Outside the dish pit door, the restaurant literally roars to life with a standing room only crowd and two hundred voices all competing for the same air space. The kid and I share a look, a sympathetic combination of fear, regret, resignation, frustration, and sheer, abject numbness. I grip him on the shoulder on my way past and whisper "Good luck" as I walk by.

Why not? It's Thanksgiving, after all.

Or should I say... Treesgiving Eve? Suddenly, 'chasing Christmas' has never felt so good...

THIRTY-ONE

SHAY

"Thanks, y'all. I couldn't have done it without you two today."

Glenda raises a plastic cup full of red wine. And I mean full. When Benjy and I gently clink cups with her, some spills on her fingers. She licks it off before sipping.

Always the lady.

I chuckle and sip the cheap champagne from my own plastic cup. We had a few bottles left after the dinner special and I talked Glenda into opening one for our shift drinks.

Under protest, of course.

I settle back into my woven deck chair and take a sip. It's cheap. Kinda sweet. But it's cold and it's free and just perfect for the end of one very long, very shitty day. "You actually couldn't have."

Benjy puts his cup down. Stretches. Yawns. Looks adorably rumpled in the aftermath, hat crooked and shirt half-tucked and one crew sock puddled around the top of his left shoe. "Yeah, not with half the staff calling out."

"Well, it wasn't half the staff, but being down three whole servers sure felt like it at dinnertime, that's for sure."

We grumble about work for a good ten minutes or so. Maybe fifteen to twenty. Okay, an hour. Tops. As always, we talk about who did this. Who said that. Who said this. Who did that. Which guests were the best. Which ones were the worst. Which kitchen guy made the best smoked turkey. Which one dried out the yams.

It's late. Coming on midnight. But it's the kind of day where you've been going since six am and won't crash until an hour or so after you get home, so why not cap off all that energy with good friends and better conversation?

The wine and champagne and conversation and complaints flow like barbecue sauce over an endless smoked meat platter. Sometime around midnight, the first Christmas song comes on. One minute it's country twang like white noise in the background and the next it's suddenly all jingles and bells and we stop, mid-sentence, glancing up at the hidden speaker above like Pavlov's dogs. We chuckle collectively.

Benjy groans. "Turn it off. Turn it off."

Glenda grins playfully. "I can't. You know that. Corporate turns that stuff on the day after Thanksgiving from the home office and won't turn it back off again until the day after New Year's."

I grin and sip my champagne and privately enjoy the shit out of the redneck version of "Holly Jolly Christmas". Benjy catches me. Elbows my ribs playfully. "Change of plans. We should just have Treesgiving here and save the—"

"You're still talking about that Treesgiving shit?"

The three of us glance over, as a group, like hungry cats when a bird flies by. Cara stands just inside the back entrance to the side deck. Hip cocked. Hands on hips. Eyes in a permanent roll. She is making her version of a GRAND ENTRANCE. I think half of her actually expects canned applause from a live studio audience. Naturally, she looks resplendent even in yoga pants and a Florida Eastern University sweatshirt.

Her hair is pulled back, casually, raven black bangs still expertly curated above her thick, rich eyebrows. Her eyes glance around the scattered deck table, taking us in one by one as if gauging our responses on a sliding scale. The muted, lackluster expression on her face says we're failing.

Big time.

I feel her glance linger on me, eyes smoky and curious and somehow slightly knowing. My face burns to think she might already sense that something between Benjy and I has changed. Then again, it already had long before we finally, well, you know.

Benjy is the first to speak. A croak, actually. "Cara?"

She cocks the other hip. Her eyes glint expectantly in the light of the gently swaying strings of bulbs just overhead. "Who'd you expect? A turkey?"

God, so corny. I roll my eyes. She never did have a great sense of humor, no matter how hard she tried. And she always tried. Like, really, really hard. I mean, she literally probably practiced that line six different ways as she drove into the Pig-Out parking lot. That's why I could never see her and Benjy together. He's such a cutup, constantly spewing sarcasm, and witty, wry observations from the moment he gets up 'til his last breath of the day, and she was always so very, very dry. It always felt wasted on her.

He's half-sitting, half-standing, like he's not sure what to do or how to do it or even when. Hands clenched around the arms of his chair like a gymnast on those hanging circle things. My glass is frozen in mid-sip, still processing the fact that she's. Actually. Here. And what that's gonna mean for the next three days.

He stammers, finally rising the rest of the way out of his chair, legs squeaking with the effort. "N-n-no, I just... You said you weren't coming home."

She rolls her eyes. I forgot how bitchy she always was to him. Especially in front of an audience. Some guys are into that, I guess. "It's called a joke, Benj. What? You seem disappointed."

More stammering as he finally launches himself from the chair as if making some kind of decision. It scoots over, practically knocking the glass out of my hand. I recover and sip greedily, eager for any chance to blot out the sudden screaming in my head. I share a quick glance with Glenda as Benjy grovels. She, too, looks eager to distance herself from the suddenly awkward interaction.

"No, no, not at all. I mean, I'm stoked. Obviously." He straightens with every lie, until he stands at his full height, radiant and young and positively beaming. Or maybe they're not lies, after all. Maybe he really is stoked to see her, and I am really, truly, and suddenly forgotten and all of that, everything that happened between us, and not just the apocalyptic, liberating sex, was just killing time.

She smiles at last. Radiant white shark teeth to match the predatory gleam in her smoky, cryptic green eyes. "Obviously."

They wrap themselves in an awkward hug. It's all bending and shifting and sharp angles and patting hands. I've seen political rivals share more intimacy before a heated debate on live TV.

Then again, who's complaining? It would have been even more awkward watching them dry hump or something after three-plus months apart. Either way, it buys Glenda and I time enough to glance over at each other, eyebrows arched to full extension, our expressions recreating human versions of that one teethy face emoji. We rise slowly as well.

Cara always knew how to kill a vibe.

She spies us from over Benjy's shoulder. Fluttering her long, effortless lashes and pushing him away playfully, but not entirely. She kept him on a tight leash all through high school, junior college and right up until she left in late August. Her long, elegant fingers still cling to the hem of his faded Thanksgiving t-shirt as if he's a balloon that might somehow float away. "Get over here, you two."

I wanna say, "There's two of us and one of you and we're the ones who worked all day. You just drove a few hours sitting on your tight ass, you skinny bitch. You come to us." But, of course, I don't. Even Glenda drifts dutifully into Cara's awkward, bony clutches before she is released after an obligatory squeeze, and I just as awkwardly take her place.

Cara leans closer. Whispers in my ear. "Surprised, babe?"

I push her gently away. Study her eyes. Smoky and mischievous and shimmering in the shadows of the side deck. Mysterious. Sexy. Vaguely evil, but playful as well. Like she can't make up her mind whether to stab me with her car keys or give me a friendship bracelet. I still can't tell if she knows about Benjy and me or is just generally fucking with me after being away for so long. I fix on a smile either way, too tired to play games even if she isn't. "Not at all, Cara. This seems exactly like something you'd do."

She laughs dramatically. I'd forgotten how specific that sound was. How not entirely pleasant it is. It's like certain servers who've never mastered their table voice and always laugh a little too artificially, a little too loudly, a little too abrasively, at something they're not supposed to. Or maybe I've just gotten used to life without her. The comfortable silence. The drama-free days and restful nights and easy, wash and wear companionship Benjy and I share when she's not around. "Well, you always were the smart one. Right, Benj?"

As if struggling to break the awkward silence, I hear Glenda behind me. Gathering up her things and hoping the sound of her purse zipping and car keys rattling will somehow mask the disapproving tongue clucks she's making with every syllable. "Right. Anyway, Shay, we should probably let these two have a proper reunion, huh?"

I have never been so very, absolutely, positively thrilled about Glenda's normally unwanted intrusiveness. "Oh, absolutely!"

Cara looks slightly disappointed. Or relieved. I can't really tell. "Are you two sure? It's been so long?"

Glenda literally drags me along. I couldn't have stuck around even if I wanted to. And I suddenly realize, I definitely don't want to. "Oh, we're sure."

Benjy looks confused. Also? Envious. Like we're not the only ones who want to escape this suddenly awkward reunion and flee to somewhere quiet and remote to talk shit about it and analyze it to the nth degree like a table full of Karens or bad tippers. "Don't you guys want to hang out some more?"

I get the hint. Hear the desperation in his voice. Ignore it. Utterly and completely. "Absolutely. Once you guys get caught up, we'll hang and chill over the holiday weekend."

Cara shrugs casually, obviously happy for our abrupt exit. "I mean, if, you're sure."

Glenda is a step out in front already. I pause. Glance at Cara. Play it cool. Flutter my lashes and beam my smile and nod reassuringly, like I would at a rowdy table full of middle-aged businessmen who've just asked me to meet them at the club after I get off from work. "Sure, girl. Absolutely."

She beams back at me, as if playing the same game. "You don't mind about Treesgiving?"

I'm about to follow Glenda out. Freeze in place. Turn slightly. "Trees…giving?"

"I mean, we'll need at least a day to catch up, right Benj?" She turns to him for reassurance. Wink, wink. Nudge, nudge. Gross, grosser. "So, we'll have to take a rain check on your magical new holiday, no hard feelings, right?"

Benjy looks at his feet. "Benj? Right?"

He looks up at her clipped, demanding tone. I wince. He nods. "Yeah, sure." Won't even look my way. Or hers, for that matter. I'll give the chicken shit that much, anyway.

I try to keep the croak out of my voice. Wave my hands. Nod too hard. Make big, exaggerated expressions as I squeak out a master class in being pathetic. "Sure thing. Absolutely. I mean…pffft. It's just…it was a silly idea anyway. My take-off on that old TV show celebration."

Cara chuckles. "You think?"

A tone replaces my croak. The bitch. Our eyes meet as a grunt, "Yeah, remember? I just said so."

"I mean, it's not like a greeting card holiday or anything, right?" Cara huffs, as if my life is just ever so silly.

My voice grows chillier, despite the unseasonable weather. "I…I never said it was. Just, it's fine."

I avoid Benjy's downcast eyes as Cara and I face off in the first 7.5 seconds of her arrival. Wow, that didn't take long. "Good, because, you know, snuggles with boo?"

I add, so that it's clear just how not hurt I am, despite the tremor in my voice and quivering tone, "I really didn't expect either of you anyway!"

Cara's eyes glow flinty at the unspoken challenge. Cocks

her hip just slightly. Arches that famous eyebrow. Freezes her lips in a quietly dangerous grin. I feel suddenly transported, like I'm back in high school. Then remember, just as suddenly, that I'm not. In high school. Not even a little. This is *my* side deck. At *my* job. And crummy as it can be sometimes, she's still a guest here. She tosses out the last word like I'm not standing there withering. Then makes me wither just a little more. "I mean, maybe if we get bored, we can stop by? Late afternoon?"

I wave a hand. Incredibly, it's shaking. Somehow, I keep my voice level as I shoot that little idea down. "Don't bother. After everyone else leaves, I'll head out for sushi somewhere."

Her eyes light up. "Ooooh, even better. Hit me up, girl. Maybe we'll join you."

I stifle a cluck of my tongue. Wonder how this ever used to work, the three of us together, this awkward and vaguely grating dynamic, me following along like a third wheel and never once complaining. I find it hard to imagine myself ever doing that again. Start to drift away behind Glenda as we leave the two lovebirds behind.

If I stay any longer, I'll just say something I'll regret. Or she will. Sometimes, retreat is the only way to win the battle. Even if it is just with yourself. "Naw, you guys catch up. I'll see you whenever. Probably when you're here on Christmas break, Cara. Snuggles with Boo and all that, right?"

She finally gets the hint and isn't happy.

I smile with a glint of satisfaction and ignore her for one last jab. "Later, Benjy!"

I hear her mutter, "Suit yourself." Smile with a slight grin of satisfaction. She always did like to have the last word.

"Girl," Glenda nudges me quietly. She waits for me as I unlock my bike. We can still hear them muttering on the side deck. Quietly. Just below the cover of the jaunty country Christmas music. Murmur. Chuckle. Murmur. Laughter. Murmur. Then another soft, sultry giggle that sounds like we were meant to hear it. I tug the bike from the rack with a huff and a grunt and walk it beside her as we drift gently away.

We wait until we can't hear the Christmas music anymore to look at each other. Eyes wide. Walking closer than we normally would. Glenda takes a deep breath. "Was she always so catty?"

I shrug, wondering myself. "I guess. I mean, maybe I just forgot since we haven't hung out in a while."

"Damn."

"So, it wasn't just me?"

Glenda makes a throaty chuckle. "Girl. No. That...that was downright uncomfortable. Shoot, I'd rather work Thanksgiving all over again than relive that five-minute nightmare."

"Right?"

We chuckle. A quick burst of pent-up anxiety. I feel instantly better. Not just about the moment, but everything. Work family, there's nothing like it. "You think she knows?"

Glenda pauses slightly. "Knows what?"

I freeze. She freezes. "Wait, you... I thought I told you."

She makes her skeptical face. "About what?"

I literally bury my face in my hands. "Shit."

Glenda chuckles again. Nudges me. "You mean about you and Benjy?" I glance up. She nods knowingly. "You didn't have to tell me but seems like you just did."

"I didn't. I honestly thought..."

She puts a motherly hand on my forearm. "Girl, it's fine. I already suspected it."

"I assumed I'd told you."

She rolls her eyes. We drift closer to her car. "No, it must have been some other cool ass, grown-up individual you confided in about your scandalous little sex life."

I think about Hub and nod. "Yeah, pretty much."

"So, what? I'm sloppy seconds?"

I pretend to think about it until she slugs me playfully on the arm. "No. Never. But there are first people you tell things to in life, and first people you tell things to at work."

"Still sounds like I come in second."

"You shouldn't, since all I do is work."

We're at her car. She juggles her big black purse until she fishes out her big fat ring of keys. Clicks something. Her door swings open. I stand back, as always, impressed. She stands in the doorway, bathed in the interior light, but doesn't sit yet. "You gonna be okay?"

"I'm fine."

She puts a hand on her hip. Cocks it. "You're not the least bit jealous?"

I glance behind me. Toward the side deck. The only lights on in the entire barn shaped building are the swaying strings of exposed bulbs. I imagine Cara and Benjy, standing beneath them, eyes aglow, doing whatever they do when no one's looking. Shrug. Turn back. "Actually, now that I've had him, I could care less."

She looks doubtful.

Surprised, even.

Then, appropriately judgmental. I'd be disappointed if she hadn't. "Well, that doesn't sound right."

Truer words have never been spoken. "I know. But it feels right." I search my soul for something even remotely feeling like jealousy, and find only a numb, inky blackness. "Maybe I'm wrong. Maybe that just means I'm so jealous I can't actually feel jealous. Maybe I've just got nothing left."

She makes scary movie fingers to match my dead inside aesthetic. "Ooooh, so wise coming from a child's mouth."

I ignore her withering sarcasm and finally slip onto my bike. My body feels as numb as my soul. "Anyway…"

She gives me another good study. "You sure you're going to be okay?"

I give her a wry smile, as much energy as I can muster at the moment. My eyes are dry now, but probably won't be for long. I grip the handlebars tightly to camouflage my still trembling hands. All the same, I can't hide the croak in my voice. "I'll be fine. Just been a kinda long 48-hours, you know?"

"I wouldn't, actually. Been awhile since I've had this kind of drama in my own life. Or excitement, for that matter."

I snort. Kick up the stand and start to drift in short, lazy circles around her gleaming sedan. "Me too, usually."

She nods like maybe that's correct. "I can't tell if I'm jealous that I'm not you right now, or happy I'm not."

I nod again. "It's crazy that, once you finally get what you thought you wanted all along, you just kinda wish you could go back and un-have it, you know?"

She narrows her eyes at me. Nods. "Do you, though? Would you really un-do everything that happened just to not feel this way right now?"

I slow as I pass her. "Not really. I just wish things were different, somehow. Not so…icky."

She nods. Watches me take another loop around her car. Sees me going slightly dark and tries to bring me back to the light. Brightens like the soft glow of the streetlamp over-head. "Listen, Shay, forget all this drama and just have fun tomorrow." She watches me circle her. Still standing in the doorway of her big, fat ride.

"You, too."

"You didn't cancel Treesgiving, did you?"

"Hell no. I just didn't want her bony ass showing up."

I hear Glenda cackling even after the big, heavy door to her spaceship car is shut. Then the big engine growls to life and finally drowns her out. I circle the car once more, just to make her smile. She honks the horn on her way out of the parking space, a foghorn in the vast, dark, empty parking lot. I wave long after her taillights have faded into the warm, soft night.

Wait till I'm halfway home to finally start crying.

THIRTY-TWO

BENJY

"Surprised, baby?"

"Shyeah!" I have zero hesitation responding truthfully to that question, let me tell you. Pleasantly surprised? Now, that's a different matter. But surprised? Technically speaking? Yes. Oh. God. Yes.

She grins knowingly. Wriggles her finger to draw me even closer. Wraps me in what feels like a genuinely tender hug, tight and firm and suggestive. Kisses me warm, wet, long, and hard, but not tender. Even as I lean into it with a soft, grateful murmur, I can tell it's by rote. Something a borderline sociopath thinks she should do when seeing her boyfriend for the first time in three months after being mostly a dick to him that whole time.

Pushes me away playfully, the way she does when we both know I'm going to get laid later and we're just kind of doing a little dance until then. I feel a strange stirring I wasn't expecting, something more than just the sexy sting of anticipation. I feel bad, suddenly. Unexpectedly. Sorry. Ashamed. Guilty.

Shitty, really.

Really, really shitty.

We're nervous around each other, suddenly. I'm not sure why. I mean, I know why I am but what the hell's *her* problem? I avoid her eyes, then she avoids mine. And back and forth and on like that we go.

It's not like her. Me? Maybe. Kind of. She was always pretty intimidating, and never more so than when we hadn't seen each other for a hot minute. Like that one time she went away to cheer camp for the weekend, and I didn't see her until Monday morning, and we had to kind of start all over again, standing there in the hallway shuffling from foot to foot while she opened up her locker before homeroom. And this is a hotter minute than either of us has ever experienced before.

She sees the empty bottle on the tabletop where we left it. A stack of red solo cups next to it, as neat as we could muster after a long, fifteen-hour day. She always did have an eye for the little details. Arches a perfectly manicured eyebrow and murmurs, "Save any of that for me?"

I've never been so glad for anything that came out of her mouth in my life. Even though I was over it literally thirty seconds ago, suddenly I'm thirsty all over again.

"Actually..." I drift away, glad for a little distance so my heart rate can return to normal, and I can hopefully reset the awkward vibe a tad. "There was one last bottle we just couldn't stomach anymore."

She drifts closer, all hip bones and mascara and her severe black ponytail swishing against the shoulders of her baggy yellow hoodie. "It was a long drive, so I wouldn't mind a little bubbly to celebrate."

I pull the last bottle out of the ugly white pickle barrel we used as an ice bucket and wink, curling the cheap gold foil off the twist-off cap. "I'm suddenly a little thirsty myself."

She makes a low, throaty chuckle and then neither of us really know what to say after that. I grin nervously because it's kind of like starting from scratch. She watches me open the bottle, both of us wincing when I twist off the cap. Then it just kind of comes off and we both laugh longer than we should at something that was never all that funny to begin with.

I get her a new cup and refill my old one and we stand, closer, to toast. "Happy Thanksgiving, boo," she murmurs when I don't take the wheel soon enough and stand there, silently, drinking her in. I sigh with relief, having nothing much to say beyond "Wow, you're really here" over and over and over again.

"Here's to catching up," I add before we clink red plastic cups, but only because I know she expects me to say something. Even if it is kinda lame.

She sips. Winces at the cheapness of the bubbly like I knew she would. Makes me smile to remember how dramatically bitchy she could be, wondering how I ever found it so cute before. Wonder if I still will now that she's back. She barely swallows before correcting me. "I mean, we're pretty caught up, right? We talk most nights."

Ah, just like the good old days. I give a secret smile she takes for flattery. Murmur, "I mean, don't you have any good gossip for me? Like creepy professors who are always hitting on you or annoying roommates who snore or the high price of textbooks or what your favorite restaurant is in town?"

She makes a *mean girl's* face like I just belched at a dinner party she was really, really looking forward to. "What are we, girlfriends?"

I literally take a step back. The fuck is that even supposed to mean? I stare at a fresh speck of barbecue sauce on my sneaker for a good minute wondering if maybe I'm spoiled by the way Shay and I talk.

Or, rather, gossip. It's basically just part of our DNA now. The running patter that's so easy and free flowing and constant, like the country music on the hidden speakers above our heads. The nonstop narration of our workday. This idiot and that clown and that boomer and that skank and that dipshit and that nerd. I guess we do kind of talk like girlfriends, or at least... friends.

I wonder, now, if Cara and I were ever that. I mean, friends? We had to be, at one time. My memories of her are too warm to think we never got along. Ever. I just think it's been too far, too cold, too estranged, for too long for me to feel all warm and fuzzy now that she's suddenly material- ized, scattering our cozy little work family like a deranged clown with a chainsaw at a kids birthday party. From the laser strength building up in her cool, green eyes, it looks like I'm not the only one who feels that way.

I sigh and stare slightly past her, just over her shoulder. In the dim light of the swaying rows of exposed bulbs, beneath the brim of my crooked work cap, I guess it could be considered eye contact. "I dunno. I just thought you'd have more to say about college life, that's all."

She shrugs and sips fully from the cheap champagne. "It's kind of like me asking is anything new around here?"

I struggle not to snort and choke and swallow and spit. *Honey, if you only knew.* "Not exactly. I mean, you worked here. You know the drill. Same shit, different table. Other than what I see on your phone when I call, I don't know dick about where you go or what you do or who you do it with or..." I let my voice trail off because now I've done it.

She glances away as if counting to ten. Bites down on her lip. Then blasts me anyway. "What is this, an interrogation?"

I struggle to remain objective. She's so good at gaslighting. I'm always feeling guilty just for asking what I feel are pretty average, basic, objectively reasonable questions. I mean, is "How's school going?" really that much of a stretch after seeing someone for the first time in three fucking months?

I take a sip and count to ten myself. "Nope."

She waits for more. I got nothing. Nothing except a dull sense of dread in my stomach. The kind you feel before something really shitty happens and you're powerless to avoid it. Or just too numb to try and even prevent it. Either way, I have a sense that this... this is not going well at all. Not even a little like I expected it might when she crashed our little post-Thanksgiving gossip fest just a few minutes earlier.

There's a waist-high railing separating the side deck from the bike rack and, beyond it, the vast, wide, big empty parking lot. The wood is purposefully distressed, like the rest of the big barn of a restaurant, but actually quite sturdy. She's leaning against it, legs gently crossed at the ankles. She's got on little yellow anklet socks to match her hoodie, and sleek black running shoes to match her dark grey yoga pants.

By hook or by crook she's taken possession of the green bottle of bubbly and tops off her glass. Again. Doesn't offer to hit mine up. I offer a wry grin. Just like old times. They say absence makes the heart grow fonder but sheesh. I dunno. All it's done for me is to bring into laser focus all the things I used to overlook about my girlfriend I suddenly can't anymore.

She takes a nice, long sip. Full lips around the cup's rim. Sets it down on the railing like she's a guest waiting for a table during high season and gives me a moist grin. "Let's start over, boo. I...I shouldn't have surprised you like this. You've had a long day."

I grin. Maybe she's not the devil after all. Maybe this will all work out and she and I can pick up where we left off and she doesn't have to know about Shay and me. Or maybe I'll tell her. Or maybe I won't. "No, I'm glad you're here. It's... it's what I wanted all along."

She cocks her head and squints, like she already knows the answer. "Is it, though?"

"Of course, it is. Who's been bugging you to get your ass home since Halloween?"

"You have, baby, but you're making me feel a certain way now that I'm actually here."

I grin and inch closer. "I hope I am."

She puts a hand up before I even reach her. "Stop, boo, you know what I mean."

"I do. We just need to get reacquainted, that's all."

Her hand presses against my chest. Firm, but yielding. I inch closer anyway, until our lips graze and she murmurs, "You're incorrigible."

I chuckle and glide my hands down to the small of her back, press her body against mine to make sure we still fit like we used to, puzzle pieces that lock in all the right places no matter how mismatched the picture might look when they're together.

"Oh, what? You're back for five minutes and you're already using big college words?"

I must surprise her. She laughs. Warm breath like sweet champagne as I smother her chuckles with warm, sloppy kisses until I feel her yield and press gently against me. We stand there, like the old days, gently swaying with our bodies glued together and lips firmly puckered. She pushes away first. She always does. That's kind of her thing.

Licks her lips. Seems genuinely surprised. "I've forgotten what you tasted like."

"I haven't."

She sighs and meets my eyes. "No, Benjy, you probably haven't."

I wait for her to explain what that means but, instead, she grabs her keys from one of her hoodie pockets and waves them. "Dad's out of town on business for the week-end. Shocker, I know. So…my room in twenty?"

We both glance at my bike at the same time. "If I don't beat you there first, hot pants."

She snorts as we drift from the side deck. "On that old thing?"

"Hey, she's stuck with me this long. She'll get me there in record time, trust."

Cara rolls her eyes as I climb on top. "At least it'll give me time to take a shower first."

I tug at her sleeve as she starts toward her car. "Don't, babe. I want you just like you are right now."

"Gross. I've been driving all day."

I follow her to her car, itching to get pedaling. "And I've been working all day. We'll be a perfect fit."

She's whining now, only half-joking. "But my sheets will be clean and…"

I silence her with a kiss before leaving her, breathless and leaning back against her car, as I zoom off. I wait for her to say something cute, or fun, or even sexy as I pedal away, still well within earshot. But she doesn't. I hear the engine turn over, smooth and solid, in the sports car her daddy bought her for graduation.

It glides by, sleek and satiny under the rows of orange streetlights overhead. No window down. No little wave. Just a quick, almost quiet toot of her horn and she's off, brake lights winking as she leaves Restaurant Row without another sound.

And, so help me God, as horny as I am, as eager as I am to use every short cut in town to get to her dad's house up on the bluff in ritzy Pelican Pointe, is it wrong that the first thing I want to do is swing by the Salty Seagull and tell Shay all about it?

THIRTY-THREE

SHAY

Fuck it. I can't take it anymore.

I plug in the lights on the tree.

They glow a radiant, brilliant white. So radiant and brilliant you can't even tell the tree is fake. I mean, it should be frickin' radiant. I have something like eight strings of lights on the damn thing. I put it up last night, or this morning, or whatever time it was after I got home fuming after Cara and Benjy and a holiday weekend ruined. I hadn't planned to put on all the strings of lights, maybe just two or three like every other year, but I was so restless and wired and frustrated and bored and sad I just kept winding and winding until I'd used every box I'd bought.

I thought it might look barren and stale without any baubles or doo-dads or balls or bows, but now that I see it glowing and warm, I'm happy I left off all that other junk. When all this first started, I was going to invite a lot of people from work. Have them each bring an ornament and hang it as they walked through the front door. But then time got away from me.

One minute it was Halloween and the next, bam,

Thanks-frickin-giving! That and, to be honest, no one knew what the hell I was talking about anyway. "Treesgiving? What?" And then they'd make that stupid question mark face that made me want to punch them in their nose. Everyone was working. Or already had plans with their families, yada yada. I don't like half of them anyway, so yeah, no ornaments.

I don't really mind, actually. You would think I'd want a ton of company around, 24/7, to distract me from the fact that my own family could care less, but I find it harder to endure people I don't really like than to simply be alone. I care about the people I work with, even have affection for most of them, but I give everything I have at work, and then some. When I'm home, by myself, I never feel quite lonely.

The friends I had back in school are gone, organically speaking, off to college like Cara or moving way for careers or romance. I've got Hub next door and Benjy most nights a week and, well, that's enough. For me. For now. Even with my own little made up holiday, I'd rather spend it alone, being cheesy and corny and utterly myself, than to apologize for 'chasing Christmas' and pretending like I'm not cheesy and corny in the first place.

I step back from the tree. Admire the glowing radiance. Smile at the way it sits, just so, in the middle of the picture window by the front door. Take that, haters. I don't care if it's still 92-degrees out there and November isn't even over yet. Treesgiving is here, and here to stay!

It's slightly overcast, which fits my sour, dour mood. The kind of day where it could be 8 AM or 8 PM and you can't really tell the difference. The grey haze outside helps to make the tree glow even brighter in the open window, muslin curtains gently flapping on either side. I grab the snowman coffee mug from the windowsill where I've paused, mid-pace, and sip the lukewarm peppermint schnapps spiked cocoa inside. Smile at the indulgence as it warms me inside and out.

Drift toward the coffee table and snag a Christmas cookie from one of the matching snowman trays on top. Nibble it slowly before drifting back to my outturned barstool at the kitchen counter. Sit down and stare, unblinking, at my tree.

It's early afternoon. The complex is quiet for a Friday. But then, it's not just any Friday. It's Black Friday. The day after Thanksgiving. The whole world's out there, shopping for last-minute bargains as the holiday season finally gets officially underway. I sigh and sip and nibble and try not to feel lonely and pathetic in my crappy little apartment with my crappy little tree and my crappy little dollar store cookies and off-brand peppermint schnapps and my sad little attempt to be cool and hip and with-it like all those perfect chicks I follow on Instagram who made *Friendsgiving* such a big thing. So, I wanted my own version and came up with Treesgiving instead!

In all the hubbub of trying to make my fake holiday trend, it never occurred to me why I thought it up in the first place or, later still, why it's become so important to me, period. I suppose, in a way, it's *my* way. My way of taking back the holidays and making them my own. Holidays are for families, warm memories, home baked pies and secret recipes and annual traditions and, when you grow up with none of that, absolutely nada, I suppose you tend to want your own. To start from scratch.

Christmas has never been really special to me, not with my family tree splintering like it had been struck by lightning. And most years I work Thanksgiving and all the other holidays, so in a way I suppose I wanted to make something for me. And my friends, if they wanted to be a part of it, too.

But mostly for me. My day. To do my way, full stop. That it fell like a wet Christmas stocking doesn't faze me so much. It's kind of fitting, I suppose, after all that's happened this week. The secrets that were shared, to say nothing of the bodily fluids and emotions, and the way it all kind of fell flat when Cara came back.

Karma, I suppose?

The record player scratches merrily between songs. Drags me back into the world of Charlie Brown and his own bittersweet Christmas reflections. The scratchy, lo-fi holiday music fits the mood and I sit, alone, at a table heaping with Christmas treats I guess I'm supposed to eat all by myself.

The tree comes in and out of focus as the gray day slowly oozes by. I gaze past it to the soft, monotone sky outside and listen for the sounds of splashing in the pool downstairs. Or, perhaps, Hub shuffling by in his lazy flip flops for the sixth time, trying to get my attention with a cheap bottle of champagne or brandy to mark the occasion.

Nothing. Nada. Zip.

I sigh and consider the rest of my day. The handful of scratchy Christmas vinyl I found at the thrift shop on the way home from work last week. The cheesy holiday movie playlist I have lined up on YouTube. The stack of dog-eared Christmas romance novels from the library by my bed.

Sigh and reach for the schnapps when a shadow passes just past the tree. Pause, mid-sip, like I've just been caught doing something dirty. Feel a jolt of energy as the shape slowly takes form. It's not Hub, though that would be great. It's slightly taller, slightly leaner, much younger. It could be a passing delivery boy. That wouldn't surprise me. Mrs. Johnson in 3-B getting takeout after a long, lazy Thanksgiving doing nothing.

But the shape stops. At my door. There's a long pause,

like maybe he's reconsidering, then a face pokes around to peer in the window. Catches me watching him. Waves me over with a grin. "Hurry, Shay, before I chicken out!"

He chuckles as I open the door. "Nice shirt."

I glance down at the jolly Santa on the front of my soft, clingy grey tee. I'd forgotten I even had it on, even though I spent about six hours online one night picking it out. The slogan next to it reads, "I do it for the Ho's." I smirk. Thought no one but me was ever going to see it. Wriggle just a little. Slide the door open wider.

"Yours, too." I tug playfully at his own soft red shirt. The gingerbread man with the broken leg. "Oh, Snap!" Corny, a bit played out, but still cute. Kinda like him. He blushes slightly.

"I thought you didn't believe in all this Treesgiving stuff, Benj."

"I don't."

"So, what's with the shirt?"

"Believe it or not, I guess you're not the only one 'chasing Christmas' this year, Shay. They were already selling them at the store when I picked up snacks for today."

I stand, still in the doorway, literally gobsmacked. Smacked by gob, I tell ya. "Already? Benj, they've been selling them for weeks. You just haven't noticed."

"Maybe because I wanted to give Thanksgiving its due?"

"Yeah, right. What are you, working for Perdue Turkey Farms as your side hustle?"

He ignores my flat joke. He's not wrong, it wasn't very funny. But I'm nervous, suddenly. He's making me nervous with his sudden and unexpected appearance, even though it's secretly what I've been waiting for, hoping for, all morning.

Glances in before taking another step. "Wow, Shay. You... you weren't kidding."

I follow his gaze around the carefully choreographed living room. The flickering jar candles every which a where. Snow globes and nutcrackers scattered hither and yon. Pom pom garland over the scratchy, jazzy record player. And, of course, the tree. "What?"

He breezes past, finally. I glance out onto the walkway, empty now but waiting for Cara to appear at the top of the stairs. Thin and haughty and with nothing Christmas-y about her impeccable outfit. At all. The scrape of a paper bag rustles against my thigh as he steps inside.

Alone. I try not to feel relieved.

He stands, mid-floor. "You really did it."

"Did what?"

"Put the tree up before it was even December yet."

I roll my eyes. He puts the paper bag on the kitchen counter. I wait by the door. He looks back at me, still straddling the doorway. "Aren't you coming in? I mean, it is *your* party."

I frown, still waiting for the other shoe to drop. "Where's your better half?"

His face dampens ever so slightly. Makes a clucking sound. A side effect of working with Glenda a little too often, I suppose. Turns away and drifts a little farther inside. Toward the kitchen. "I'll tell you later. I'm starved. Can we eat now?"

I shrug. Shut the door. Try to hide my relief. "Sure. Take your pick. I've got sugar cookies, candy canes, gingerbread men—"

"I mean real food."

My face sags. I start the record over to stop the needle scratching on the end of the last track. It's been doing that for a while now. It was kinda bugging me, but I'd been too comatose to get up and do anything about it so I just kept listening. "Well, you were supposed to take care of that. Remember?"

He grins. Tears open the brown paper bag. "For once, I actually did."

"Wow, it really is a Treesgiving miracle!"

He ignores me. Starts pulling out the contents of the bag, one by one. Inside are wedges of cheese in all shapes, sizes and colors, a whole rustic sausage, a few boxes of fancy-ish crackers, the kind with sesame seeds and cracked wheat, two bottles of champagne of dubious design and origin. He nudges me with his big, broad shoulder. He lets it linger until it's something slightly else. Our eyes meet briefly above the spread. "You slice. I'll pour?"

I nod. The candles flicker. The tree glows. The music jingles and jangles, light and comforting and familiar. We stumble merrily around the tiny kitchen. Feet crossing. Hips nudging. Reaching for things at the same time and pulling our hands back and snorting joyful, relieved snorts. Music jazzy and soft. I arrange the sausage and cheese on a snowman plate. Sort the crackers in a tree-shaped serving bowl. He pours the cheap bubbly in paper Santa cups. Hands me one. Our eyes meet again. He blushes slightly. Quickly. Raises his cup. It looks tiny in his long, tender fingers. "To…Treesgiving."

I chuckle. Tap his paper cup with mine. Sip deeply, suddenly grateful for something a little less peppermint-y and chocolate-y. "Mmmmmm. That's good."

He winks. "Only the best for Treesgiving."

"You don't have to say it like that. Every time."

"Like what?"

"Like you're making fun of it."

He arches an eyebrow like the villain in some vintage Saturday morning cartoon. Leans a little closer. Too close. "But... I am."

I kick him playfully in the shin. But in bare feet, it ends up hurting me more than it does him. He grins at my pain. I slug him on the shoulder, and he grins all the wider.

The space is too tight, suddenly. Too intimate. I grab my plate and drift past him to the couch. Luring him away from the tight, claustrophobic space. Outside of the tiny kitchen, I can already breathe easier. He follows. Reluctantly. We nestle in amongst the spray of new throw pillows.

One tumbles over onto his lap. He holds it up. Examines the cheesy reindeer face on the front. Taps the fuzzy little red ball for his nose. "Jesus, Shay. I'm about one snowflake away from an intervention here."

I chuckle. "Okay, so maybe I went a little overboard."

He glances around the room. The plastic tree glowing like a bonfire in the dingy, overcast gloom. The single stocking on the hook on the back of the door. The Christmas cookies piled high on Christmas plates resting on carefully triangulated stacks of Christmas napkins on top of a matching Christmas tablecloth. "A little? I mean, how many people did you invite?"

I shrug. "Some people at work. A few from the track team back in the day. Glenda didn't know when she'd get off and she may still drop by. So far, you're the only one who's showed up."

He leans over slowly. Grabs a gingerbread man. Nibbles it thoughtfully. "So...what was your plan if I didn't come?"

"Nothing. Sit here and nibble and relax and unwind."

"Alone?"

"Yeah. Kind of like the way I've lived for the last year."

He washes the cookie down with some more champs.

Tops off our paper cups with the dark green bottle. Leans back amidst the tower of throw pillows with a contented sigh. "Oh, yeah."

I snag a piece of cheese and sausage on the end of a reindeer toothpick. Wave it at him before sliding it in my mouth. "Anyway, thanks for the snacks. I needed a little savory to go with my sweet."

He reaches for the bag. "Shit. I almost forgot."

I nibble a cube of cheese, tangy and musky, while he roots around in there, long arms going all the way to the bottom like some magician reaching into his hat. The cheese is good. Filling. Savory. Robust. The first non-sweet thing I've had all day.

I glance up from picking another cube to find him holding a present. He's smiling. Proudly. Like he wrapped it himself. I can tell he did as he hands it to me, all crooked edges and three big lumps of tape holding it all together on the bottom. "Happy Treesgiving!"

"What's this?"

"A...Treesgiving present."

He glances around the room. Even over under the tree. Like maybe he's waiting for his? I explain the concept patiently to him. "It's not that kind of a holiday."

He snorts. Sees the writing on the wall. Shrugs and sips some champs to drown his disappointment. "Who says?"

"I do. It's kinda my holiday, remember?"

"Well, it's a bullshit holiday, so anyone can add a new rule and I say it's a gift giving holiday. So..." He nods to the present over the lip of his cup and gives me a big, cheery wink. "Happy fucking Treesgiving, Shay!"

I snort and hold the present awkwardly. It's flat but at the same time kind of bumpy and also just a little thick. Not thick enough to be a book, unless it's one of those comic style manga things the kids are always reading at work. But why? "I didn't get you anything."

He wags his red plastic cup. "That's what you think. You can bet your ass I'll be taking this little baby home with me when I leave today, so...thanks!"

"Well, anyway, I appreciate this."

"How can you appreciate it if you don't even open it?"

"I was gonna save it."

"For what? We're already at Treesgiving? It's not a Christmas present."

I wag it close to his face. "Well, it's wrapped like one."

He chuckles despite his anti-Treesgiving indignation. "Just. Open. It. Already!"

"Okay, okay, sheesh."

One tug at the clump of tape on the bottom and the thick pile of snowman wrapping paper pops open like one of those fancy 3-D greeting cards. I slide it away to reveal a frame. A haunted house frame, to be precise. Inside is a picture. A Halloween picture. Well, kinda. It's definitely a Halloween party picture, that's for sure. Then I look closer and all the feels come rushing in. "Aw, Benjy! Where did you get this? Holy shit! I've never seen it before!"

"One of Cara's friends sent it to her and, before she could delete it, I sent it to myself and had it printed."

"Why would she delete it? This is so awesome!"

"Cuz she's not in it, duh."

"Of course, she is." I squint and tap the corner of the frame. "That's her shoulder right there. Did you show her this?"

He looks positively, adorably mortified. "No. Screw that. I ignore that part. It's our picture, Shay. That's us."

"I know it. Jesus. I know it. I mean..." I notice a fine layer of dust on the glass part of the frame. And gathered in the nooks and crannies of the haunted house's orange and green gabled roof. And on the black paint of the hovering bat in the corner. "Is this used?"

He nearly snorts out his champagne. "It was mine. I wanted you to have it."

"What? You got tired of looking at it?"

He pauses with the red cup halfway to his lips. Looks thoroughly indignant. "I...I could never get tired of looking at that picture, Shay. I literally look at it every day. But I thought, after what happened the other night, I guess I was feeling sentimental and thought you might be, too."

"I totally am." I want to tell him just how sentimental I've been feeling since the other night. How disconnected and detached and untethered and floating, still struggling to come to terms with what happened, and how, and when, and with whom. I want to tell him all of that but figure it's slightly easier to gush over his very thoughtful present instead. "This is such a sweet surprise."

I lean up and hug him. The frame is still in my hand. It comes between us to make for a very awkward hug. Our lips meet, but just to the side, not quite matching up and when he tries a little tongue action it glances my nose and I snort, like a dog with fresh cut grass and we chuckle, leaning back as if relieved. "Okay, well, thanks for this. It's my new favorite everything."

I set it on the counter to prove what I say is true. Even though secretly I know I'm going to move it to my room after he's gone because the Halloween theme clashes with the Christmas stuff. I mean, obvs. He looks proud. Reaches for a cookie. I grab another cube of cheese and join him.

We eat. Heartily and noisily. Like we always do. And I think of how often we do. Shift meals and burger joints and sitting on sidewalks in front of convenience stores on our days off with our skateboards stacked beside us or in our favorite booth at Chopstix and more shift meals than I could actually ever really count.

I smile and push my plate away before I'm actually full. Sit back amidst a pile of Christmas pillows and sip surprisingly good champagne from a paper Christmas cup and tap his thigh with my bare foot.

"So, are you gonna tell me about Cara now? Or are we gonna drag it all the way out to actual Christmas?"

THIRTY-FOUR

SHAY

He sits back, too. We're at opposite ends of the couch. A wall of Christmas pillows, soft and fuzzy, between us. His soft cotton shirt flatters him, hugging his sharp edges and lean curves. Red always does. Pairs well with his worn khaki shorts. Frayed slightly at the hem, but not on purpose. He pours us more champagne from the bottle on the coffee table.

Takes a deep breath. Drops the A-bomb like it's no big deal. "We broke up."

I kick his thigh again. Pillows topple onto his lap and then drizzle to the floor. Brand new or not, I literally don't care. "Get out!"

"No, for real."

"What? Why?"

He looks back at me. "You have to ask?"

"What? Because of us?"

He looks confused. Like, duh. "Uh, yeah."

I try to back away on the love seat but there's not much room and the trendy wooden arm stabs me in the small of my back. "Whoa, whoa, whoa..."

He leans forward. Puts his cup down. Grabs a hold of my thighs. "Shay, I thought this was what you wanted."

I squirm from his grasp. Squeeze myself into the farthest region of the couch that I can. Not nearly far enough. "Benjy, just tell me what happened first. Let's start there. Did you tell her?"

"About us?" He looks visibly ill. "No, I'm not that stupid."

"Phew." I literally say "Phew." It sounded a lot better in my head. Drain my paper cup. Go to refill it. The bottle's empty. Of course, it is. I unfold myself from the stabbing arm rest and pad to the kitchen, grateful for a little distance from him. Open the second bottle. Pour a glass for myself. Stay where I am. "So how did you do it? Break up, I mean."

"I didn't do it. We kind of did. Together. At the same time."

"What? Like, mutually?"

"Basically."

"Tell me, Benj. This is major. Tell me everything."

Avoids my eyes. "You don't want to know everything, Shay. You know?"

I cross my arms, all indignant like. "I'm pretty sure I do."

"You don't." He makes a face. And suddenly I know what he means. Like, exactly what he means.

"Gross. You had sex first?"

He winces. "I mean, duh. I hadn't seen her in months."

An awkward pause follows. I nod, as if to scrub the mental image of them together, naked and writhing, out of my head. My voice is surprisingly clinical when I can finally speak. "Where?"

"Shay, stop."

"I mean, your place? Her place? What?"

"You really want to know?"

I brace myself with a fresh shot of champagne. "Actually, I'm kind of generically curious. This is basically relationship apocalypse, so might as well go for broke, right?"

"That's still kind of awkward."

"What isn't awkward? About this whole sitch, I mean? Not that long ago you were sitting on that very couch with a big boner about to poke through your Spidey boxers and today you're sitting in the same spot telling me you broke up with Cara, so…"

My voice trails off. He shrugs. Nods. "True. Anyway, her dad was out of town on business, so we went back to her place."

"Her place? Like you did it in the living room? On the kitchen floor? In the pool, what?"

He chuckles. "Come on, Shay. Gross."

I wave my cup at him like it's a gun. Growl playfully. "Tell me, perv!"

"Anyway, we went back to her room. Like always."

I cluck my tongue. Picture her stupid girly-girl room, more throw pillows and artsy black and white prints and shelves full of trophies and awards. Pour some champagne. He raises his cup. I drift just close enough to top him off, then distance myself once more. Pace around in front of the coffee table. Wave the champagne bottle around like a baton. "So, what? Like afterward? You're lying there in the wet spot and just… Hey, so, I want to break up?"

"It was more like during."

I pause mid-step. Make a face. "What?"

"Yeah. Like, mid-thrust she—"

"Oh." I cringe. "God." Pause. Only half-pretend to hold back a stream of projectile vomit in his general direction. "Please. Stop. Benj."

He looks almost happy with himself. "You asked, remember?"

"I did. You're right." Shiver. Start pacing again. "I just, the whole thrusting thing took me by surprise." Wave the bottle like a starting gun. "Proceed."

He chuckles. "Anyway, she kinda just pushed me away and her stupid bed's so small I kinda had to stand up to keep from falling down, so I grabbed a pillow and covered up and kind of sat on the windowsill while she broke it down for me."

"Why would you cover up?"

"What?"

"I mean, you were being intimate two seconds before, why cover up now?"

"Really?"

"Yeah, really. It just seems odd."

"What part about me telling you about being kicked out of bed by my gf with a raging bone-on while you sit there squirming and acting all Sherlock Holmes isn't odd?"

I chuckle even as I clench my chin, Holmes style. "Accurate. Proceed."

He starts to. Even opens his mouth and everything, then pulls up just short of talking. "Wait. Where was I?"

I moan, suddenly eager to see where this story was headed. He never could tell a proper story. "You said she was breaking things down for you while you covered your bone-on. Broke *what* down, Benj?"

I can practically see the light bulb flicker back to life over his head. "Oh, yeah! Basically, her reason for dumping me literally during sex over Thanksgiving weekend."

"I thought you said the breakup was mutual."

"Yeah, but you know Cara wears the pants."

Our eyes meet. I remind him. "Or wore, as the case may be."

He makes a kind of face. Kind of gives me two gunshot fingers pointed at me. Winks. "Good point."

"And the reasons were…"

"The usual, I guess. Us. Her. School. Work. Her maturity level versus mine. Dreams. All hers. Aspirations. As in, I have none. The future, something else I guess she thinks I don't have. The past. That kind of shit."

"And what? You're leaning against the window, covering up your dingdong with a pillow the whole time?"

He smirks. Waves his glass for more bubbly. I oblige cautiously. "If I can offer an observation, Shay? You seem way more interested in what I'm not wearing while we broke up than how we actually, you know, broke up."

"Not at all. I'm just trying to picture the scene is all. Proceed."

"With what?"

"How you broke up?"

"I just told you."

"That was it?"

Shrugs. Sips. Swallows. "I mean, once I got the gist of where she was going, realized she wasn't going to change her mind and that nothing I could say was gonna change anything, I kinda quit listening."

I frown. He picks up a cookie. Nibbles it. Puts it back on one of the Christmas napkins. Sighs. I top his glass off. If only to get his attention. "You don't seem too surprised, Benj."

"I'm not. Frankly, I kinda knew the minute she bum rushed our shift drinks at Pig-Out last night we were done for."

"Really?"

"I could just tell."

"How?" I'm, like, genuinely curious.

Shrugs. "Just, every time I called lately, she was either never there or making an excuse to get off quickly."

I glance at the tree. "Same."

"It wasn't like that when she first moved away, you know?"

"Yes, Benj. Yes, yes, I do."

Another long pause ensues. He sighs. "It was time, Shay."

"Still, you were high school sweethearts."

He makes a "pfft" sound. "Please."

"Benjy, stop. You were." The words come out sincere, but I can't help but think that maybe I'm rewriting history just a little. There had always been a little bit of tension between the two of them. Hell, between the two of us. It was just easier to ignore, maybe even forget, with Cara out of the picture for a few short months.

He bites his lower lip, puffy and moist from a recent sip of bubbly. I try to ignore how slick and sensual it looks. He nods, none the wiser I suppose. "I mean, I guess. I'm not gonna say I regret all that time because we spent it together and no one put a gun to my head, but honestly?" He pauses, as if maybe convincing himself. Or me. I'm not sure which anymore. Then again, I'm not sure about just about anything anymore. "I'm not sorry it's over."

I'm still pacing. Bare feet on the hardwood floor. The record's scratching again. Fucking Charlie Brown already. I busy myself with starting it over. Fumble around like I've never done it before. He watches me. I can feel his eyes on me, on all those places I want him to see, and when I turn around, he lets them linger there.

Softly.

Achingly, like he did the other night. His hunger is like a third presence in the gaily lit room. I lean against the other side of the couch. Not far from the record player. Farther from him, thank goodness.

He grins. "In other news, I'm not wearing any underwear."

I snort despite myself. "Benjy!"

"What?"

"What even… What does that mean?"

He turns. Inches closer. Grabs my hand. "I'm free, now. I came here right away. I can't wait to make up for lost time."

I slip my hand from his gasp. Instinctively. I'm not even sure it's what I wanted to do, but I've already done it and I couldn't have stopped myself if I'd tried. And… I didn't really try. I back away, as far as I can, almost bumping into the wicker bureau where the record player sits. That's all I need is another scratch on my only good Christmas album. "Whoa, whoa, Benjy, I told you. I warned you, that was a one-time thing."

He looks crestfallen. I finally know what that word looks like now. Voice cracks as if he's just reached puberty. God, I've known him so long. Wanted him for almost as long. And here he is, wide open and free balling and puffy-lipped and hungry and I… I flinch at the slightest contact.

What the hell is wrong with me?

He's still yammering. "What? Why?"

I cross my arms over my chest, lecture style. "Because it was wrong, Benjy. What we did."

"Maybe then, Shay. But not now. Not anymore."

I turn. Bite my lip. Then my thumbnail. "Benjy, I mean… I thought you understood."

He stands. Takes two steps on his long, gangly legs and

is suddenly in front of me. He smells breezy, musky, manly. Grabs my arms. Squeezes them for emphasis. I look up at him. "Shay. I came, like three times that night."

I stare back at him, somewhere between flattered and nonplussed. Push him away. Half playfully, half "back off, dude!" Pick up the half-empty champagne bottle and start pacing again. "Because. You. Had. Blue. Balls!"

He stands near the tree, watching me carefully. "They weren't *that* blue!"

I roll my eyes. Can't believe we're calmly discussing interrupted thrusts and blue balls and bare balls and multiple orgasms on poor little Treesgiving! "Plus, we were at it for, like, hours. If you hadn't come that many times, I'd have been disappointed."

"Still, I've never done that with anyone else."

"How many girls have you slept with? Exactly?"

"Counting you?"

"Obviously. Jesus."

"Three."

I pause, mid-pace. That was not the answer I was expecting. "What? Who was the third?"

Winks. "You, dumbass. I'm counting you twice because it was so awesome."

"Gross." But I smile, just the same. Despite myself. Despite everything I've said up to that point.

I've drifted to the kitchen, somehow. He's followed me as far as the other side of the counter. Slumps down into a barstool. Looks about ten years old. "I don't get it."

"Get what? The fact that I don't want to be sloppy seconds."

"But it's not like that."

"You're sure making me feel like that."

He frowns. Fiddles absently with the hem of a snowflake placemat on top of the counter. Nibbles another cookie. I never realized he was such a nervous eater. "You sure didn't feel like that the other night."

I sigh. Heavily. Slump back against the countertop behind me. "Look, Benjy. The other night was an anomaly."

"The fuck does that even mean?"

I reach for his hand. He pulls it back. I sigh and sink back against the counter. I mean, I can't exactly blame him. "It's not like a mistake, exactly, but…"

He's huffy now. Puffing up slightly in his creaky wicker barstool. "Sounds like a mistake to me."

"Then you're not listening to me, Benjy."

"Oh, I think I hear you loud and clear."

"Look, what happened, happened. I'm glad it did. Obviously, I enjoyed the hell out of it myself. And I wanted the hell out of you. Have for years, actually. And I can't believe that, after wanting you so much, for so long, I'm the one pumping the brakes right now."

"So why the hell are you?"

"I don't know, Benj. I honestly don't. This is all new to me, obviously."

"Me too. You think anyone's ever broken up with me before?"

It would sound pretty vain coming out of anyone else's mouth, but in this case, he's just stating facts. One girlfriend equals one breakup. He's literally never had anyone do that to him before. I try to put this thought on a big mental billboard for him. "That's my point, Benj. This is uncharted territory for you. You're messed up about it all. You're not thinking straight and, what's worse, you're not giving yourself time to lick your wounds and consider your options."

Our eyes meet over the counter. He puts down another

half-nibbled cookie. I glance at the napkin in front of him and count six. Six half-nibbled cookies. It's like a raccoon has taken over his body. "I've never thought straighter, Shay. I've wanted this for as long as I can remember."

"Me too, actually. Very, very, very much so. But I guess... I guess I'm not ready for it to happen the same day you break up with Cara, or even the same day you slept with her, dude. I mean, you've still got her musk all over you, you know? Think about it."

"I told you we didn't actually..."

"That's making me even sloppier seconds, Benj. You didn't get to finish with her so now you come sniffing around here for your happy ending?" His head is vaguely cocked like I'm speaking a third language. "I mean, you get why I might be a little resistant to that idea, right?"

He clearly doesn't. "No."

"Then you're not listening, Benjy. Or worse, you just don't care how I feel."

"So how do you feel then? I'm listening." His words say he is, but his tone, flat and deep and empty, says he could care less. His posture, defensive and stiff, is even less welcoming to new ideas.

"Don't take this the wrong way, Benjy, but... I feel like you're just wanting me for sex right now."

"And?"

"You are?" Shit. I was hoping I was wrong.

"Fuck yeah. Waddya think?"

I shrug. "Like I'd rather eat cookies and cuddle by the tree right now, is what I think."

He's nodding eagerly, like this might really happen. Like his gross primate talk might really, actually work. "Sure, yeah. I mean, after."

Wow. Just...wow. Was he always this pervy? How...how

did I miss that? Was it because, until I had him, I was just as big a perv? "Okay, anyway, I just—"

"I can't believe this."

"Clearly."

"I mean, honestly this is absolutely perplexing to me right now."

"Believe it."

"I thought… I thought this was what you wanted."

"I told you, it is. I also told you just not today. Or maybe not even this week or this month, Benj." He sits there, picking up and putting down his half-nibbled cookies. Looks just like a kid who's just been told he can't leave the table until he eats his vegetables. "Why is it so hard for you to understand I don't want to snatch you off the market the minute Cara kicks you to the curb?"

"I don't know, Shay. But it is."

He turns. Abruptly. Takes a long, slow step toward the door. Walking, but walking slow. Like he wants me to follow him. Or stop him. Screw that. To both. I stay put. "Where are you going?"

"I don't know that, either. Just… I'm only making a fool of myself staying here, that's for sure."

"Benjy, don't be like that."

He turns, slightly. Sees that I haven't moved an inch. His face looks like putty, his normally high coloring pale. "How else should I be?"

"I get it. You're hurting. I'm here for you. Just… let's chill, okay? We've waited six years. You can't wait a little longer?"

He pauses at the door. "I guess that's the difference between you and me, Shay. I honestly can't wait. And not just for sex. I'm… I'm sorry you don't feel the same way."

"I positively do, Benjy. If you would just stop and listen

to what I'm actually saying instead of just hearing 'no' every time I open my mouth. That's why I'm trying so hard to—"

But he's gone. Slams the door so hard my silly elf shoe stocking sways from side to side in tune with the retro jazzy Christmas music still oozing scratchily from my sad little record player in the corner.

THIRTY-FIVE

BENJY

I stop a few blocks away from Shay's place. At a food truck called Moo's. Not because I'm hungry. At all. I just can't go home. Not yet. No doubt Mom will be up, tapping out a fresh contract on her laptop, grilling me about where I've been and when I'm going to move out and why I'm not a brain surgeon by now and how come I always liked Dad better than her and I just can't.

Not tonight.

I can't go to Cara's, obvs. She's probably sitting there, all sexy in front of her bedroom vanity, ripe and smooth and naked except for that silky tan robe she wears sometimes, swiping up and down and sideways on some dating site, not that she needs it. Either way, I'm the last person she wants darkening her doorstep right about now.

I'll usually stop at the beach when I'm feeling this way. Not that I've ever felt this particular, rock bottom, freefalling, no end in sight way before, but even though the beach accesses are empty and sandy and inviting, my heart's just not in it. I'm both restless and tired, draggy but wired, sad and scared and I'm not sure where to go or what to do about any of it.

But I need to get off the road. I can hardly think straight, let alone see straight. Not just that, my whole body is shaking. My knees, my legs, probably even my toes. I go to scratch my nose, or some other stupid automatic thing and my hands are trembling like I'm being interrogated by the Feds or something.

So, I find myself standing in front of Moo's, getting off my crappy bike with shaky legs and winding my crappy lock through my crappy tire around the weathered fence post out front with my trembling fingers.

Usually crowded, if not standing room only, today the food truck-slash-ice cream parlor looks like a bomb went off and they had to evacuate. I'm half convinced they're closed until I walk up to the window in the middle of the converted Airstream trailer and an older woman I've never seen before smiles from behind the cash register.

"Can I help you?"

"Are you guys open?" I glance around for emphasis, as if she might not already know every table and inch of space around the food truck is deserted except for my sad, shaky ass.

She chuckles a smoker's grunt and glances over my shoulder at the empty half dozen or so picnic tables mapped out around the grassy lot between her and the fence along the sidewalk where my bike rests crookedly on the sandy concrete.

"Yeah, but probably not for very long. I thought we'd do gang busters with everyone in town for the holiday weekend, but I guess no one's in the mood for mint chocolate chip shakes and French toast breakfast cones after stuffing themselves yesterday, you know?"

I brighten up for the first time since Shay shut me down, lock, stock, and barrel. "I sure am!"

Another smoky chuckle. "You sure are what?"

"Up for what you just said, the thing about a chocolate chip shake and French toast cone."

She seems genuinely startled. Like maybe she thought I was just here to ask for directions instead of actually ordering something. "Okay then! Coming right up."

She glances at my torso as I go to pay. Nods at my shirt as I fumble for my wallet. "Cute," she says in an absent way, like maybe she's just trying to make small talk.

"Oh this?" I glance down at the cheesy broken-footed gingerbread man. Blush. I'd totally forgotten I'd worn it. I'd bought it just for the day, just for Shay really. Now I can't stand it. Like, right now? It is legitimately making my skin crawl. I glance behind her at the stack of folded up Moo's t-shirts she's probably never sold once in her life.

"Do you have any of those in large?"

She looks predictably surprised, then turns lazily, giving the stack a quick study. After a while she nods and reaches for one. Hands it over. It's light purple, the color of cheap grape taffy, with a smiling black and white cow on front licking an ice cream cone. It's their logo, I guess. I've never paid it much mind until I was holding one of their t-shirts right in front of my face. I drag my stupid Christmas shirt off my shoulders and tug on the Moo's shirt instead. It's a little stiff but soft too and I know one wash will make it just about perfect. I hold the balled-up tee in my hand.

"You want it?"

She kind of backs away, with her hands up, eyes big and lips pursed like maybe I've turned into a crazed Thanksgiving weekend psycho stalker after all. She's not necessarily wrong. I guess I didn't really think through the whole dragging my shirt off and changing right in front of her vibe I'm giving off.

"No kid, I'm good."

I chuckle at the sheer, utter absurdity of it all. "I meant for, like, your son or something." Shakes her head. "Grandson?" Now she just looks offended.

Fuck it. I can't win this weekend.

I shrug and toss it in the dented metal trash can next to the straws and napkins. Like everything else in, near or around the food truck, it's painted a vague light purple, like someone mixed Pepto Bismol with grape soda and smiled at the result. She goes to hand me my change for the shirt and the meal, and I wave it off.

"Keep it."

She makes another face. I'm half convinced she's reaching for one of those silent alarm buttons under the cash register like you see in bank robber movies. "Kid, that's like a 240% tip."

I snort. If she only knew. I live at home, I'm a server who walks out of work every night with a tip apron bulging with crumpled bills and I do nothing but work, sleep and work some more. If there's one thing I've got, it's plenty of disposable cash and nowhere but empty food trucks on the day after Thanksgiving to spend it.

"It's all good. After all, it's Treesgiving right?" She makes another face but pockets the cash quickly before I can change my mind. Turns and sets about whipping up my meal.

I stand there awkwardly. Usually you pay at the window, go find a seat and one of the two or three pimply high school kids behind the counter brings it out to you when it's ready, but I can tell she's already sent everyone else home, is probably alone, so I stand and wait to take the tray myself. I look at the menu above her head, find about six things I probably would have liked better than what I ordered, but, oh well.

I probably won't taste any of it anyway.

She turns back around fairly quickly, a tray of heaping goodies I didn't order plus what I did sliding across the counter my way. On a pink-purple tray, natch.

"What's all this?"

She shrugs. "You'll probably be my last customer of the day, so it's just stuff I would have had to get rid of anyway."

"But…"

"Besides, it'll make me feel less guilty about taking your big tip." Chuckles her smoker's laugh. When I don't say anything, when I can't really say anything because I'm still shaky and about to cry for some stupid reason, she shoves the tray a little closer, so I'll get the hint and vamoose.

Fixes on a smile. "Enjoy."

"I will." I say it too loud. So loud she actually flinches and takes an involuntary step backward. She's still smiling though, but I know the feeling. It's a restaurant thing. You're smiling so your face won't give away what you actually feel inside, which is, "Holy shit, buddy, just take your stupid French toast cone and new shirt and trembling fingers and leave already!"

I start to thank her again, to make up for it, give her a big grin, but it's awkward now after the big tip and me taking off my shirt right in front of her and talking too loud and probably shaking like a jitterbug this whole stupid time.

Correction. I've *made* it awkward. So, I shrug and smile and walk away, find a picnic table way over in the corner by the fence where I can keep an eye on my bike and still hear the roar and crash of the ocean across the street.

I go to take a sip of the shake but it's still too thick to make it more than halfway up the straw, so I set it aside to melt a little in the smoldering grey Florida humidity. It won't take long. Nibble on my French toast cone, which is basically just a piece of oversized French toast wrapped around scrambled eggs and bacon bits under a light sprinkling of cinnamon sugar and syrup. It's overly sweet. Too sweet by far. But I nibble it anyway just to be polite. Besides, all I've had all day are stupid Christmas cookies at Shay's, so I'm already sweeted out.

There are other things on the tray, fried Mac and cheese wedges, curly funnel cake fries and some kind of pumpkin spice cupcake thing with one of those candy corn flavored thick, hard pumpkins squashed on top. I take bites of each dutifully, shoving them down on top of my nervous stomach, just so in case the old lady behind the counter glances over she'll find me nibbling on them and not seeming ungrateful.

Eventually the shake loosens up enough for me to slurp it through my straw. It's just sweet enough, savory enough, chocolate-y enough, creamy enough to revive my weary soul. I finish it quickly, ignore the inevitable brain freeze and shove the tray away before I can take another bite and ruin the fleetingly blissful moment.

I know it won't last long before the sadness, the finality of it all, kicks in so I savor it like the aftertaste of cold mint chocolate on my tongue. The crash of the waves across the street. The grey in the air. The vague, moist warmth of a late and growing later Florida afternoon. The empty streets and quiet sidewalk and hum of quiet neon in the signs bordering the food truck parking lot.

The bench beneath me is worn and weathered and I kind of sink into it. Sag, maybe, is more like it. This... this is not how I expected my day to end. Alone. Cinnamon sugar on my fingers and syrup on a pinkish, purple-ish tray with a 70-year-old cashier for company.

It wasn't just the sex I thought we'd be having. I mean, sure, obviously, but I wish I could have found the words to tell Shay it was so much more than that. It always was, even when we were having it. It always has been, even when I was dreaming about it, fantasizing about it, all those years.

I don't blame Shay. I mean, how can I? I was crazy thinking she would go for it in the first place, but... that's just the point. She makes me crazy. Like, legitimately, certifiably crazy. Always has. I just... I should have stuck around longer, that's all. Listened to what she had to say. Heard the words she was saying instead of what I was hearing. Which was, basically, "No."

No, I won't sleep with you right now.

No, I won't hop right into bed with you this moment.

No, I won't date you.

No, I won't be your girlfriend...

So...now what? I stare off, into the distance, the neon blurring and the sound of the crashing waves like white noise in the background.

The gray gets grayer, and the day gets longer, and the waves crash, and I sit, surrounded by my half-eaten goodies with napkins balled up on top of each half empty plate so the old lady doesn't feel bad about giving away the store. I feel lonely in a way I never have before, and not just because I'm at a table for one.

Although, I suppose, that's actually a pretty big part of it. For the last few months, I haven't eaten anywhere without Shay sitting nose to nose across from me. Fidgety and flirty and funny and sexy and smiling and serene, completing the picture in a way I never even knew I needed until today.

Now, suddenly, who am I going to eat with? It's more

than that, obvs, but the break-up and the shakeup suddenly take on a more realistic shade of gross. It's bizarre to think how long I've waited for Cara to break the news that she was over me when I've already known for twice as long. And even more bizarre to think that my backup plan, the one that brought me even more comfort, is suddenly pulled out from under me as well.

Thoughts of a life without Shay, or, at least, the way Shay and I used to be, race through my mind. Like, how is work going to work, without my favorite work buddy? Who will I ride home with at the end of a shift? Share snark with from the moment we clock in 'til shift change?

Like, will I have to change my schedule and only work days when she works nights and vice versa? How gross will that be? And what happens the next time some older, bad boy bartender hires on and flirts with her and I want to stab them both in the throat with a steak knife? Hell, for that matter, maybe Moo's is hiring? Or one of the other dingdong big chain eateries on Restaurant Row?

Literally, I'd rather work with a bunch of boring strangers every day than risk watching Shay work her whole flirty, hair twirling, fake laughing, hip nudging sexy vibe on some random new guy in the conceivable next few weeks or months when we start to hire for the busy season. The very thought turns my already queasy stomach, as if it's already happened.

I think, for a fleeting second, about beating her to the punch. About going in to work tomorrow and picking the first cute waitress I see and really laying it on thick, but that seems even grosser than watching Shay do it with some random new guy. No matter what she just said or did to me, I couldn't do that to her.

Even now.

For once, for perhaps the first time, I am lost and adrift, with no plan or compass to guide me. Glenda has asked me a million times over the years what my plans are for the future. Where I see myself in five, ten, even twenty years? Why I'm not interested in going corporate, like she keeps asking during my annual review every year. And, when I decline, what else I might be interested in, moving forward. Moving forward? I know she means college or a white-collar job or something that uses my brain, but how do I tell her that my only plan, ever and always, was just Shay?

Where is Shay? That's where I'll be. Period.

Still at Pig Out? Good, so am I.

I can't tell Glenda that, of course. And maybe, one day, I'll take her up on the offer. Become assistant manager, start contributing to the IRA program, maybe even get transferred to some other non-Shay working restaurant in the Pig Out chain, but now? That seems distant, far away and not the least bit attractive to me.

I could have gone to community college with Cara, instead of dropping out after that first semester the way I did. I could have even taken online classes or gone at night so that we both got our AA degrees at the same time and could go away to college together. But truth be told, if only to myself I suppose, I couldn't bear the thought of not being wherever Shay was.

Yet now the thought of being in the same room with her makes me so queasy I can't even stomach a French toast cone or free Mac and cheese bite. Maybe I should have used my words, instead of my hands, to tell her how much I cared about her that night, but honestly, I couldn't have stopped myself if I tried. I thought she felt the same way. I guess I thought she always would. To find out she didn't, to find out that we weren't on the same page the way we've always been about this one thing, about this most important thing, has left me stripped and stupid and stranded.

A scratch on the pavement startles me. I glance up, half hoping it's Shay reconsidering. Fat chance. The old woman is standing there instead. The cashier.

She has a ball cap in her hand?

"Here." She shoves it at me. Awkwardly. I flinch and back up a little, kind of like she did when I offered her my cheery "Oh, Snap" tee. She grins. Yellow smoker's teeth to match her croak of a laugh. But the smile is kind and, in this case, generous.

"Sorry," she says, still holding it out. "I… I'm closing up, but I still feel bad about that big tip you left me. I thought you could use this."

"What? Why?" I'm halfway between amused and offended.

She nods at my head. Grins a little, like maybe she's addressing her grandson after all. "You look like you haven't slept and, when you got up from not sleeping, forgot to comb your hair."

I chuckle and take the hat. It's stiff and flat-billed, not curved and worn in and weathered like the ones we sell at Pig-Out. I'll probably never wear it again but shove it on now just to make her happy. "Thanks."

She nods. Says nothing for a moment. Shifts awkwardly from foot to foot. "Listen, uh, I'm going to head out now so…" She nods toward the crooked, leaning gate a few feet from where I've locked up my bike. "If you could just lock up after you go."

"Seriously?"

"No, I mean, there's no lock, just don't camp out here overnight, you know?"

"Of course not, but…" I glance past her to see the food

truck all boarded up. The service window closed. The condiments and napkins all shut away, safe inside the converted trailer. "You sure I can stay?"

She shrugs. "I mean, unless you're gonna toss a picnic table over your shoulder and cart it home with you, what can you get away with?"

"I suppose you're right."

She smiles once more, already backing away. "Well, have a good night, kid…"

I grin and wave the hat. It's so stiff it hurts going on and off again. I struggle not to wince. "Thanks again, for this."

She pats her pocketbook, tan and cheap looking and clutched to her side as it hangs from a weathered strap. "Thanks again, for this."

I grin and probably blush a little. She side steps a little more, then nods and kind of turns and that's that. The gate clacks a little as she opens it, then clicks a little as she closes it and, in seconds, she's gone. I watch her bristly grey hair bob and weave down the sidewalk to a scruffy little parking lot until a strand of stubby palms blocks my view. A car engine starts in due time and, a few seconds later, a beat-up compact car wheezes out into the street and chugs away in the other direction. Trailing behind it on the salty breeze, I hear classic rock chugging out the window. Because… of course.

I sigh and sit back, feeling like a trespasser and wondering, you know, why she didn't even take my tray and throw it away. What? I'm supposed to do that, too? The ballsiness of it all kind of makes me chuckle.

It's something all of us at Pig-Out have wanted to do at least a thousand different times, but never could because there are about a million more moving pieces involved to closing a high volume, upscale barbecue chain than, you know, closing the window on a food truck and asking your last customer to not steal everything in sight.

Still, I give it up for grandma. Nana's got balls.

I linger only a few minutes more. Sure, it sounded fun at first, the idea of being alone at someplace other than Pig-Out after closing time. But now, suddenly, I feel like I work here, and it's taken a smidge of the fun out of loafing in my own private food court. I take my trash to the pinky-purple can and dump it on top of my stupid early Christmas shirt. I mean, she didn't even empty the trash. Did she do any of her side work? I sigh and leave the tray on the ledge beneath the closed tight window. Glad, I suppose, that my hands are no longer trembling.

I glance around, one last time. Evening has fallen, somehow, some way, and the last remnants of sunset linger on the horizon, casting a pale orange glow beneath the encroaching darkness. I realize, as I slide through the creaky gate and swing it tightly shut behind me, that I've barely slept since Cara got home. I've grown suddenly weary, glad for the fact that home—and bed—are just a few blocks away.

I unlock my bike, fingers spinning through sludge as I expand the last of my energy climbing onto my bike and gaining just enough momentum to keep it upright on the wide, clean sidewalk as I pedal silently away from Moo's. And still, tired as I am, I crane my neck every few feet to see if maybe, just maybe, Shay is somehow chasing right behind me.

Of course, she never is...

THIRTY-SIX

SHAY

"Red or white?"

Hub leans over the second story railing. The cheap Santa hat on his head flops to one side. The fuzzy white ball on the end sways with the motion. He's got a bottle in each hand. I try not to grin. Fail miserably. "White, I guess? I started with champs, so..."

He grins back. "I have champs. Gimme a sec."

I stay put. Arms stretched out on either side of me. Legs extended as I lounge in the shallow end. Hear the door open and shut, then open and shut again before he drifts down the stairs, a champagne bottle in one hand, two plastic cups upside down on top.

He's in a pair of baggies and a white v-neck t-shirt. Bare feet. Hair stubble hidden under the jaunty Santa cap. Looks casual. And seasonal. Clean. Sober. The very sight of him warms my heart after Benjy's angry words, closed mind, stiff body language and abrupt, dickish departure. I'm still... still trying to process it all. Wonder if I ever will.

I nod as he approaches. "What's with the hat?"

He waves the champagne bottle up toward my apartment. In the waning twilight, the glowing tree in front of the open window looks even more radiant than ever. It might as well be up in Rockefeller Center, for how beautiful it is. "It's Treesgiving, isn't it?"

I narrow my eyes. "Did I tell you about that?" So much has happened in the last twenty-four hours, I honestly can't remember.

He sets the bottle down on the pool tile beside me. It makes a familiar clinking noise. Reaches in the back pocket of his baggies. I've never seen a guy actually do that before. Use those back pockets, I mean. I always thought they were just for show. Pulls out a crumpled maroon envelope. Instantly recognizable. The top is torn open. "Not in so many words, but I got the message."

I smile at his resourcefulness. Flattered, somehow, in a way I can't fully express. "But, how?"

"I saw you slinking away the other morning. You had this little sucker in your hand on the way down the steps, but not when you snuck out to your bike, so I put two and two together and did a little dumpster diving..."

I blush. Suddenly, it all comes back to me. "Hard to believe, seeing how distracted you were."

He pops the champagne bottle. Pours us both a red plastic cup full. Drifts closer to the stairs. His expression has a gentle tone of defensiveness, with subtle hints of apology mixed in there somewhere. "Hey, we all celebrate in our own way, you know?"

I shrug. "I'm not judging."

Looks doubtful. "Yeah, well you sound predictably judge-y."

I chuckle. He's in the water now. Making little ripples that drift just over my breasts as he wades closer. The sensation is, let's just say, not unpleasant. Hands me the cup. It's cold and full. "I'm honestly not, Hub. You do you, you know?"

He chuckles. Soft little lines around his kind, gentle eyes. The only time he really shows his age. "Wow, so wise. Must be the time of year."

I shrug. Hoist my cup toward his. "Speaking of Happy Treesgiving, Hub."

His eyes grow soft. He inches closer. He's definitely in my space now. Warm, gentle, almost sensual ripples preceding him like the prologue in a racy romance novel. At the moment, I'm not entirely complaining. His voice is low and smooth to match the mood, sending shivers everywhere the ripples couldn't reach. "Happy Treesgiving, Shay."

We tap plastic cups. Sip. Keep eye contact. "Wow, you even said it right."

He grins. Sinks down in the corner next to me, but still vaguely facing me. Arms outstretched. Fingers almost touching mine. Looking tan and radiant as ever in the softening twilight. "Well, I should. I've read the invitation enough times by now."

"That's kind of sweet." Then I nod up toward his apartment. The window dark and silent in comparison with my glowing tree extravaganza next door. "What, you mean while Tiger Butt was asleep?"

He struggles to get his sip of champagne down before choking. "Shit. You think she wanted to hang around after the beer and smokes ran out?"

I roll my eyes. The champagne is good. Dry. Cold. I've felt vaguely buzzed all day. It's the kind of day where, no matter how much I drink, or what, I'll never get less or more buzzed than I am at this very moment. "Tell me more, Hub. How did you feel about that?"

"Stop."

"I'm serious."

"Me too."

Shrugs. Sips. "I felt relieved in one way, and lonely in another."

I nod harder than I mean to. Buzzed isn't the only thing I've felt all day. Lonely was right up there as well. "I can see that. Is she good company at least?"

Shrugs some more. "Good enough to pass the time, I suppose." He pauses, then adds: "Watches a lot of TV, though."

I snort. "That's kind of an odd observation. Waddya mean?"

"Like, a lot. Of TV. Like, it's all she talks about. Literally, everything I brought up conversationally was somehow relatable to a show she watches. Or just watched. Or wants to watch. Or her friends watch. Or she just re-watched for the umpteenth time."

I chuckle, vaguely enjoying his obvious discomfort. "Sounds like a bad blind date."

He grunts. Nods enthusiastically. Waves his cup. Swallows. "There you go. I've been trying to think of a way to describe it ever since she left and that's the best one yet."

"Kind of an occupational hazard for a man whore, I suppose."

He snorts and chokes again. "Man, you're on fire today, huh? Is this some kind of a Treesgiving tradition? Roasting your neighbor mercilessly until he caves and slinks away to the deep end to lick his wounds?"

"I'm sorry, Hub. I really am." I reach out. Touch his strong, veiny forearm. Pull my hand away slowly before either of us can get the wrong idea. "It's just been a shitty day."

He nods. Goes quiet. We both manage to glance up at the

tree at the same time. He nudges me gently. It feels good. Too good. "But it's Treesgiving."

My turn to snort and choke on cheap champagne. "Benjy broke up with Cara today."

Hub makes a face. Practically sticks his tongue out trying to do all the mental math. "That's the boy you've been crushing on before you finally slept together and his actual girlfriend who was away at college and possibly cheating on him at the same time?"

I nod, marveling at how much we know about each other's significant others.

"So, isn't that what you wanted? Sounds like a Treesgiving miracle if you ask me."

"I thought so."

"And now?"

"Now, I'm not so sure."

He nods. Grins. "Kind of an occupational hazard for a brazen hussy, I suppose."

"Screw you, Hub."

He arches an eyebrow.

I roll my eyes. Know what he's about to say. "Don't even, stud. Not today."

He chuckles. Polishes off his champagne. Sets the empty cup on the wet pool tile behind him. Tugs off his cap before he drifts beneath the water and swims, underneath the surface, all the way to the deep end. Surfaces with a splash and a deep breath and grins. "You coming? Or you just gonna sit there and watch your tree glow all night?"

A while later, I say, "Thanks again for the champagne."

He peers in the open window. The tree is still aglow.

"Thanks for the invite."

I keep the front door closed. He gets the message. Lingers anyway. It's kind of nice. Late as it is, tired and confused and surreal as I am, I'm not quite ready to be alone. Then again, I'm not quite ready for Hub to come inside my house yet, either. I'm… I'm still not sure why that is, but it's definitely a deal breaker for whatever reason.

He notices. He always notices. Everything. All the time. Every time. "Maybe you'll let me in on actual Christmas, huh?"

I linger with my back to the door. Pivot from foot to foot, keenly aware I'm in a small, wet bikini. I mean, I might as well be naked. I suppose I could have worn a one-piece, or even something a little less skimpy. Then again, I suppose I knew Hub would drift downstairs eventually and maybe, I dunno, maybe I wanted someone to see me half-naked today at some point. To ogle or absorb or at least notice something other than my Christmas tree.

"Maybe."

He nods toward his door. "My place is always open and I'm not a rude bastard, so you're welcome there anytime. Holiday or no."

"Oh, don't I know it?"

He leans back against the railing. Suddenly in no hurry. Fine. That's great. Me either. We're both leaning back. No worries. He narrows his eyes. "Is this what's known as playing hard to get?"

I smirk, drinking in his sexy beach bum vibe. "What? No one's ever said 'no' to you before?"

"Oh, plenty have. More and more as the years go by, actually. But none that I really care about."

"Well, if you care about me, you'll recognize how hurt and wounded I am right now and back the flip off."

"What? Like I'm not hurt and wounded here?"

I put a mock fist under my chin and mimic my best therapist voice. "Who hurt you, Hub?"

He chuckles at my antics, playful despite my life falling apart all around me. "Besides you?"

"You're not hurt, Hub. You're just a… a collector."

"Of what?"

"Of experiences."

He nods. Kinds of mulls it over. "So, you think that's what I'm after with you, Shay? An *experience*?"

"Oh, sure thing. And after the experience is over, then…"

"Then what?"

"Exactly."

"You didn't answer me."

"You know how it would go, Hub. Great for a night and then you'd slink back home. Probably before the sun even rose. Definitely before I got up and could nag you into staying just a little longer. Nothing would change, but everything would change."

"If nothing would change…"

"I mean, you'd be back to your old tricks the next night. With Tiger Butt or some other rando chick. And I'd get jealous, hearing you through the walls and it would make things awkward, so…"

He holds up both hands. Chuckles. "Fine. I get it. I respect that. It's not entirely accurate, but close enough for Treesgiving."

He stands gradually. Stretches. I try to ignore the slow, predatory way his masculine body unfolds until he's standing there in front of me, dripping and rippled and resplendent in the dim shadows cast by the light of my tree, just on the other side of the open window. "Speaking of… I should probably get home."

I nod. Turn slightly from the door. "Me too. Thanks for showing up."

"Wouldn't have missed it for the world."

He's facing me now. Full dead on. I'm facing him. "It was an experience."

He winks. "Not quite."

"Oh, no?"

He inches closer. Even with our bodies damp from the pool shower I can feel the heat wafting off of him in a singularly delightful shimmer. His own personal heat wave. "I heard it's not quite Treesgiving until you've kissed goodnight."

I snort. But don't back away. Hope my voice doesn't tremble the way my body suddenly is. "Oh yeah, where'd you hear that?"

He pretends to look up. Frowns. "Not sure. But since it's an entirely made-up holiday, anyway, does it really matter?"

I shake my head silently. Consider the option. Struggle not to lick my lips in anticipation. "Actually, that sounds like a nice tradition."

He seems surprised. Like maybe I'd put up more of a fight. I might have, usually would have, if I hadn't suddenly embraced the absurdity of this very weird, very particular, very life altering day. "It does?"

I nod quietly, dipping my head momentarily and taking a deep, precautionary breath. Just out sight, before I glance up at him again. Fix him with a vaguely coy but openly honest gaze in reply. "Yeah, actually. I don't know if you knew this or not, but I'm a fan of experiences too."

"I didn't. Know that, I mean."

I nod. He inches closer. There's nothing left to say. Not with words, anyway. My hand is still on the doorknob, but only as a prop. I wouldn't dream of going in just yet. He leans in gently. Slowly. Inevitably. His kiss is soft and tender, slow, and wise. I was expecting a chaste, goodnight kiss but lose myself in the soft, tender warmth of this unexpected and most welcome surge of unfiltered passion. In fact, he pulls away too soon but, somehow, instinctively, I know enough not to lean back in for more. Instead, I merely smile. Smile big, wide, and sappy. Sag back against the door like some romcom dweeb and finally lick my lips. "Now *that* was an experience."

He grins. "Thanks, Shay. For that, I mean."

"Thank you. I think that was just about perfect."

He nods eagerly. Almost boyishly. Very un-Hub-like. "Now I know, and that's enough for me."

"Know what?"

"That something could've happened between us, eventually, sometime."

"Sure, it could have. Jesus. Did you ever doubt it?"

"Every day."

"Stupid. I've flirted with you every day since I moved in."

He chuckles. "That was flirting?"

"I thought so."

He chuckles. Gently drifts away. Apparently, he knows a thing or two about playing hard to get as well. "Good to know."

I grin. Lick my lips again for good measure and turn the knob. Glance over at him doing the same. He sees me. Smiles. Nods. "Hey, Shay?"

I flutter a little inside at the way he says my name. "Hey, Hub?"

Winks. Points a gun finger at me. "Best. Treesgiving. Ever!"

THIRTY-SEVEN

SHAY

I chuckle, throaty and overwhelmed and already wistful about what I've just turned down. Watch as he drifts inside, the fuzzy white ball on his Santa cap swinging to and fro before the door shuts forever on our soft, quiet Trees-giving experience.

I'm still smiling as I twist the knob. Go to push the door open and hear a throat clear just to my left. Jump two feet into the air. At least. "Jesus! Cara, what the actual dude?"

She's grinning. I'm talking from ear to ear, every damn tooth visible. Enjoying herself. "God, Shay, could you be less aware of your surroundings?"

I glance toward Hub's door. Hope he's stepped outside to see what the commotion is all about. Looking for a little distraction, even saving, from this sure-to-be unpleasant encounter. But his doorway is dark. I'm alone. With her. "Sorry, I was a bit distracted."

She glances past me to apartment 2-C. Grins. Purrs. "I saw that, Chica."

"You did?"

"Sure did."

"How long have you been standing there?"

"Long enough to hear you psychoanalyze your poor neighbor there half to death and totally, like, totally cock block yourself out of one very age-inappropriate fuck."

My blush is immediate and severe. I can feel my face burning, bright as the Christmas tree just on the other side of my door. "Sorry, I'm not normally so talky but we've got some baggage."

"I guess." She already looks bored because I've been talking about something other than her for too long. "I think he kissed you just to shut you up."

Ouch. I'm about to huff but then, magically, I laugh. Hard. Deep. Somehow, she's grinning as well. Standing in the glow of my tree, just outside the open window, I notice more details as my blush starts to fade. Her unkempt hair. Big, smeared raccoon eyes. The same too-big Florida Eastern University sweatshirt from the night before. She looks like the album cover of some hipster emo band's new solo EP. Something twee and bitter with a name like "Sad Girl on the Steps" or something.

She's kind of sagging against the windowsill. I've never seen her look so defeated. So thin and pale and frail. I mean, sure, she's normally all those things. That's been her aesthetic since as long as I've known her, but there's usually some kind of radiating glow from inside that pulls all those individually wan and lackluster things together and makes her literally shine. I'm not digging this deconstructed version of her and, from the looks of things, neither is she.

I inch closer and, before she can protest, wrap her in a hug. I'm stronger than her. Much more so. She's like skin and bones. She cries gently, quietly against my shoulder. Bare and soft in just my small bikini. Finally pushes me away and sniffles. "Quit it."

I chuckle again. Grab a hold of her sweatshirt sleeve and drag her gently inside. She drifts along like a rag doll. The tree is the only light on in my apartment and the living room is legitimately aglow. Like, if we weren't both such dysfunctional skanks, I could honestly believe this was what heaven must look like.

She stands in the middle of the room, taking it all in. I drift toward the record player and start Charlie Brown Christmas over again because why the hell not? Its retro cheery jazzy flow has been working its magic all day, so let's play it till the end, shall we? Maybe the bittersweet piano and swishy drum swipes will wipe the slate clean after Benjy's abrupt middle finger of a departure.

I drift inevitably toward the kitchen. She follows me. Slumps down on the same barstool Benjy did, however, many hours ago. At least it's not still warm. That would be embarrassing. And something she'd notice right away, even in her slump shouldered, raccoon eyed haze.

I could picture Cara, narrowing her eyes and peppering me with laser-focused questions, all of which I'd have to answer honestly because...

"Was someone just here?" she would ask with a wriggle.

"A guy someone? This heat in my seat definitely feels like guy heat, huh?" She might even press down on the seat, more evidence for her "a guy was just here" line of questioning.

Finally, her imaginary "aha" moment as she'd announce, triumphantly: "Wait a second. This feels like just the amount of warmth Benjy's butt gives off. Was...was Benjy just here?"

When she doesn't interrogate me, at all, I heat up water in a kettle on the stove instead. Pour packets of cocoa in two fresh snowman mugs. Grab the peppermint schnapps from the cabinet above the microwave. Wriggle it at her. She perks up at last, the wicker of the barstool creaking in gentle anticipation. She always did like a good, stiff drink. I guess that's one thing, maybe even the last thing, we still have in common. "Yes, please."

I glance absently at the glowing letters on the microwave. 1:22 a.m. Then look a little more closely because that can't be right. But in my soul, in my weary bones, I know it is. Holy actual shit, where the hell has the time gone? With all the major breaking news that has happened, the break-ups and come-ons and the let downs and the free-balling and bikinis and chaste kisses and denied embraces, I feel like I've lived two lifetimes in this day already. And yet, I still feel as wired as I had when I woke up that morning, restless and unable to sleep another minute longer.

I put the bottle of schnapps between the snowman mugs. "Well, you'll be happy to know you've officially missed Treesgiving."

Despite the mousy appearance, her sarcasm is suddenly back on point. "Oh no! You mean. I have to wait a whole year to celebrate some made up fake-ass holiday my BFF created out of thin fucking air. Whatever shall I do with myself until then?"

I sigh, willing the kettle to steam already, dammit. The awkward silence, the unspoken drama, the simmering revelations, are collectively killing me. She swivels slightly in her chair. More wicker creaking as her inner bitch gently revs its engines as Cara finally shifts out of neutral. Her smile is saucy, even if her lipstick is faded. "At least you had fun."

I grin. "I did." Then immediately regret it.

"Wanna know how I spent my stupid made up, fake-ass Trees-fucking-giving?"

I bite my lip. Just then the kettle whistles. I hope she can't hear me sigh with relief over the jittering, clanging lid.

I pour hot water in the cups, expensive dark chocolate cocoa frothing to life amid the steamy bubbles as its rich, almost decadent aroma fills the stilted air between us. Add a healthy dollop of peppermint schnapps in each. Healthier than I should add in the middle of the night, but hey. Trees-giving only comes once a year, right? Set her cup down in front of her. Hold mine by the handle. Fix her with an apologetic frown.

"Will you be upset if I already know?"

Her eyes shimmer to match her wicked frown. "Fucking Benjy. I knew that immature windbag couldn't keep it to himself."

I stifle a snort at her colorful, and spot on, interpretation. "I'm sorry. I wasn't going to say anything, but then I knew he would eventually, and it would be weird if I didn't and…"

She deflates again, more wicker creaking as her body sags, folding itself around the cheap, cheesy snowman mug nestled between her two pale hands. "It's just… I wanted to be the first one to tell you, you know?"

I cock my head. Do the mental math. Glance pointedly at the digital numbers on the oven behind me. "Then, why'd you wait so long?"

She snorts. "Fuck if I know. I've been crying and napping and crying and napping all day. And night, I guess? I mean, I wasn't gonna leave my bed at all today, but I just couldn't take it anymore. I had to tell somebody."

I cluck my tongue. "So, I'm just… somebody?"

She stifles me with a glare over her frothy mug. "Shay, honestly, can we not make this about you right now?"

I choke down a snort because, seriously? This bitch? Has it ever, in all our years, ever been about me? But I'm feeling just guilty enough to cut her some slack and not poison her next spiked mug of cocoa. "Sure, yes, of course. I just…was I at least your first somebody?"

She grins. Lies, probably. "Of course."

Clink her mug with mine. "I better be."

When it's clear she's going to make me draw this shit out of her tonight, I offer a generic greeting card effort. "Cara, you're just feeling down on yourself right now."

She gives me Grade-A "duh" face. "You think? My boyfriend just dumped me, Shay."

I snort. I can't help it. Make a wince-y face. Stretch out the syllables of my response to let her know the sarcasm is real. "Did he though?"

She doesn't get the irony. Never does. About herself, anyway. "Uh, yeah. Basically. I mean, what else am I supposed to think when he can't even get it up the first time we're together in—"

I nearly drop my snowman mug. First Benjy with his "mid-thrust" BS and now this? Are these two creating erotic *FanFic* together now or something? "Whoa! Okay, now, just… whoa! Cara, come on dude. That's not fucking cool. At all."

"Sorry, it's just freaking me out, you know?"

I moan with TMI overload and blow on my cocoa until it's cool enough to sip. Savor the sweet, chocolate-y goodness and the warm, soft spike of peppermint as if either will ever scrub the thoughts of my two BFFs mid-thrust with erectile dysfunction from my already oversexed brain.

Use the mug to hide the smirk I'm wearing to think of Benjy omitting that little piece of juicy gossip about his own saggy self. To say nothing of the fact that, well, he certainly hadn't had that problem with me. If anything, it had been almost impossible to keep that bad boy down! "Is that a first? For you two, I mean?"

"Uh, yeah. I mean, he's been sexting me basically nonstop since I moved away and the first time we're together he's like a limp noodle? The hell is up with that shiz?"

Even the oversized snowman mug can't hide my jaw dropping. "Oh. My."

"Oh, stop being such a prude already. It's Benjy. It's not like I'm talking about some college boy hookup."

I take another strong swig to brace myself for the inevitable. Then swallow and swing for the fences because, once you've finally kissed your neighbor and your BFF has told you about her boyfriend's limp noodle, what's stopping you? "Are you... I mean, were you going to talk about some college boy hookup?"

She ignores me. Sips her cocoa. "Damn, that's good." Takes another sip. Makes a flat line with her plump lips. "Could be better, though." Tops it off with another hit of schnapps. Sips. Sighs dramatically like she's rehearsing a TikTok video for later. "Perfect." Glances up at me from over the top of her mug, nestled picturesquely between her two little hands. "What were we talking about again?"

I roll my eyes because she knows damn well what we were talking about and was just buying her time with all that bullshit preening to figure out if now was the time to finally come clean. "College. Boy. Hook. Ups."

She puts her mug down. Winks suggestively, like maybe the schnapps has finally kicked in. Or maybe she's just finally tapping into the whole dysfunctional Treesgiving spirit going around lately. "Yeah? What about 'em?"

"Have you had them?" She glances away at a scratchy part on the Christmas album. I lower my voice and reel her back in. "Be honest now." I play it off like girl talk, hopefully hiding the pounding of my heart as I anxiously await her answer.

She turns back from the smattering of Christmas lights dancing above the thrift shop record player. Meets my eyes. Doesn't blink or play cute. "Them as in plural?"

I nod. Wait breathlessly for her response.

She finally shrugs. No big deal. "Yeah, a couple."

Wow. Okay. I… I wasn't expecting that. Pizza Frat Boy? Yeah, that one I expected. But plural? How many pizzas was this Ho getting hand delivered every night? Damn! "Jesus, Cara."

She looks vaguely disgusted with me. "What? When did you join the fucking nunnery, Shay? Jesus. We used to talk about guys all the time back in school."

"Yeah, guys we'd wanna hook up with, not guys we had."

She wriggles her shoulders as if shaking off my mock virginity. "Yeah, well, things change."

I roll my eyes because I'm tired of her making me feel like some redneck townie with every stupid sarcastic sylla-ble. "In three months? How many are we talking here?"

She avoids my eyes, but not the question. "Enough, Shay. Okay? Just, stop slut shaming me."

"I'm not, Cara. I'm not doing that. At all. I would… I would never do that. I just…if we're girl talking, you know? Middle of the night? Just you and me and the Christmas tree? You're not shy about talking about limp noodles and sexting and whatnot. Why can't you just say a number already?"

She looks vaguely irritated. "The number doesn't matter, okay? What matters is I'm free, and it feels good, and I don't feel bad about any one of them. Not a single one. Isn't that enough?"

"Yes, of course it is. Of course." I'm blathering, alternating between raising the mug to my lips and mumbling some inanity and then putting it back down, unsipped.

She glances up. "Aren't you even the least bit happy for me?"

I nod. "Of course, I am. I mean, part of me is, anyway. You know I want you to be happy, but..."

"But what?"

"But the other part of me is a little bit sad?"

She cocks her head, like Benjy does. Makes me wonder which one of them is copying the other. And for how long. And who started it in the first place. "Sad for who, exactly?"

"Both of you, in a way. I mean, sad that it took you so long to be happy and sad that, now, maybe Benjy isn't gonna be for a little while."

I nudge her mug gently with mine to get her attention. "Aren't you? A little? Sad, I mean? Isn't that why you couldn't get out of bed today?"

She nods reluctantly, as if embarrassed to be showing actual human emotions. "Sure. Fine. I mean, I was. But now that I've had some fresh air and a little boop-boop, I'm... I just needed a little time to process everything, is all."

"Is one day enough, though?"

She frowns. Fiddles with some cookie crumbs on the countertop. The ones left by her ex-boyfriend and his insatiable carb loading appetite. Jesus, what a day. And she thinks I'm the prude? Sister, listen...

I try to shift gears a little and get back to the heart of the matter. "Does he know?" She bites her lip in response. Avoids my eyes. Sips her cocoa. Adds more schnapps. Jesus, I hope she rode her skateboard. Chick's gonna be lit after her first mug full. "I mean, did Benjy know? Before you came home? Is that why... is that why maybe he tried to slide you the limp noodle earlier?"

Jesus, now they've got me talking like a junior high erotica author already. She chuckles. "Gross. No, he didn't know then and he still doesn't know. I owe him that much at least."

THIRTY-EIGHT

SHAY

"Jesus."

"Don't you Jesus me, Shay Marigold Witherspoon."

I chuckle. She hasn't used my full name in years. Wasn't even sure she remembered all three of them. "I'm just saying, that's kind of epic, don't you think?"

"Epic to try hooking up with new guys? Epic to try having sex sometime other than between 8 and 10 p.m. on a weeknight? Epic to have more than one orgasm a year? Yeah, I'd say so!"

Jesus, I thought the 'limp noodle' part was bad! "Oh. Wow."

"What wow?"

I don't know where to start unpacking all the baggage in that one sentence, so I start with the mostly obvious. "If you were that unhappy with Benjy, for that long, why didn't you just dump him before you left for school? Make a clean break of it, you know?"

She's back to whining again. Her nerves are so frayed, her emotions so raw, I wonder if maybe she's had as much sleep this holiday as I have, which is to say, none at all. "I tried. You don't think I tried? But every time I started to broach the subject this past summer, he got those puppy dog eyes, and I figured, screw it, what he doesn't know can't hurt him."

I reach for my mug and sip. Strong, sweet, hot, and heavy. My energy is waning vaguely, and she doesn't seem like she's going to crash anytime soon so I'm trying to use whatever I can to cross the finish line with whatever I have left in me. Which isn't much at this point. "So, I mean, you knew ahead of time you were going to, uh savor the college experience, so to speak?"

I flinch in advance, waiting for the inevitable dustup. The scowl. The sigh. The grunt. The snap back.

She smiles instead, slow, and sultry like she's been waiting to tell me the *Whole, Damn, Time*. "The college experience." She mulls it over in her mouth, as if savoring each syllable. "I like how you put it."

Then, nothing. One big awkward silence. So, I have to ask again. "Sooooo, did you? Know you were going to stray in advance?"

She sighs. Glances around. Nods. Looks back up at me. "Shay, to be honest, I knew I was going to stray three months after we started dating. It took everything I had not to stray back in high school."

I take another big gulp, surprised to see my mug is almost empty. "Jesus, Cara. Why haven't you said anything until now?"

She shrugs. "I mean, there's girl talk and then there's, like, revelations about yourself you're not even ready for, let alone your best friend, you know?"

I nod. That actually makes a lot of sense. Mutter, "wow" and don't even realize I'm doing it until she calls me on it.

"Stop saying that, Shay. You're making me feel bad."

"I don't mean to, Cara. I really don't."

"Well, you are."

I ignore her hypersensitivity for once. "So, just to be clear, you left Crescent Beach and the whole way to school you were, what, wriggling in your seat with anticipation about who your first D was gonna be with?"

I'm literally imagining her doing just that. She does it now, biting her lower lip as if reliving the moment. "Kinda, yeah. It was like, every mile I left in my rearview mirror was one mile closer to getting laid and, well, it was pretty liberating, I'm not gonna lie."

I start to say "wow" again and hold my tongue. But not for long. "And so, you get there and, what, turn into a man eater?"

She snorts. "Not quite, but it didn't take long, I'll tell you that."

"Jesus." I'm picturing her, or trying to, but can't see her with anyone else but him. "Are they all like Benjy?"

Nearly spits out her cocoa. "What? Goofy and shy and awkward and funny and sweet and charming and adorable?"

I smile and nod because she's actually describing him to a "T" and not cutting him down for once. "Yeah, actually. Like that."

"Now, why would I leave one gangly high school kid to run off to college and find six more versions just like him?"

"I dunno. You always said Benjy was just your type."

She nods, like maybe she's forgotten. Or just outgrown him. Possibly, even, outgrown us as well. Shrugs. "I guess, after eating vanilla for four years, you want to try another flavor, you know?"

I frown. It feels like she's talked herself into that. Like maybe she's forgotten, conveniently, all the fun they had.

The fun I watched them have. The fun I envied and wanted for myself.

"So, not even one of them was like Benj?"

"Not even one. They're, not even all like each other. College is like a buffet, and I didn't realize how hungry I was until I started taking a bite, you know?"

I realize I've been pacing a bit, like a caged animal, up and down the length of my admittedly small kitchenette. Maybe…maybe I had more energy than I thought, after all. I suddenly slump back against the counter. Like I had earlier in the day. With him. Suddenly, this little spot feels like a confessional. "I don't know, actually. I feel a little jelly, I guess."

She looks vaguely surprised. "You shouldn't. I mean, you've been single the whole time. All those sexy busboys and waiters and bartenders at work and you're telling me you haven't been nibbling on a little sampler platter yourself all these years?"

I blush vaguely, more for the fact that I haven't than that I have. "Not really. I mean, not with the same kind of slutty gusto you're describing."

She pauses, as if considering asking me something about myself, then seems to reconsider. Because why would she? This is clearly her moment, her time to revel in her own self-pity, swallowed up in her oversized hoodie with her smeared mascara and a whip cream moustache and enjoying every sad, pathetic, dramatic minute of it. She fixes me with a knowing gaze and smirks. "Shame. You're missing out, girl."

I jut out my chin. "I'm fine, thanks."

She nods, like maybe I am. "That's true. You haven't had someone holding you back for years like I have."

I bristle. "Okay, listen. He's my friend, too, you know?

He wasn't holding a gun to your head, Cara. I mean, you could have broken up any time you wanted to. You know you always wore the pants anyway."

She sits there. Takes it. Then frowns a little, like maybe she's feeling actual emotions for a change. "It's weird."

Then doesn't finish the thought, so of course I have to prod her dramatic ass. Like always. "What is?"

"You. Talking about Benjy and me. In the past tense, I mean."

I offer a wry, sudden grin. Because she's right. "It is, actually. I...I don't know how to feel about it all just yet, either."

"*You* don't? How do you think I feel?"

"Like the one who made the decision, Cara. Remember?"

She makes a face. "Did I...did I tell you that? Or did he?"

I freeze, for just a moment. Wondering. "Both of you did, I feel like. And either way, I can be happy for you and sad for him, you know?"

Snorts. "Sorry if I didn't consider your feelings first before I made a major decision that would impact my life, Shay."

"You know what I mean, Cara. This...this affects me, too."

"How?"

"Once you're gone, back to your boner buffet, who do you think's gonna be left here, consoling our little buddy until he's over you?"

She snorts, ignoring or perhaps just avoiding, the obvious. "Boner buffet. You always did have a way with words, Shay."

I grin a little, thinking of the thousands of rapid-fire snippets of conversation I engage in all day at Pig-Out. "Comes with the job, I suppose."

She fixes me with those big, sad eyes. I'm out of things to say. Maybe, just maybe, please God more than maybe, she is, too. Either way she lets the pause grow, staring me down until she finally breaks the silence with a doozie. "Speaking of the job, does Benjy know?"

Not for the first time, I pause mid-sip. "Know what?"

She perks up again, eyes growing fiery to match her crooked smile. "About you and the silver fox next door, obvs."

I sag with relief. "There's nothing to know." I wait a beat. "And besides, we're not together."

She arches a wicked severe eyebrow. "You could've fooled me, Shay."

I offer a wry, secret smile, savoring what Hub and I had shared on my welcome mat. "It was an experience."

"Yeah, I heard all about it. If he'd kissed you any longer, I was about to have an experience of my own crouching there on the steps, if you know what I mean."

I literally blanche. "Gross."

She wriggles some more. "Just sayin'."

I frown. "Where is all this sex talk coming from, anyway?"

"I dunno. I just feel...liberated. You know? At Eastern State I was able to start fresh. Nobody watching me. No curfew. No judging eyes. I could go where I wanted, with who I wanted, do the walk of shame the next morning and never feel the least bit ashamed, you know? It was...it was like being a virgin all over again."

I lean back against the oven. Hold my mug with both hands. Grin vicariously. "Sounds kind of nice, actually."

She responds with locker room gusto. "Fuck yeah it is. You should try it, Shay."

"What? Sex?"

She chuckles. "I mean, for a start." She nods at my bikini bottom. Soft and blue beneath the gauzy, loosely tied wrap still clinging loosely to my hips. "You better start using that thing before it seals itself shut."

I roll my eyes. *If you only knew, ho. If you only knew...*

THIRTY-NINE

SHAY

I frown. Listen to the crickets chirping in the weeds surrounding the dumpster downstairs. Try to keep the relief out of my voice. "I wish I didn't have to work the rest of this weekend."

She rushes to correct me. Or herself. I'm not sure which, but either way she can't let the moment go looking like she flattered me with some kind of invitation. "This was fun. We should do it again sometime. Not right away. But sometime. You know?"

I grin anyway, because…what the hell? In a few days she'll be gone again, out of the picture for another month or so and by the time she comes back for Christmas, this will all be resolved. One way or another. I hug her. Hard, strong, and tight. Then push her away playfully. The skateboard rolls slightly under one foot. She rolls it back.

I tell her. "I'd like that."

She seems vaguely surprised. "You would?"

"Of course, I would. Why would you say that?"

"I dunno. We've been kinda distant lately."

I'm surprised she noticed, frankly. Thought she kind of

preferred it that way. "I guess. Work, you know?" She shrugs. Keeps looking at me like she's waiting for something. I say something more just to give it to her. "Plus, you've had all your extracurricular activities."

Shrugs again. "I guess." Then she gives me a look. Chin out. Eyes wide and knowing under the soft orange streetlamp. "Then again, Shay, I wasn't the only one."

I freeze with my foot on her skateboard. "What's that supposed to mean?"

"You weren't gonna tell me?"

My heartbeat, strong and sudden, pounds in my ears. "Tell you what?"

She rolls her eyes. And the skateboard. Takes it from underneath my frozen bare foot and slides it back and forth under her one high-top sneaker. "Benjy already told me, Shay. It's fine, really."

"What? Is?"

We both know what she's talking about but on the off chance she's bluffing, no way in hell am I going to be the first one to cave and fess up.

"You and Benjy. I get it. I don't blame you. I stole him from you once, Shay. It's only right you steal him back at some point. Took you long enough."

"He…he told you that? I mean, we weren't sure if…"

She chuckles. Slugs me not-so-playfully on the arm. "Hell no! He didn't say shit, but you just did, you fucking slut!"

"Cara!"

She is thoroughly enjoying herself now. Back to her old ways, standing tall and model thin, eyes aglow with relish beneath the weak streetlight. Gone is the mousy mess I had to drag into the apartment hours earlier. "God, you're so easy. You always were. I can't believe you fell for that shit. That…that's like Gaslighting 101, ho."

"Come on, Cara. It's not funny. It's been eating me up inside."

"So why the hell didn't you tell me yourself then? Why make me trick it out of you?"

"I was waiting for the right time."

"Which would have been when, exactly?"

I chuckle. Groan. "I dunno. Over the phone. Two months from now when I wasn't smack-dab in the middle of a 48-hour panic attack."

She chuckles low and dry. "Chicken-shit."

"Yeah? So?"

Then: "You knew, didn't you? About me and those other guys?"

I nod. "I mean, just the one guy. Pizza Boy?"

"Pizza Boy?"

"Last time we FaceTimed. A week or so ago? You said you had a pizza coming and called the guy 'babe' just before you hung up."

"Oh, Dante? That dud."

I laugh. "He didn't sound like a dud when you were cooing at him in your dorm room doorway."

She shrugs. No big deal. "So, what? You figured I had a side piece, might as well finish what you started all those years ago on Bridget Carlson's porch?"

"What?"

"I mean, we're dishing here, right? Just you and me, a little girl talk under the stars. Might as well come clean about all of it then, right?"

I glance around the parking lot, empty cars and the crash of ocean waves a block away. "You couldn't have saved all this drama for upstairs?"

"It's like you said, I was waiting for the right time."

I glance around for potential witnesses. "Now? Now is the right time?"

"I'm not sleeping on it another night, Shay, so...yeah."

We stand there, face to face in the deserted parking lot. The skateboard rolls back and forth between us, wheels on warm pavement. Waves crash on a distant beach. Water laps, gentle in the breeze, in the pool just behind us. From my window just upstairs, Charlie brown serenades us quietly. She cocks a hip. Crosses her arms over her chest. Juts out her chin. "So? That porch? That slutty Little Red Riding Hood cape? That kiss? Am I wrong?"

"You saw us?"

"Shay, I always saw you. Not just then, that night, but all the secret glances you two shared. All the time. The easy way you two had about each other. The inside jokes and scary movies and stupid, lame lo-fi chill trance Goth bands you'd gaga over and your dumb bike rides and all of it. I saw it all. It used to drive me crazy."

"So why wait until now to break it off with him? Why be with someone who drives you crazy?"

"I dunno. Jealousy, I guess? Laziness? Pettiness? All of the above?"

"You know that's seriously fucked up, right?"

"It was always gonna be fucked up, Shay. You. Me. Benjy. The three of us. It started fucked up, it stayed fucked up, might as well end fucked up too, right?"

She might be a straight up evil sorceress, but the bitch has a point every now and again. I nod. Put my shoe firmly on her skateboard and shove it back her way. Hard. She notices. Grins. "I dunno, Cara. It kind of feels like a new beginning to me."

"Yeah?"

"Yeah, I mean, it's kinda like a weight lifted off of my shoulders."

She nods a little bit. Shoves the skateboard back my way. I shove it back hers. "I guess so," she says. "Now I can go back to school and ho around, guilt free."

I snort. "Good for you." Then: "May not be the same, though."

"How so?"

"I mean, sometimes the guilt is the funnest part, you know?"

She winks. "I dunno about the funnest part, but, yeah, my anticipation level for the boner buffet has definitely gone down a notch, that's for sure. Now that I'm not starring in my own episode of Drama Dorm, I'm just like every other ho on campus."

"I mean, not every other ho. Sounds like you're pretty good at it by now."

While she chuckles, long and hard, I think back to the night I shared with Benjy. The longing, the hunger, the craving, the urgency, the absolute and utter want of it all. And wonder if it would have felt the same if we'd been free to get together. I know the answer, instinctively, is no. And I suddenly feel a little guilty about that, too.

She laughs again anyway. Sighs. Says nothing. It's late. I know the moment, however unexpected, is ending. I take my foot off the skateboard. Glance at her under the orange glow of a flickering streetlight. "So, you're really not gonna beat me up over all this?"

She rallies, suddenly. Hops on her board and scoots away. Out into the middle of the empty street. Makes a grumpy old man face. Whizzes by with a clenched fist. "Oh, for sure, bitch. One day, you'll never know when, I'm gonna whoop your sorry, cheating, whoring ass, girl. You just wait!"

I laugh until I cry. And then just keep laughing. When I finally stop, I can hear her still cackling halfway down the street, little chuckles over the sound of her skateboard wheels scraping the pavement. And the sadness I feel watching her tiny figure retreat into the darkness makes me miss the days when she was being a catty old bitch and not a person with actual feelings and a sad, twisted, dysfunctional, shitty little narrative all her own.

FORTY

BENJY

"You're not even gonna stay until Sunday?"

Cara shrugs. I reach for the duffel bag and drag it off her shoulders. It's like a carefully choreographed dance and, in this, at least, we're still partners. She's got the back door of her sports sedan open, and I slide it across the leather seat next to a bunch of wrapped presents. Arch an eyebrow suspiciously. "Who are those for?"

She sighs. Shuts the door as if I might dig a little deeper, possibly even flip over a gift tag or two and read the names printed there in Shay's predictably perfect handwriting. "Me, dummy. Dad already had my Christmas presents wrapped and waiting for me under the tree when I got home, Benjy."

I frown. Literally scratch my head. "Is the world ending or something? Did I miss the memo? Why is everyone pretending like it's already Christmas?"

She frowns back. Leans against the car like she's suddenly in no hurry to leave. Quite a switch from literally five seconds ago when she couldn't wait to rush me out the door and lock it behind us before my feet were even on the welcome mat. The Christmas welcome mat. "Well, it is Thanksgiving weekend. That's traditionally when a lot of people put up their trees."

"Like who? I've never done that."

Dad was always big on Christmas, or so the few pictures I still have of him would indicate. Frankly, those are the only pictures I still have of him: Dad playing Santa, me on his knee, big blond curls poking out from beneath his cheesy crooked Santa cap. Dad teaching me how to ride the new bike he got me for Christmas, wrapping still stuck to the banana seat. That kind of thing. Therefore, Mom is staunchly against Christmas.

We still decorate, vaguely that is, just in case one of her coworkers stops by to drop off a contract or some other paperwork and has to come inside for some reason. Mom calls it "keeping up appearances" and that's exactly what it is: not an ounce of spirit in any of the tinsel or generically red and green ornaments hanging from the fake tree branches in the living room. No stockings, no Santa mugs, possibly a throw pillow or two leftover from some house Mom's been staging in December but I suppose when Dad left, he took Christmas with him.

"Like my dad, for one. And Shay, for another." Cara points across the street at grassy green lawns full of unsightly candy canes and inflatable snowmen and winking snowflake lights hung from garage doors. "And the Johnsons. And the Harolds. Lots of people, actually."

I frown and gently rock from foot to foot, nervous for some unknown reason. Sad for many more. It's true what they say about the holiday blues, I suppose. Most years I just ignore the holidays, but this year there's so much more to celebrate. So much more to be sad about, too.

"Let's face it, Benjy," Cara says. "Our families aren't exactly…traditional."

I cluck my tongue. Think of Mom, listening to anything *but* Christmas music while she's tooling around in her new sedan, ignoring the seasonal displays all over town and focusing on the properties she's selling, as if it's just another month out of the year. And Cara's dad, off on a business trip the first weekend his daughter's home from school. Then there's Shay's mom, out in California doing who knows what with who knows whom while her only daughter dukes it out on her own back home, so used to being alone she might as well be an orphan.

"What families?" My voice is deep and droll and judge-y.

Her eyes match my tone. "Exactly."

I glance at the presents in the backseat. "So, what'd he get you?"

"Probably the new laptop I asked for. Some stuff for the dorm room. A few hundred bucks on a gift card. The usual."

"You opened them already?"

"No, he's just pretty predictable."

"Well, what if you come back for Christmas? Will you get more presents then?"

She smirks, half-evil, half-amused, all sexy. "Why would I do that?"

"I mean, it's Christmas."

"You're the only reason I came home for Thanksgiving, Benj. And if we're not even, well, why would I bother?"

"But what would you do instead?"

"Not sit around this depressing town all weekend wondering what you were doing and who you were doing it with, that's for sure."

I finally laugh out loud. Who is this bitch kidding? "Cara, please. I don't know if you've been reading romance novels up there or something, but... Will you even really miss me when you go back?"

She blushes vaguely. Avoids my eyes for a tick like she's just been caught. Then surprises me with some calm-voiced real talk. "I know I wasn't always the best girlfriend to you, Benj. I can be a bitch sometimes. A lot of times. Demanding. Bossy. All that unpleasant shit. But I don't regret a day we spent together, okay?"

"Really?"

She looks vaguely pissed I would question her. I feel slightly relieved. It was as if an alien had inhabited her body for a moment there. A nice alien, at that. She takes a play slug at my arm. Only half-connects. "Yeah, really. What the actual?"

"I just—. It never felt like you liked me all that much."

She doesn't necessarily deny it. "Do I strike you as someone who does things she doesn't want to do? With people she doesn't want to do them with? For years at a time?"

"I guess not, but you do strike me as someone who couldn't wait to get out of this town and took your first opportunity to do so."

She makes a face like the whole town just farted. "Can you blame me?"

"Come on, Cara. It's not so bad."

"Jesus, Benj. Don't start thinking like a townie, okay? We both know you're better than that."

"What if I'm not, though? What if I like it here? What if I actually belong here?"

"Then you're crazier than I thought."

"Yeah? And?"

We both snort. I can feel her getting antsy to get on the road again. Surprised she even agreed to see me when I texted her at the last moment. Just to see if I could come by, one last time, before she left. All the same, I've already kept her longer than she probably wanted to stay.

In more ways than one.

She glances around her posh street. Florida suburbia at its finest. The towering palm trees and manicured lawns and pastel paint jobs on million-dollar homes beaming in the late morning sun. "I can see the charm, kinda. But at least get out for part of your life, Benjy. If you want to come back, fine. If you don't, all the better."

Her superior tone reminds me of all those times she made me feel like the school janitor back in the day. I push back. "Jesus, you act like you go to school in Manhattan, Cara. I hate to break it to you, babe, but Florida Eastern is still in Florida."

"But it's a path, Benj. To somewhere else. A few more semesters there and I graduate and go on to design school anywhere in the country I want. It's a world away from here, Benj. Trust me."

I don't trust her, though. She always did have a skewed view of reality. "Maybe I'll jet one day, Cara. Maybe I won't. Being a townie isn't all that bad."

Her face responds before her lips do, and both share the same message: "Gross."

I chuckle. "Well, they say opposites attract, so…"

She makes a sound kind of like a laugh but is wriggling the entire time. I get the hint. Nod toward her car door. "Well, you're probably eager to get on the road, so…"

She stands to her full height, jingling her keys with

obvious and irritating relief. "It's not that, it's just—. I want to beat the traffic."

Roll my eyes. "Well, you're ending your visit a day earlier than everyone else in the country so you should be good to go, right?"

Even she can't miss the barbed sarcasm. Rolls her eyes back. I notice, not for the first time, how pretty they've always been. "Okay, stop. Let's end this on a good note. Isn't...isn't that why you wanted to come over today, Benj?"

I nod. Step away from my bike. Inch a little closer. It's awkward. I do it anyway. "I'm good, Cara. Really. I am. I just wanted to make sure you were, too. So, are you?"

She looks sad, suddenly. Nakedly, clearly, transparently sad.

I don't think I've ever seen her look sad before. Mad? Plenty of times. Sad? Not so much.

"I thought I would be, but you really shouldn't have stopped by. I kind of wish I'd ghosted you earlier, you know? If I could have gotten away without seeing you one last time, I'd be free and clear by now. Now it's harder."

"It should be hard, Cara. Jesus. We spent six years of our life together, you know?" I marvel to think that, at twenty-two, this is me. This is my life. Standing here, the jilted lover, watching my girl head back to college after the weirdest, strangest, greatest, saddest, bestest, Thanksgiving weekend ever.

She sighs heavily. "I know, boo, and it was great. But now...now it's time to see what happens in the next few years, you know?"

I grin. A little too quickly.

She sees it. Nods. Leans forward for a quick, chaste kiss that lingers longer than I thought it would, but not as long as I'd like. "You're free, baby. Free to be with who you wanted to be with all along."

"Stop."

"I won't stop. And neither should you. We had our fun. And it was fun. And I'm glad we had it, but now that it's over, you should run to the one you really wanted all along."

"I always wanted you, Cara."

"Oh, I know, boo. Let's face it, you aren't that good of an actor to fake it all those years. But we both know you settled for wanting me when Shay was the one you really needed all along."

I bite my lip, then shake my head. "That's not entirely accurate, Cara." She seems a little surprised by my response. Or maybe it's just me using a bigger word than usual. Townies, I guess, aren't supposed to say things like that.

"Oh, no?"

"No. I cared about you. Both. And when we were together, we were together. Period."

She seems to think for a minute. Holding her keys and not even jingling them impatiently like she has been for the past five minutes or so. "I think you cared about me, Benj, for as long as you could. And I even blame myself for pushing you into her arms the other night."

"You do?"

"Yeah, I was a bitch. Impatient. Cold. I get it. You still could have waited to hit that until we officially broke up, though, you know?"

I'm surprisingly unsurprised that she knows. About me and Shay. And surprisingly cold about it. "In a way, Cara, I think we broke up the day you left for school back in August."

She doesn't deny it. Nods, even, just a little. I keep pushing, even though it's hard. "And I kind of feel like you acted like we were already broken up, too. If you know what I mean."

She takes a little step back. Or maybe I've just moved closer while talking. I'm not sure. Either way, she doesn't deny it. Any of it. "I know what you mean. And you're not...you're not wrong. About acting single while I was away."

I rock back a little. Chuckle. "Slut!"

She shoves me playfully. "Man slut!"

"When were you gonna tell me?"

"Never, if you'd have just let me leave five minutes ago like I planned. I would have burned rubber and ghosted you and never looked back and that would have been the end of it. But oh no, you had to show up and ruin things, as always."

I know, even though her tone is light, she's only half-joking. "Who?"

"Like it matters? You wouldn't know them anyway."

"Them? As in more than one? Jesus, Cara. What the fuck?"

"I suck. What can I say?"

"You're sorry? How about you start with that?"

"I might have, if you hadn't slept with my best friend, bud."

"I might not have slept with your best friend if you weren't screwing everyone in your study group every time I called!"

She frowns, a sly smile still curling up the ends of her thin, pale lips. "Not everyone, but I strayed. And I actually am sorry."

I sigh and scan the horizon, the green grassy lawns with snowmen and reindeer under the warm Florida sun, my ex and I casually talking about who we've been boffing while she was away at school. It would be almost comically surreal if it wasn't so weird and sad and tragically scarring. "When were you going to tell me?"

"Never, if I thought it was going to hurt you."

I frown and murmur and stare at my feet.

"Well, does it? Hurt you, I mean?" Cara asks.

Our eyes meet. For once, she doesn't look away. I don't, either. "Not as bad as I thought it would, I guess. I mean, I kind of already knew or I wouldn't have acted the way I did."

"Oh, so it's my fault?" She uses her clucking tongue for punctuation.

I cluck back. "No, I get it. I'm grown. We both are. It was a dick move, what I did, I just don't feel so bad about it anymore, you know?"

She's jingling her keys again. I smirk. She does, too. "We're both dicks, bud. Let's face it and move on, okay?"

"Just like that?"

She opens her door, but doesn't get in. "Yeah, Benj. Just like that."

I shake my head. Stick my hands in my pockets. Pull them back out. "I'll give you this much, Cara. You sure know how to say goodbye."

She chuckles. Long and loud. She always did laugh the loudest when we were talking about her. "Look at it this way, Benjy. Now you won't be sad about me leaving anymore, you know?"

She slides into the driver's seat, like that's her big exit. I grab the door so she can't shut it yet. "That's just it, Cara. I'm still sad. About everything. All of it. Especially the way it ended."

She sighs. Getting a little impatient now. "You'll get over it, bud."

"What? Like you have?"

She looks up at me. Slides her sunglasses on. All ready to go now. "I'm not over it, yet. But by the time I get back to school, I'll have put it up high on a shelf, you know? Like a picture in a frame. And I'll take it down every once in a while and think about it and you know what I'll do then, bud?"

"Puke?"

She snorts humorlessly. "Stop. I'll smile, Benjy. I'll smile about it all. Proms and homecomings and weekends and you in wet baggies on the beach and weekend booty calls and movie nights and every single bit of it. Even...even the end, you know?"

I glance away for a moment. Over her roof. Past a palm tree and the sunshine and the green, shimmering lawns of her neighbors, glowing blurry with emotion.

She snaps me back to life. "Are you crying?"

I shrug. Glance down at her, dry-eyed. Well, mostly, that is. "Not yet. Maybe later, when the dust settles and you don't text me back for a day or two and then only with a 'hey, what's up' and no fun little emojis and I realize it's really, finally over. Maybe then."

"So, I'm smiling at the end while you're crying?"

I grin. Shut her door. Wait for her to slide the window down before replying. "I'll smile after a good sniffle or two. Then I'll put you on a shelf and smile some more."

She nods. Turns the engine over. It purrs, smooth as ever. "That's all I want, Benj. For you to smile when you think of me." As if to prove the point, she slides the window back up, sleek and tinted like a mirror in the late morning sun.

I'm smiling again. Even as she pulls away.

She's not the only one eager to get a jump on the day. I watch her taillights blink down the street, barely pausing at the stop sign before turning right and screeching away without so much as a honk of her horn.

I grin and start pedaling, cruising down her street and out of her subdivision and down the hill to find the real reason I don't mind living in Crescent Beach.

And never will.

FORTY-ONE

SHAY

I see his shadow before I see him. Glance up from my edamame. My surprise is genuine, impossible to hide, but so is my insanely sincere happiness. "How did you…?"

Benjy shrugs his broad shoulders. Slides into the booth across from me as if it was made for him. "I went to all your favorites until I saw your bike in the rack out front."

I nod. Don't say anything right away. Not on purpose, it's just between the sake and the Asian string vibes chilling overhead I've just been zenning out and am not currently in a particular hurry.

He must take it for me being aloof. Rushes to add: "I don't know why I didn't start here in the first place, you big sake lush."

I snort. Reach for my sake cup as if to prove it. Lean back in my booth. Sip it slowly. Savor it. And the moment. And his gushing, glowing, uncertain young face. "That's vaguely romantic."

He seems somewhat surprised and adorably sweaty. "Is it?"

"I think so."

He chuckles. "Me too, actually." Glances down at the cluttered table. Sees the little white cup in front of his otherwise empty space. Glances around the deserted restaurant. Back to me. "You expecting someone?"

I reach over and pour fresh, warm sake into his cup. When I glance up from my labors, our eyes meet over the little white carafe. My voice is deep and unmistakable. "You, eventually."

He grins. "What if I didn't come?"

I shrug. "What if? Then I would have wasted a perfectly good little white cup, but since, in this scenario, you wouldn't have come anyway, you would have never known about it. I'd feel stupid for a day or two, then get over it. That's what."

He frowns. I tap his foot under the table. "But I knew you'd come."

He perks up. I like him perked. I like him...period. "Yeah? How?"

"Call it a Treesgiving miracle, I guess."

Rolls his eyes. Reaches for his cup. Is about to take a sip. I'm about to razz him for not toasting first. He catches himself just in time. Blinks bashfully over at me. "Sorry. Here's..." He taps my glass. Gently this time. No spilled sake. He's catching on. "To starting over?"

I blush. Everywhere. Inside and out. I don't realize how much I've missed him until I finally see him again. "I couldn't have said it better myself."

I feel like I'm being extra sultry at the moment, but it's not on purpose. I'm just moving slow and low, voice and hands and eyes included, and it must be coming off that way. He looks confused and vaguely impressed and a little unsteady, so I'm kind of glad even though I'm not currently in control of just about anything that's going on at the moment.

In due time, the server comes. The server goes. In a few minutes, the sumo wrestler curtain rustles and she emerges with more sake. A big beer. Two fresh, cold glasses. Sets them down between us without a word. Turns away and swishes off in her dusty black polyester slacks as if she already knows the score.

I'm glad she does because at the moment, I don't know what's about to happen next. And maybe, just maybe, that's part of the fun? Or, if not the fun, at least the excitement?

Benjy busies himself pouring the big beer into the two frosty glasses. Taking his time, waiting for the foam to go down so they come out evenly. Glances past our table at the retreating server. "Something I said?"

"No, there's some kind of drama going on in the kitchen. She's been like that ever since I got here."

He chuckles. "I guess every restaurant's got some drama, huh?"

"Pretty much."

"Speaking of drama… You and Cara okay?"

"Good as we'll ever be, I guess. You?"

"Same."

I sip some sake. Sip some beer. Sit back and grin at him. He looks doubtful and asks, "What?"

"You look cute, is all."

"Come again?"

"You heard me, Benjy. Don't make me say it twice just to flatter yourself."

He looks adorably doubtful. I can't say as I blame him. I'm even more confused than he is. "What the hell is this now?"

He looks at the two white carafes standing next to each

other. Dusted with carp and cherry blossoms to match the little white cups. "How long have you been here, anyway?"

"Long enough to know I'm glad you didn't give up on me."

Raises his little white cup again. I sigh and reach for mine and clink. He says, "On us, Shay. Right?"

I nod. Sip. Set the glass down. Nod at his shirt. "Where'd you get that?"

He glances down like he forgot what he's wearing. Lifts it away from his chest a little until the chunky cow logo comes into focus. Grins. Lets the soft cotton drift back to clinging to his smooth, sculptured chest. "Moo's, obviously."

I nod. Touche to the little smartass in the cute little purple cow shirt. "The food truck?"

"Duh."

"I guess I meant, when did you get it?"

"Yesterday? Today? This whole stupid weekend is running all together."

I narrow my eyes at him like I'm doing some bit from that old Columbo show. "Okay, so let's try it this way. *Why* did you get it? I mean, are you gonna start collecting random food truck t-shirts now?"

"I dunno. Maybe."

"What for?"

His sigh of exasperation is endlessly amusing to me for some reason. "Maybe that's my Treesgiving tradition, huh? Maybe every year on your stupid made-up holiday I'm going to pick a new food truck in town and sit there and gorge myself and then buy a souvenir t-shirt to remind myself never to go back again, okay?"

I shrug. Picture the two of us doing just that together next year. "I dunno. Sounds kinda nice, actually."

He looks disgusted, suddenly. With me. Himself. With this whole situation. "Trust me, it wasn't."

The silence that follows isn't necessarily awkward, just silent. And I didn't set out an extra sake cup to just sit there and be quiet. "So, what now?"

He chuckles. Puts his little white cup back down on the table. Grabs the table like he's bracing for impact. "Well, for starters I want my picture back."

I snort. Shake my head. Lower my voice slightly to make it clear how very, very serious I'm being at this particular moment. "Listen, cute or not? You're not getting it back. I love it. It's mine now. You gave it to me. Remember?"

"Yeah, but that was before you broke my heart and now that you have, I don't want you to have it anymore."

"If I broke your heart then why would you want to look at it anymore?"

"Who says I want to look at it? Maybe I want to burn it in a ceremony."

My surprise snort-chuckle turns into a burst of laughter I can't contain. I glance around the empty restaurant to make sure that none of the people who aren't sitting there noticed. "What do you know about ceremonies? What are you, Wiccan all of a sudden?"

He's smirking, struggling not to laugh, but not giving up on his crazy idea, either. "What do you know about Treesgiving? It was a Treesgiving present, and I want it back."

I think for a minute. Stare him down. He wilts like he always does because he's full of shit and a big fat wimp to boot. "I tell you what, we'll compromise and make it a Treesgiving tradition."

"What? To break my heart?"

"Stop. I'll give it back to you next Treesgiving. Then you

give it back to me the year after that. And so on and so on. That's what will make it a tradition."

"Screw that. I don't want anything more to do with your stupid Treesgiving and if you think I'm going to celebrate that shitty holiday anymore you've got a second thought coming."

"Stop, Benjy. This isn't you. This isn't us. We're gonna figure something out and if it takes us all year to do it, then all the better."

He looks thoroughly exasperated, like a hungry kid who can't open the new cookie jar no matter what. "Why do you want to figure something out if you don't want to sleep with me anymore?"

I literally groan. "Ugggggghhhh, just because I don't want to sleep with you anymore doesn't mean I don't want to figure something out."

He juts out his chin. "How about you figure something out while you're sleeping with me? How about that, huh?"

I can't help but laugh. "Why are you so horny all of a sudden? You just got laid like, two days ago? That's more than you've gotten in the last four months and now you can't keep your hands off me?"

"Yeah, so? I just don't understand why we can't be friends with benefits, that's all."

"Stop, Benjy. You and I don't say stupid things like that. Those are the things the kids at work say."

"Hate to break it to you, but we *are* the kids at work."

"Maybe, technically, but we don't say things like 'friends with benefits.' Or 'read the room.' Or 'lots to unpack here.' Or 'you do you.' We don't say things like that period. It's not us."

His eyes are challenging even if his scruffy chin is vaguely quivering. "I don't think there is an 'us' anymore."

"Then what are you doing here, Benjy? Why did you ride all over town looking for my bike if you didn't think there was an 'us' anymore?"

"Fuck if I know!"

I laugh again. I don't want to, but he keeps making me. "Listen, Benjy, I don't know what's gonna happen between us, but if you really want that picture back, you're gonna have to wait a year and I'll wrap it up and give it to you next Treesgiving."

"That's so stupid but fine, God, yes, fine, whatever."

I beam. Literally. Beam. "See, that wasn't so hard, was it?"

"Yeah, actually, this is really fucking hard. But what choice do I have?"

"Look, it's hard for me too. Like right now you're really being charming. Stupid, but charming. Sexy even."

"So, what is the fucking problem then? Let's just be sexy together and call it a day?"

"It's not that easy, Benjy. You just broke up with Cara. No matter what you think, she is hurting about that. And no matter how much I want to be with you, and you already know that I do, the last thing I want to do is hurt her even more after being such a shitty friend in the first place."

He looks back at me like he's never thought of this before. Or maybe like he's thought of nothing else since. "I mean yeah, obviously you're right, but she won't even know."

"Oh God, Benjy, don't screw it up now. I'll know. You'll know. That's the point. That's what makes it so hard to figure this all out right now."

"The point is that it doesn't have to be so hard. It's actually pretty simple. You and me together, finally, after all these years. Simple, see?"

"Benjy, I say this in the nicest way possible, but what if...stick with me here...what if the reason we were so hot for each other that night? For these last four years? What if it's because we knew we couldn't be together? What if it's because it was dirty, naughty, forbidden, wrong and maybe that's what made it so sexy?"

"Or maybe it's just because you're sexy? Have you ever thought of that?"

"Are you buttering me up? Is that what you're doing? Did you read that in some book about how to get chicks?"

He is effortlessly, even hilariously, cocky. "I obviously don't need a book on how to get chicks, Shay. I just had two in the last forty-eight hours, remember?"

I flick a piece of edamame salt at him. He doesn't flinch. He seems actually wounded. Like something's broken inside. I know the feeling, but I also know I'm sticking to my guns this time no matter how cute he looks sitting there all slumpy and broken.

"And maybe you'll have two more in the next forty-eight? Who am I to say? Maybe now you've unleashed some crazy sex beast inside of you and you'll need to get all the single ladies out of your system? Am I supposed to be the next girl you cheat on?"

The cocky jut of his chin softens and sags to reveal the sad glisten of his mopey eyes. "I would never do that to you, Shay."

"I bet you said that to Cara at some point, too."

"You act like I'm the bad guy here. We're both bad, remember?"

"I do, Benjy. That's what I'm saying. I feel like, if we start hooking up right away, I'm still going to feel like the bad guy until we stop."

"So what? You're going to start dating other people now?"

I literally laugh out loud. Long and hard. I think I needed that. "Benjy, stay with me here. I could always date other people. Remember? You were the one who was with someone. And now you're not. And you might really, really like that feeling and I don't want to get hurt watching you sleep your way around Crescent Beach while you make up for lost time."

"What if I do that anyway? You're still gonna be watching, right? Like what if some hot new waitress applies to work and we start going out and you're on the sidelines watching us? What then?"

"I don't know, Benj. I mean, I've watched you and Cara together for practically forever and it sucked every time. I guess I'm used to it by now."

He frowns like banging every chick in town is some kind of bad idea or something. And I don't think I've ever met a guy like him before. "Besides, you might find Mrs. Right along the way."

He reaches over, across the table, presses one of his fingers down against mine gently. It's unlike anything he's ever done before. Unlike anything anyone's ever done before. Unlike anything I've ever even felt before.

Now it's his voice that turns low and deep and sultry. "What if I already have? What if it's you, and I've been waiting all this time and now I have to wait even longer?"

"Benjy, I feel the same way. Trust me. I do. But if it's right, if we really are meant to be together, then this will all wait. It'll still be there a day from now, a week from now, a month from now, even a year from now at next Treesgiving."

He sits back and crosses his arms over his chest. "It better be, ho, because I'm not giving up on you."

"You better not."

"Are you crying?"

"No. I just got some rock salt in my eye. Duh."

"Bullshit. You're crying. It's your stupid rule that we have to wait and you're the one crying?"

"It's not my rule Benjy, it's just my decision. And I've made it. So, stop trying to change my mind."

"Screw that. You're not the boss of me. I'm gonna spend every day for the next year trying to change your stupid mind. Even if it takes me all the way until next stupid Trees-giving, you're gonna see I was right all along."

When I don't answer right away, when I can't answer right away with my stupid throat choked up shut, he juts his chin back out. His eyes gleam, like this has somehow already happened. And maybe, who knows, it already has. He senses my vulnerability and leans gently forward, a predatory gleam in his soft brown eyes.

"So, this is how it's going to go, okay?" When I start to reply, he waves a sake sticky hand to silence me. For once, it works. "Starting today, but not today, since you already shut me down, I'm going to start randomly just asking you out. Day, night, weeknight, weekend day, working, not working, text, phone call, in person, whatever. I'm just going to keep asking, okay?"

"And?"

"And one day, Shay, you're going to say 'yes' to me. And that day, will be just the best ever, okay?"

I shrug and nod at the same time. Possibly pull something in the process. "What if I never say 'yes,' Benjy? What then?"

"Listen, failure is NOT an option here, okay?"

He's so fervent, so earnest, so refreshingly demanding, I nod. I reach for my sake, and he pounces, snatching my hand up and forcing a shake. "There, that seals it. Challenge accepted."

I nod, gently, then stubbornly slip my hand from his grasp, feeling the warmth of his fingers long after ours part. He grins, as if knowing it. Sits back. Looks me up and down the way he does sometimes when he thinks I'm not looking.

"How about them apples, huh Shay?"

I sit back. Reach for my little white cup before he can attack my hand again. Wriggle back in my booth like I've got all day. Then remember that, yeah, I actually do. All day, all month, all year if that's how long I need. Or just till tomorrow, if that's how it all shakes loose, and I finally cave the first time he asks me out.

I take a long, warm sip of sake and glance back at him, lips still wet. To match the gaze I'm no longer hiding. "I like them, Benj. I like those apples just fine..."

FORTY-TWO

SHAY

I smell the smoke at the top of the stairs. I'm only halfway up, face feeling sun-kissed and warm from the slow, easy ride home from Chopstix. Try to hide my telltale smile before I reach the landing, but it's still there by the time I hit the last step.

Hub glances up from something on the little table between our apartments. Looks relieved. Like, genuinely, earnestly, sincerely relieved. "Bout time. Jesus."

I grin, vaguely buzzed and slightly flattered. "Have you been waiting long?"

"Long enough."

I nod at his faded green collar shirt, paired with a basic pair of khaki slacks. He looks so different in his work uniform, like some vaguely neutered version of himself, making me feel a little bit sad for the sexy Lothario who nonetheless has to run a cash register and stock dingy shelves at some dollar store to pay the bills. "Bull hockey. You just got home from work, didn't you?"

He grins. "I was going to change but didn't want to miss you."

I'm still kind of standing near my door. "You could always just knock." Then I knock, rapping playfully on my own door.

He chuckles. Shakes his head. Sips a can of generic soda called Bolt. They sell them at the Dollar Time where he works. He brings them home for us, occasionally. I probably have four or five lying around in my crisper drawer for when the real stuff runs out. "What's gotten into you?"

I sigh, reliving my cozy, familiar, coy but most of all romantic lunch with Benjy. "Oh, about a carafe and a half of sake, I guess."

He rolls his eyes. Nods at me, still in my Pig-Out uniform. "Rough day at the office?" Nudges the chair across from him out a little with his sneaker.

I wasn't going to sit down. Between a busy day at work and Benjy's overwhelming presence at the sushi bar, it's been a long day. Still, Hub is hard to resist so eventually I do. Only then do I notice the second can of Bolt soda on my side of the table, not to mention a giant box of chocolates between us. "What...what is all this?"

He pauses nibbling one to explain. "We've started getting the first of the Christmas candy at work and, gosh darnit, this one got damaged right off the truck. So... I volunteered to bring it home for us."

He waves the dented box top at me for proof, a cozy Victorian Christmas scene with snow and dreary streets and gas lights and little people bundled up against the cold with their hands stuffed in fuzzy muffs. In the corner of the box top is a tiny, almost unnoticeable "dent" that looks surprisingly like his fingerprint. "For us?"

He grins. "Sure, I mean, it's cheap dollar store chocolate, but it's chocolate."

I can't argue with that logic. I crack open the can and

take a sip. It's warmish, but crisp and sweet. I'm not really hungry after sushi, but I spent most of the time bantering playfully with Benjy and not eating so I'm not too full to reach for a piece of chocolate. It's soft and smooth and melty, the way cheap chocolate gets, but gooey and caramelly in my mouth. I chase it with another sip of warm soda and, bam, instant energy.

"Not bad."

He nods. Reaches for another piece like a little kid on Halloween. "Right?"

We nibble and sip for a while, the afternoon growing soft and warm and orange as the sun drifts down, casting soft, pleasant shadows on the second-floor breezeway. Then he grunts, amusingly, and slides the box of chocolate, already half-eaten, in my general direction. "Ugggh, enough!"

I chuckle at his vaguely girly outburst and savor the bite in my mouth before doing the same and pushing it back at him. Then he pushes it back. "Stop, Hub. Just put the lid on already."

He looks surprised, like it's never occurred to him. "Oh, yeah, good idea."

"You think?" I watch him slide the cover on and then inch the box against the wall beside us. I consider asking him for the box cover 'cause it's kind of a cute picture with the whole Victorian London aesthetic, but it folds slightly when it hits the wall and I realize it's cardboard and no thanks.

Dumb idea anyway. I mean, what was I gonna do with it? Frame it? I glance up from admiring it a little too long I suppose and find Hub glancing at me curiously. "What are you doing?"

I glance back and shrug. "I just had a whole moment with your candy box top."

He gives a little merry snort, laugh lines around his soft, gentle eyes. "I saw that. What? Do you want one?"

"I mean, if it was a tin or something, but..."

"Okay, look, it's Dollar Time, not Tiffany's. You want a tin for your chocolates you're gonna have to go to *Dollar General*, okay?"

"I dunno, maybe I'll take a picture of it and use it as a screensaver?"

Hub looks vaguely, adorably dumbfounded. "Wow, this...this is not why I waited this long for you."

I picture the scene. Hub in his very official assistant manager collar work shirt, looking all slicked back and mature like a substitute teacher. The half-melty chocolates and warm soda and cock my head gently. "Okay, so what *did* you wait out here for?"

He grins, looking me up and down. "We'll get to that, but first sake?"

I have to blink for a moment because even though I just got home, Hub has created a whole mood out here on the landing, so it already seems like forever ago. "Yes. Sake? What about it?"

Looks vaguely suspicious. "You went and got sake alone?"

I grin and sit back in my chair a bit. "So, what if I did, huh?"

He wears a knowing grin. "It would be a first, that's all."

"Well, this is a weekend for firsts, right?"

He waves a hand. "So, you went with some girls from work then?"

I cross my legs, then re-cross them. Glance away. "Sure. Yup. Right."

He grins. "You know, you don't usually seem this breathless and gushy when you come back from a girl's day out."

I make a "pfffttt" sound. "When's the last time I did that?"

"Yeah, never, so, I'm guessing Benjy found you?"

"Found me?"

"He swung by here awhile back sniffing around the bike rack before scooting off in a huff. Figured he was looking for you." Hub sits back, too, like he's just solved a major case squad crime or something. "Looks like he found you."

I jut out my chin playfully. "So, what if he did?"

"Nothing, I just…what's going on with that?"

"Nothing, just trying to figure things out."

Hub leans forward playfully, pretending to glance toward the stairway and then craning his neck for a better view of the bike rack downstairs. "So, is he coming over later, or… will I be getting some sleep tonight?"

"You can rest easy, Boomer. I'll be sleeping alone tonight, thanks very much."

For all his playfulness, Hub looks visibly relieved. "For now, you mean?"

I give him a sly grin, reliving my sake lunch with Benjy and squirming just a little. The day is warm, my belly's full, the sugar is in my veins and Hub is my neighbor and waited for me to get back from lunch. I'm suddenly on flattery overload and not quite sure what to do with it all. "For now, yeah."

"And your college friend? Cara?"

"Gone."

"Back to school?"

"Yup."

He grins. Sips some soda. Winces at its warmth. Glances around the walkway as the shadows lengthen. Lands back on me with another, soft, kinder type of smile. "So, the future looks pretty bright for you now, huh?"

I shrug, touched by his kindness. His softness. His observational skills. His generous, patient, mature nature. "I think so, once the dust settles."

"I'm happy for you, Shay."

"Thanks, Hub. I'm...pretty happy for myself."

He pauses, eyes drifting gently away. I watch him, his slowness and gentleness turning vaguely awkward, and grin. "You good?"

"I'm great."

"I guess I meant to say are *we* good?"

He looks surprised I'd ask. Or, perhaps, notice. "Good? Sure. Great."

I chuckle. "You're...you're jealous, aren't you?"

"Who? Me?"

I reach over slightly and poke the faded mermaid tattoo on his wiry forearm. "Admit it, just a little?"

He sighs. Sags. Nods. "Maybe. Yeah. I guess I just liked the old Shay."

"The old Shay?"

"Yeah, sure."

"I'm still the old Shay, bro. I just have a few more options now than I did this time last week."

He leans a little closer. Smiles softly. Gentle lines around his eyes. "I guess I just liked it best when I was one of those options."

His macho tunnel vision makes me snort. "So, now you know how I feel every time I see another tipsy tramp stumbling in and out of your doorway at all hours of the day or night."

Rolls his eyes. Then meets mine. "I guess things are changing for us too, then, huh?"

I glance away, then slowly back. "I wouldn't say that, Hub."

He chuckles dryly. "So, what would you say then?"

I mull it over gently before grinning. "Well, I'd say our relationship is still evolving."

He winks and reaches down beside him. I hear the crinkling of paper and something scraping gently along the wall and then he slides a present over across the table. It's big. Not boxy, more like tall. Tall, long, and wide. I kind of have to shift in my seat a little to accept it.

"What...what is this?" I take possession of it, see the cheery, cheesy Santa faces on the bright red wrapping paper.

He stands, gently. So gently I don't even realize he's doing it until I have to glance up to look at him. The present is awkward, so I stand, too, if only to get a better grip on it. "It's your Treesgiving present, silly."

"What? No, no, I don't... You didn't have to do this, Hub."

He stands, watching me curiously. I'm holding the present in both hands because it's that kind of present. Otherwise, I'd be waving them in his face.

"Of course, I did, girl. It's still Treesgiving weekend, remember?"

"It's NOT a gift giving holiday!! I haven't given anyone anything!"

He leans forward and, gently, chastely, with my hands in no position to defend myself, plants a most innocent kiss on my forehead. Soft and chaste and warm and brief. Then he leans back, smiling, before gently backing away toward his apartment. "That's not true at all, Shay. I mean, you've given me eleven months of you. Of us. Of greasy takeout food and late-night swims and cheeky bikinis and crooked smiles and fun conversations and experiences. And I wouldn't trade that for the world, Shay."

He's practically at his door now. Hand reaching for the

knob. I hold up the gift. It's light and the paper rustles gently in the breeze like he didn't do such a great job of wrapping it. "Don't you want to watch me open it?"

He looks suitably horrified. "God no. That would be too embarrassing. Just..." He waves me away. "Wait until you get inside to open it like a civilized person, please."

"Are you sure? How will I thank you that way?"

He chuckles. Swings the door open. Still standing on the mat. "Pretty sure we'll run into each other soon enough, Shay. You can thank me then."

"Well, I'll just thank you now, in advance." I call out to his retreating form. I've never seen him bolt so quickly before! He waves a silly little wave before the door shuts gently behind him.

I stand there, surrounded by soda and chocolate and twilight. But now I'm all curious so I dip inside my apartment and there, in the darkened hallway, tear the paper open. Frown at the back of a frame before turning it over. Then I grin, big and wide, and step on the little extension cord bulge that turns my tree on. By the shimmering light I gaze at a painting.

It's vibrant and bright, and not just because of the eight strings of lights illuminating it from the tree. It's of a girl. Young, tan with copper colored skin. Her back is turned, no face in sight. Hair straight and brown and damp beneath a trickling shower head, the details of the gently falling spray and streaks in her hair almost lifelike. Banana leaves frame her on either side, big and green, giving it a tropical, boho vibe I'm into immediately.

She's wearing a yellow bikini, softly crooked to expose the vaguely sexy hints of tan lines, pale and sandy. Instant, reflexive humility wants to believe it's not me, could never be me, not with the flattering curves and glowing hair and sleek, glistening girlish figure, until I see the vague shimmer of a rainbow tattoo peeking out of the cheeky bikini bottom.

I grin and blush and approach the living room wall where a random rainbow tapestry hangs above the record player. I never regretted buying it, per se, but it always felt kind of like a place holder until I found something just right. Now that I have, it's time to scoot. I take it down and replace it with the painting, stepping back to admire how well its tropical, bossa nova vibe fits with my boho sensibilities before leaning back in to straighten it a little bit this way, a little more that, until it's just right.

While I'm in the general vicinity I put Charlie Brown Christmas back on because, after all, it's still Treesgiving weekend. Take a step or two back until I feel the loveseat gently graze the back of my calves and then sink down, heavily, staring at my gift until the tears blur Hub's signature, soft and blue in the corner of the print.

Despite its vaguely racy nature—I mean, butt cheek glistening in the sun decked out to masterpiece detail, hello—it feels like an ending, of sorts. A cap off to something we shared, maybe even a sendoff to sharing it ever again. It feels, mostly, honestly, like a souvenir of our "experience" the other night.

A not-so-chaste kiss followed by a soft, bittersweet, quiet goodbye and then I could picture Hub sitting in front of a canvas, paints by his side, a spliff gently curling smoke into the air while Marley plays in the background as he knocked this puppy out, stroke by stroke, grin by grin.

It has the air of a final moment, frozen in time, never to be repeated again no matter how many bags of Pig-Out onion rings I bring him, no matter how many late-night swims and tall-boy ciders we share or, for that matter, how many times he watches my rainbow tattoo, wet and glistening under the pool shower.

Something about that, the finality of it, the frozen moment and sunny memories and joyful bliss of what could have been, help me put a thing, some very specific thing, to bed.

Once and for all.

Some certain things to be savored and admired and remembered and recalled, always fondly, whenever I look at the painting. But something vaguely dangerous and tempting that, now that Benjy and I are on a more forward leaning, even official trajectory, I can't entertain quite the same way I used to.

And I wonder, vaguely, almost regretfully, how that will feel the next time I'm softly, effortlessly buzzed and feeling Hub's eyes all over me as I step from the shallow end and onto the wet pool tiles. Will I still feel flattered? Coveted? Wanted? Or will those same, hungry eyes feel threatening? Dangerous? Or even…unwanted?

I shrug and smirk and lean back into my half-dozen Christmas throw pillows. Let the thoughts drift away, to the back of my fuzzy, overloaded mind. Vow to sort them out some other day, when I'm not feeling so flattered and special and, especially, definitely hopeful. And then I whisper hoarsely to myself, finally believing every word, "Best. Treesgiving. Ever!"

Don't miss out on your next favorite book!

Join the Satin Romance mailing list
www.satinromance.com/mail.html

THANK YOU FOR READING

Did you enjoy this book?

We invite you to leave a review at the website of your choice, such as Goodreads, Amazon, Barnes & Noble, etc.

DID YOU KNOW THAT LEAVING A REVIEW...

- Helps other readers find books they may enjoy.
- Gives you a chance to let your voice be heard.
- Gives authors recognition for their hard work.
- Doesn't have to be long. A sentence or two about why you liked the book will do.

ABOUT THE AUTHOR

 Alex Winters is the pseudonym of a busy restaurant manager whose curious young staff would love nothing more than to follow him around the dining room reading his steamiest, most romantic passages aloud! When not writing romantic holiday stories of various heat levels, he enjoys long walks with his wife, scary movies and smooth jazz.

www.awintersromance.com

𝕏 x.com/awintersromance

⊙ instagram.com/a_winters_romance

ⓐ amazon.com/author/awintersromance

ⓖ goodreads.com/alex_winters

ⓟ pinterest.com/awintersromance